I0563176

PrideMaiden

Prideland Series: Book 2

Theo Mann

Invisible Publishing Company

Prideland Series

Contents

Chapter 1

The first crack of a stick struck Dina across the side of the head. She covered her head with her arms to protect herself, but too many of those beat at her from all sides. When she covered her head, they struck her body. When she wrapped her arms over her stomach, they hit her in the back.

She'd known this was coming, but she still screamed out in pain. She'd almost lost her life more than once escaping from Prideland to make it back to the *Savannah*.

The Coalition Destroyer hovered in orbit over this planet even now. She held the ship in her mind at all costs. She could take what was coming as long as she knew it was still there. She could stand whatever sorry excuse of a life she had left knowing the *Savannah* was still there.

The *Savannah* wasn't still there, though. The ship had probably already left orbit. She made her choice when she came back to this planet. Now she was on her own.

She knew better than to beg for mercy. Anyone caught trying to escape from Prideland could expect instant death. Either the village factors would beat her to death or the cats of the Pride would rip her to pieces.

They couldn't let anyone escape without suffering the consequences. That would break the understanding between the cats and the human population. No human on this planet could ever be more than a slave, a pet, and prey for hunting. That was the understanding. They could dress it up any way they liked with fancy words, but the understanding boiled down to that and that alone.

Dina didn't have time to think about that right now, though. One of the men delivered a vicious kick to her lower back and she pitched over onto a hard dirt floor. "Stop!" she screamed, but no one listened.

From her new position, she looked up at the hole in the roof above her. She was back in the village with the subsidiaries to the Pride—the village people who served the cats with tribute, obedience, and blind worship.

Light streamed through the roof hole and framed a human head looming over her. She couldn't make out the features of its face with the light behind it. She tried to blink to make out who it was, but her eyes didn't work. Her eyelids must be swollen shut from the beating.

Then the man spoke to her and she recognized the booming voice of Harmon Farley, one of the Pride's most loyal supporters. He brought his face right up close to hers and his venom breath seared her torn skin.

"You should know better than that," he snapped. "We will never stop until you're dead. You're a slag! A slag has no understanding with the Pride. A slag doesn't know how superior the cats of the Pride are to humans. If you weren't a slag, you would know how much better off you are in the Pride than anywhere else. Only a slag like you would turn your back on the Pride—and for what? For a life in the dirt in the jungle? Are you going to wander around the universe looking for a place to settle down? You'll never find a place as good as the Pride. But you're only a slag. You deserve to live in the dirt and you'll die in the dirt. That's all you're good for."

He straightened up and a rain of blows and kicks pounded Dina all over her body. She curled into a ball, covered her head with her arms, and screamed for her life. How much longer could she stay conscious?

Her body went numb. She only felt the pain from a great distance. One more good kick to her head and the lights would go out.

"Please," she sobbed. "Take me to Senator Renfroe. If I'm going to die, let him be the one to kill me. If the Pride is the best place in the universe for me and I'm going to die, at least let the cats kill me."

"You don't deserve to be in the same room with a cat like Senator Renfroe," Farley shot back. "We're the village factors. It's our job to deal with you."

"Please," Dina whimpered, "you can beat me all you like and I might be a worthless slag, but I came back, didn't I? I ran away, but I came back to the Pride. Please just tell Senator Renfroe I'm here. He'll know how to deal with me."

"*We* know how to deal with you," Farley told her and kicked her again in the ribs. "If I have anything to say about it, you'll never make it out of this village alive. In fact, you'll never make it out of this house. So you came back. You should have known what would happen to you. You ran away. That makes you a slag."

"I'm not a slag!" she cried. "I have an understanding with the Pride. That's why I came back. I want to take my place in the Pride."

A low chuckle rumbled through the room. "Even slags have a place in the Pride," a soft male voice murmured. "They have a place two meters underground." He broke into a wicked laugh that traveled around the circle of other men in the room.

Another factor stepped out of the shadows, squatted down by Dina's head, and the faint light glanced off his cheekbones and forehead so Dina could see him clearly.

"I'm disappointed in you, Dina," he murmured. "I expected better from you."

"Alexander Mathus!" she exclaimed. "Have you been here the whole time?"

He nodded and glanced around the room. "Didn't you know? This is my house."

"Your house?" Dina followed his gaze as best she could from her place on the floor. "But where are Darcy and the children?"

"I wouldn't let them stick around for something like this. They went to one of Darcy's friends' house. My family will only come back after you're gone. I wouldn't want them having anything to do with a slag like you, not even to see you come to your rightful end."

Dina's heart sank. Darcy was the only person in Prideland who ever admitted to Dina that she wanted to get out. Dina had been working to help Darcy and hundreds of others escape from the Pride, but it didn't work out that way.

Now Dina was as much a prisoner of the Pride as everyone else on this planet. If Dina died now, neither Darcy nor anyone else stood any chance of escaping.

"I would have liked to see Darcy again," Dina remarked, "if only for a few seconds. I would have liked to thank her for her hospitality the last time I stayed with you."

Alexander made a face. Of course he didn't believe a word Dina said and why should he? He stood up and kicked Dina hard in the stomach. She groaned in agony and clutched her abdomen while she gasped to catch her breath, but he only squatted down next to her again like nothing ever happened.

"You had a fine way of showing your thanks the last time we saw you in this village," he reminded her. "We took you into our home when you'd almost frozen to death in that storm and how did you repay our kindness? You ran away again. That's when I knew you were an unredeemable slag."

"I might have been a slag then, but I'm not anymore. I've learned my lesson. I've come to an understanding with the Pride."

"Do you really expect me to believe that?" he asked.

Her mind spun. She had to find some way to delay her punishment. Maybe if Renfroe found out where she was, he would come and save her. "Just give me a chance to prove it."

"Give you a chance?" Alexander snapped. "What do you think we've been doing all along? We've given you every chance to come to an understanding with the Pride. I see no reason to give you another one. You knew the price of running away and now you're going to pay it."

"I tried," she whined. "I really tried. I just didn't know."

"You didn't know?" Farley bellowed in the background. "You knew perfectly well. Didn't you go to classes and festivals? Didn't the other helpers tell you? You knew. Of course you knew."

Alexander changed his tone back to his soft, friendly, helpful voice. He could change his tone in a heartbeat when he needed to. "You're forgetting something, Dina. I was the first person in Prideland you ever talked to. I was there when you and your friends landed on this planet. I took you to your first class to teach you the understanding of the Pride."

"You beat us all up!" Dina reminded him. "How could we come to an understanding with the Pride? We didn't know anything then and we couldn't learn when you kept beating us all night long."

"And don't forget the festivals you went to in the city," Farley added. "I remember seeing you there, but you didn't celebrate the cats the way the other helpers did. You sat there stiff and sullen. I saw you, so don't try to deny it."

"How could you see me in that crowd?" she asked. "There must have been a thousand people in that building."

"Oh, I know all about you. I can spot a slag in a sea of faces. It doesn't take much when the whole crowd is on its feet, cheering and waving their arms, to spot the one person sitting there like a stone."

"I never thought...." she began.

"And don't forget that hunt I took you on. I remember the look on your face when Khalid and Hector reduced that slag. I remember how you wanted us to bury him instead of tending Senator Renfroe the way Hector told us to."

"That man was a human being," she snarled. "We just watched those cats drag him down when he was fighting for his life and the life of his companion."

"Your duty is to your benefactor. Renfroe took you in and did everything he could to bring you to an understanding with the Pride. You wanted to leave him lying there unconscious while you buried that worthless slag. Only another slag could think that way."

She opened her mouth to argue back, but Alexander raised his hand to silence her. "It doesn't matter. You've had all the chances a person could ask for. You've seen the Children's Festivals, too. Darcy and I took you to see our daughter Sonya receive the House of Man and you shamed my family in front of Lord Helion with your behavior."

Dina turned away feeling sick. "I didn't know about it then. That was the first time I ever found out about the House of Man."

"Nonsense," Alexander snapped. "You must have known about it before."

"I saw it, but I didn't know what it was. I didn't know the cats scratched the scars into the flesh of every subsidiary and helper in the Pride. I never knew before that day how they got so maimed and broken and that the cats do it to stop people from running away and fighting back."

Alexander smiled a little and shook his head. "You see? You don't have an understanding with the Pride. You're still talking like a slag."

"I'm not a slag!" she wailed. "I just didn't know. Now I do. I understand the Pride and I'm ready to live with that understanding. How was I supposed to react? Why can't you give me another chance? I promise I won't break the understanding again."

Even as she said those words, she knew it was hopeless. The village factors had their own understanding with the Pride. They had no choice but to deal with her as a slag. They had to make an example of her for the other subsidiaries and the helpers in the city. They all had to see her get her punishment.

She understood all of that. That was the understanding she'd come to with the Pride. At long last, she knew every horrible thing there was to know about the Pride, but she still came back. If she died now, she would die with an understanding of the Pride.

Farley stepped out of the gloom and brought his stick down hard on Dina's shoulder. The shock jerked her back from the brink of unconsciousness. Tears ran down her cheeks and she choked on her own blood. Blood and saliva ran out of her mouth and down her chin.

Kicking feet pounded the whole length of her body. She couldn't keep track anymore of who was kicking her where. One of them hit her in the back of the head and lights exploded in front of her eyes.

How much longer could she survive this? It wouldn't be too much longer and then she could die. It would be so peaceful and quiet once she finally drifted over the edge.

She started to drift away under another hail of blows, but she snapped alert again when the door of the house opened. She didn't see anyone come in. No human shape blocked out the light before the door closed and the light disappeared.

Her eyes took a second to adjust, and when they did, she sucked her breath in through her teeth and floundered to get up as a black panther slunk around to her left.

His gleaming yellow eyes bored into her and he panted through his parted lips to show his fangs in the dim light.

He limped on his right hind leg, and when he finally stopped and faced her, he held that foot up off the ground. She was facing Khalid, the panther she'd fought and injured in her final battle to get off the planet.

He swung his head around toward the factors and growled low under his breath. "Leave this one to me. She attacked me with a weapon and she tore my leg open breaking out of Prideland. You all know the penalty. She's mine."

The men backed away. "We know. We only wanted to do our duty."

"You did your duty. Now leave her to me. I owe her my teeth around her throat."

The men retreated to the outer edge of the room. Dina struggled to get off the floor, but she couldn't move her legs. Every particle of her being hurt too much. She couldn't fight Khalid again—not like this. She had nothing to fight him with but her bare hands.

His lips and nose twitched and his nostrils flared to catch her scent. He must be able to smell her fear. He paced right and left eyeing her with intense scrutiny while she floundered and choked on the ground in front of him.

He dragged out the moment just to delay the inevitable. She would die in his clutches, not under the sticks of these worthless subsidiaries.

He finally took another step toward her and she tried to close her eyes, but her swollen eyelids wouldn't close. She had no choice but to watch her fate close in on her.

Every fiber of her being screamed for her to get up, at least to fight back if she couldn't run away. Seeing him toy with her sparked a wave of rage that immediately switched to murderous hate. If she couldn't fight or kill him, she had to hurt him another way.

She flipped onto her stomach and pushed herself up on her hands to glare at him. She could just imagine how hideous she looked with blood running out of her mouth and her face smashed to a bloody pulp.

As soon as she faced him, her hatred for him overflowed in malicious laughter. "Does your leg hurt, Khalid? I'm surprised you came here to fight me. You wouldn't want to do anything to risk injuring any of your other legs, would you?"

He growled under his breath. She wouldn't have recognized a cat's laughter if she hadn't spent four weeks in Prideland. "You—fight me? You couldn't fight me now if you wanted to. This sore leg of mine won't stop me from tasting your blood."

"You're a coward, Khalid," Dina spat. "You wouldn't dare to attack me if your lackeys here hadn't softened me up for you. You don't dare to face me when I'm strong and healthy. I've seen you fight before and you've never fought a full-grown man by yourself. You better be careful if you come near me again. If you attack me, you might be able to kill me, but not before I hurt you just the way I hurt you before. I'll make sure you never hurt so much as a tree lizard again."

Khalid raised one of his paws, extended his claws, and slashed the air screeching and yowling. He hissed and spat at her, but she didn't stop. Her own anger kept her going to bait him even more. He would attack soon and then all her troubles would be over.

"Do you want to test yourself against a defenseless woman, Khalid?" she yelled. "Now's your chance. And later, when your friends ask how you hurt your leg, you can tell them you attacked a woman half your size and she drove you away to run off into the jungle. How does that sit with you, Khalid?" She opened her mouth as wide as it would go and she laughed in his face.

Something moved on the other side of the room and Farley's voice rang off the walls. "Don't let her talk to you like this, Khalid! She's a worthless slag. You shouldn't have to listen to her. Let me shut her up for you."

Khalid rounded on him and roared in fury. "Get back! Don't come near her! She's mine. I'll deal with her myself. I don't need you or anyone else doing my dirty work for me."

Dina smirked to herself when she saw her taunts hit home, but she didn't smirk for long before Khalid sprang at her.

She only had time to roll onto her back and raise her throbbing arms off the floor before he pounced. The next thing she knew, he landed on top of her and snapped his jaws in her face.

She shoved her hands against his chest, but even then, she felt her own weakness. She might as well be pushing against him with a wet rag.

He exploited her weakness to the limit, crushed her under his weight, and her arms buckled when he forced his weight down right on her chest. He opened his mouth and his jaws hung suspended over her face to close on her neck.

She dodged her head downward and to the side just in time to stop him from closing on her throat and he screamed in fury. The sound alone made her flinch and she tucked her chin against her chest to protect her neck.

His mouth closed around her face and head and the points of his teeth pricked her skin. The pressure of his bite tightened around her skull and she almost let herself relax into it. She couldn't fight anymore.

She shut her eyes as tight as she could. She didn't see the door fly open or the light flood into the room, but she heard it. The men yelled out and those two sounds made her peek out a streak of movement and a flurry of activity.

The next instant, a lightning bolt flashed across the room and some shape she couldn't make out sailed past her. A cannonball struck Khalid from the side, tore him off her, and sent him rolling across the floor.

Khalid landed across the room, rolled to his feet, and spun around to face his attacker. He flattened his ears against the side of his head, slashed his claws, and screeched and spat at an enormous object standing over her.

It blocked her view and she struggled to force her mind to think clearly enough to believe what she was seeing. Her eyes refocused and that was when she noticed the stripes on an enormous cat's underside. The fog blew away from her mind and she realized that Renfroe was standing over her.

Chapter 2

Dina sat in her old place on the stone bench by the fountain in Renfroe's garden. She gazed around at the shrubs and trees. This garden cast its old hypnotic relaxing spell over her mind and body.

The music of falling water soothed her exhausted brain. The tree lizards squeaked and squawked in the branches and jumped from one tree to another. Glistening moths fluttered through the sun's golden beams, landed on the leaves, and took off again going somewhere else.

Dina relaxed into the scene. She knew this part of Prideland so well. She understood this quiet beauty the same way she understood the other part of Prideland—the part that howled for her life and attacked her whenever she moved or tried to do anything. She could rest here. Just for this moment, she was safe.

She let herself drift into a peaceful trance. Renfroe never made any sound when he moved anyway. He could sneak up on her whenever he wanted and she would never hear him coming.

This time, though, he made some sort of clicking noise with his tongue that made her turn around. She didn't smile when she saw him standing under the portico.

He tilted his head to one side and studied her. What did he see? Was he angry at her for running away—again? She hadn't seen her reflection since she came back from the village, but she felt the factor's bruises and Khalid's bite marks. She could just imagine what she looked like.

"So you're home again, Dina," he finally rumbled.

She stared at him for a second and then let her chin fall onto her chest. She stared at her hands in her lap. She didn't look up when he paced across the courtyard and sat down a few yards away where he could watch her from a distance.

"You lied to me," he murmured. "You said you wouldn't run away and then you went and did exactly that. The whole time we laid together on the parlor floor, the whole time you kept telling me you wanted me and cared for me—the whole time you planned to run away. How can I trust you again?"

"You don't have to ask me that," she choked. She could barely speak above a whisper. "You already know the answer."

He cocked his head the other way. "I do?"

She nodded, but she didn't look up. She couldn't, so she studied the skin around her fingernails. "You know I'll never run away again."

"And how do I know that?"

She raised her eyes to meet his gaze. "You should know better than anyone. I have an understanding with the Pride now."

"You do?"

She nodded again. "You don't have to ask. You already know."

"Tell me anyway. Tell me about your understanding."

She turned away. She couldn't look at him, so she soothed her swollen eyes on the brilliant green of the leaves nearby. "I got away. I made it all the way back to my Pod and I flew away to my ship. I was back on board the *Savannah* for three whole days. Did you know that?"

He followed her gaze out into the garden. "I knew it."

"Then you know I came back of my own free will."

He stared at her, but he didn't say anything.

"I made it all the way there, but I came back. That should tell you everything you need to know."

"Why did you come back?" he asked. "If you went to such lengths to escape and you succeeded, why did you come back?"

"Don't you know? I thought it would be obvious."

"No, it isn't obvious," he replied. "If I knew, I wouldn't ask."

"I came back to be with you. There. You wanted me to say it and I said it. I came back because nothing can compare with the life I have here with you. I had a relationship with Tom on board the *Savannah*. I had a career and friends and the respect of my superiors. All of that is gone now. I have no more reason to be there than I do to be here. I have no reason to be anywhere. I have no life left anywhere. The only thing left is you."

He stretched his neck toward her and sniffed at her. He could always tell when she was lying. He could hear her heart beating and smell any change in her scent. He knew she was telling the truth.

"I told you before, Dina," he replied. "I care for you and I want you here. I want you to care for me, too, but if that's the only reason you have for coming back, then you don't have enough of an understanding with the Pride to stay here. You have to commit yourself to the Pride on your own terms. That's the only way you'll be able to stay here with me."

"But don't you understand? I have committed myself. If I hadn't come to an understanding with the Pride, my feelings for you wouldn't have been enough to make me come back. I'm part of this Pride now. I'm just as much a part of the Pride as any of these other helpers. My place is here. I have no other place in the whole universe. I have no home but here and I can live my best life here. My destiny is here, and whatever happens, I'll always have to come back here."

He looked away from her. He didn't have to question her. He could tell from her smell and the tone of her voice she meant it.

He finally let out a heavy sigh. "I didn't think I would ever get you back. You scared the life out of me. I thought I'd lost you for good."

She raised her head to peek at him. "You were scared? I didn't think anything scared you."

"Losing you scares me. You should know that by now. You say you have no other life outside the Pride. Well, I have no other life apart from you. I don't know what I'd do if you left and didn't come back."

"I won't leave again," she told him.

He nodded, took a few steps toward her, and sat down on the grass at her feet, but he didn't cross the last divide to touch her. "I'm not sure how to approach you. I hardened myself against you after you left. That was the only way I could cope with the pain of you leaving. I'm not sure how to come back to you now."

"Can't we just go back to the way we were before? Can't we just settle into each other? We had a nice way of relating before. It would be nice if we could just go back to that."

"It would," he murmured.

She put out her hand to touch him, but she stopped herself with her hand hanging in mid-air. He didn't turn around. Why did she hesitate to touch him? Didn't she just say she wanted to?

A flood of conflicting emotions overwhelmed her. If she touched him now, she would be giving herself over to him without reservation. Isn't that what she planned to do when she came back—to give herself to him, body and soul?

Giving herself to him meant sexually, too. She'd given herself to him once before, but that was to give herself a chance to escape.

She belonged to him now and she wanted to belong to him. She wouldn't run away again and being here with him meant giving herself to him no holds barred.

She let her hand fall and her fingers sank into his fur. A wave of electric shivers ran outward from her hand through his skin and he shuddered under her touch. He turned his head even farther away so he looked in the opposite direction from her.

"What's wrong?" she asked. "Don't you want me touching you anymore?"

"I want you to," he growled.

"Then why do you shiver like that? You won't even look at me."

He puffed his breath out through his nostrils, but he still didn't turn around. "I don't know."

"Thank you for saving me from Khalid. I thought I was dead for sure that time."

He chuckled low in his chest. "He will never forgive you for hurting his leg. He will never stop trying to kill you. You'll have to be especially careful when you go out of this house now. He'll be waiting to catch you alone, and if he does, there won't be anything to stop him from killing you. I'll have to go with you when you go into the city. Even in broad daylight, you wouldn't be safe alone."

"You told me before. The Pride doesn't intervene in who or what a cat can kill."

"Khalid always was a dangerous killer. Now he has a vendetta against you. He'll never rest until he gets revenge."

"I never meant to hurt him. I was fighting for my life."

Renfroe shook his head. "That doesn't matter. You're human and he's a cat. It's bad enough that you escape, but the Pride can't let you get away with attacking him. You should have been reduced on the spot for killing Fallon. Khalid isn't the only cat who wants you dead."

"You're the only thing that saved me. The subsidiaries would have beaten me to death if Khalid hadn't interrupted and Khalid would have killed me if you hadn't come. I owe you my life."

"You don't understand. I've lost my standing in the Pride for defending you. None of them will look sideways at me after I stopped Khalid from killing you. They say I've gone soft in the head. Some of them are even saying I should be driven out of the Senate."

"But you're the Chairman," she pointed out. "How could they get rid of you?"

"Oh, they could get rid of me if they wanted to. They wouldn't have any trouble with that. I'm still Chairman, but I'm only hanging on by a thread. They say I put you before my own kind. They say I've lost my understanding with the Pride and this is the first time that's ever happened to a cat. You have to admit they have a point."

"But didn't you say the Pride has no negative consequences for the cats at all? If you chose to defend me against Khalid, who's to stop you?"

"No, that's not what I said at all," he replied. "I said the Pride has no negative consequences for killing of any kind. That's why I should have let Khalid kill you. I'm the one who tried to impose consequences on Khalid for killing my helper. I shouldn't have done that."

Dina pulled her hand back from his shoulder. Maybe she shouldn't be touching him after all. "Do you regret it?"

"No, but my position in this Pride is shaky at best. I won't be able to do anything like that again. In fact, if you step out of line one more time, I might have to kill you myself just to show the other cats that I still know my own place in the Pride."

Dina's breath caught. "You wouldn't kill me, would you?"

He turned to face her at last. His eyes locked onto her and held her in their magnetic grip. "I would never harm a hair on your head, Dina.

You know that. I would protect you with my life. I just want you to know where we stand. The other cats won't put up with me making an exception of you any longer. I've crossed the line too many times already. If they come for you, they'll kill me on their way to get to you."

She dropped her eyes back to her hands in her lap. "I didn't know it had gone that far."

"If you understand the Pride the way you say you do, you should know I took a big risk bringing you back from the canton alive the first time you ran away. Now I've threatened Khalid when he wanted to kill you. You're sitting here relatively unharmed...."

"Unharmed!" she snapped.

"I said *relatively* unharmed," he returned. "You're relatively unharmed considering what they wanted to do to you and what they would have done to you if I hadn't intervened. If you understand the Pride the way you say you do, you know the subsidiaries should have killed you when they had the chance. If you had been anyone other than my helper, they would have."

"I know," she whispered.

"So you see, you're living on borrowed time. One of these days, one of the other cats will get to you before I do. When that happens, there is no power in all of Prideland that can save you. If I tried to pull the same stunt again and protect you from them, they would drag me down along with you. They wouldn't send Khalid by himself to face me. The whole Helion gang--in fact, the whole Pride--would come and they would take us both."

What could she say to that? The trickling water in the fountain marked the passing of time and she didn't answer.

At last, Renfroe sighed again and Dina glanced at him. He hadn't moved from the spot by her knee. She laid her hand on his shoulder again. "I really am grateful for what you did. I didn't know it had cost you so much, but now that I know, I'm even more grateful."

He didn't turn around. He kept staring out into the garden. "I don't want your gratitude. I did it for purely selfish reasons. I did it because I wanted you here with me."

She threaded her fingers through his fur....all the way down to his warm skin. "Then come to me. Why do you stand there with your back to me? I'm right here. Come near me and be with me."

Not even his ears twitched. "I don't think I can. I gave you my heart and you ran away from me. I hardened myself against you to get over the pain of losing you. I don't think I can come back from that."

Dina's heart skipped a beat and her throat tightened with desperate sobs. She couldn't lose him, not now, not after she sacrificed her freedom and almost her life to be with him. "Please, Renfroe. Please come back. I only want to be with you. Please, just let me be with you. That's all I want in the world."

His shoulder rose and fell with his breathing under her hand, but other than that, he stood perfectly motionless. Only his voice told her he wasn't a statue of a tiger.

"You haven't really come to an understanding with the Pride. You want me, but you don't really want to be part of the Pride. You still speak against the Pride and you use your old nasty language for the way the Pride works. You might know what the Pride stands for and the way it works, but you haven't accepted it—not really."

Tears sprang to her eyes at the thought of losing him—now, after all this time. Those tears would fall in a minute, and when they did, she wouldn't be able to stop them. Then she wouldn't be able to talk to him at all anymore.

"But I have accepted it, Renfroe," she choked. "It's only natural that I would be shocked when I learned what the Pride was all about.

You can't blame me for that, but I'm here. I came back of my own free will to live in the Pride and be a part of the Pride. I've given my whole life for it.....and who knows? Maybe, before this is all over, I *will* sacrifice my life for it. You can't ask me for more than that."

He didn't answer. He sat at her side, not moving, not making a sound.

His stillness crushed her more than anything else she ever experienced in all her time on the planet. If he didn't come back to her, if they couldn't find a way to bridge this gap between them, what would become of her? Would he send her away? If he did, she was as good as dead. Then again, if he didn't come back to her, her life wasn't worth anything anyway.

"Please, Renfroe," she whispered. "Please come back."

He didn't answer. He roamed somewhere out there at the limit of his vision, on the horizon beyond this garden. He'd already left her alone with this hopeless grief. She'd wasted her only chance at freedom and now she'd lost him, too.

Her hand fell away from his shoulder and her chin sank onto her chest. All the despair and pain of the last few days rushed back to her, only this time, she sat in his garden with him at her side.

She was safe now. No cats or their loyal human helpers would come here to attack or punish her. She could let her guard down here, but she didn't have him.

She'd lost the one person on this wretched planet--maybe in the whole universe--who cared for her and to whom she could give her heart. The empty void yawned before her, all the way to the farthest reaches of space, but he wasn't there anymore. He wasn't anywhere she could find him or ever get him back.

The ache in her throat and her heart overcame her last shred of resistance. Choking sobs broke out of her and those hot, painful tears streaked down her cheeks. She hung her head and poured out her grief to no one. No one heard and no one cared.

Out of the depths of her anguish, she became aware of a prickling sensation in her hands. She opened her eyes between sobs and looked down into her lap. Her tears spattered on her hand. She almost didn't understand when Renfroe let out another deep sigh and laid his head in her lap.

She closed her eyes and wept in pure relief.

Chapter 3

Dina and Renfroe strolled through the deserted house. She rested her hand on his shoulder, and he walked so close to her that his shoulder sometimes bumped into her knee. She smiled to herself when it happened and made no move to put any distance between them.

"Where is everybody?" she asked. "I haven't seen anyone since I got home."

"They're hiding from you," he told her.

"From me? What for? I've only ever tried to be friends with them."

"You know Buck and Belinda can't have anything more to do with you," Renfroe reminded her. "Buck is a factor. It's his job to keep you in line and punish you for breaking the understanding between the people and the Pride. He's already visited Belinda for failing to stop you from escaping. She won't want to take a chance on that happening again."

"I know, but I thought they would be around at least to do their jobs."

"They'll come out to do their jobs when they know you're not going to see you. You can't expect them to do anything else."

"Then I'll be all alone here," she remarked.

"I'll be here," he replied. "You won't be completely alone."

"I meant I won't have any other human beings to talk to. I didn't think it would be like this."

"What did you think?" he asked.

"I thought I could make up with Belinda, at least. She said she didn't want to have anything more to do with me, but I thought she might have said that in the heat of the moment after her run-in with Buck. I thought she might get over it in time and we could start over."

"I wouldn't count on that," he told her. "I suppose you don't remember much about what happened after we left the village."

She cocked her head to one side. "What do you mean?"

"I didn't think you remembered it. You were pretty far gone. After Khalid left, I ordered the subsidiaries to bring you back here. You couldn't walk so they carried you on a stretcher."

"They carried me?" she gasped. "That must have taken all night. It's a long walk from the village to the city."

"It was the only way to get you back to this house without the other cats coming after you. I had to get you back to this house as quickly as possible and I didn't want to run the risk of using a wagon."

"So they carried me. They must have been furious."

"They have nothing to complain about," he shot back. "They live in the service of the cats. I ordered it. They did it. That's the way the Pride works."

"So what does that have to do with Buck and Belinda?"

"That's the part I thought you didn't remember. They brought you in through the kitchen door. All helpers use that door and the subsidiaries wouldn't use any other door. They set you down on the kitchen floor and then they ran away. They didn't want to stick around you, either."

"Wonderful," she grumbled under her breath.

"I ordered Buck and Belinda to carry you into the parlor," he went on. "Then I made them stand side by side in front of me and I told them both that if either of them laid so much as a finger on you, I'd kill them myself. I told them you were here to be my helper, and if either of them didn't like it, they could find another position then and there. I told them they didn't have to like it, but they would do their duty to me and treat you with respect or I would reduce them myself without a moment's hesitation."

"I'm sure they were delighted with the situation," Dina snarled. "After the mess Buck made of Belinda's face, I'm sure he would have picked up where the subsidiaries left off."

"Exactly," Renfroe agreed. "That's why I had to say what I said. If I hadn't, you wouldn't have survived a day in this house. They both have a very good understanding with the Pride. They would have reduced you."

"Now I understand why they stay hidden. What happened after they left me in the parlor?"

"Nothing happened. You slept there until just before I found you at the fountain. You must have woken up in the parlor and then gone outside."

"I did, but I didn't know you put me there when I came back. I didn't know what happened."

"That's what happened," he replied.

Dina gazed at the statuary on either side of the corridor. "I suppose Belinda will go back to leaving my food on a tray on the floor outside my room the way she did before."

"You aren't going back to your old room," he told her.

Her head spun around. "Why not? I thought it was working pretty well."

"It was, but that was before. It won't do now."

"Why not?" she asked.

He turned his head the other way so she couldn't see his eyes. "I don't want you staying in that room anymore."

"But that makes no sense," she countered. "It's the only place in the house where a human can lie down and I can't sleep on the parlor floor every night."

"No, you won't sleep on the parlor floor, but you won't sleep in that room, either. I have something else in mind."

"Oh. What is that?"

He sauntered down the corridor toward Dina's old room. "I'll show you."

She followed him between the marble statues and the potted trees. Everything looked exactly the same as it did the night she left. She couldn't expect anything to change in the space of a few days, but it felt like years had passed for all the change it worked in her life.

Renfroe drew level with the door to her old room, but he walked right past it. She glanced at the door, but the room must have been the same inside, too. He wouldn't have changed it.

He led her all the way to the far end of the corridor before she realized she'd never been to that end of the house before. She'd always stayed between her own room and the main part of the house. She hadn't explored any further. She hadn't had a chance.

Renfroe stopped at another closed door, sniffed it, and then turned to look up at her.

"What's in here?" she asked.

"Open it."

She hesitated. She'd seen so many horrors on this planet. She didn't think she could handle another one. "It isn't anything bad, is it?"

"It's nothing bad," he replied. "Consider it a gift from me to you."

"A gift?" she repeated.

"I wanted to do something nice for you.....to show my appreciation for your decision to come back."

Dina's eyes flew open. The last thing she expected to come from her escape was some kind of token of appreciation from him. She ought to be punished, not appreciated.

A chill went up her arm when she put her hand on the metal doorknob, but it opened at her touch and she stepped into the room.

A big glass double door on the opposite wall let light stream through from the garden and another walled patio outside. It looked just like the one she and Renfroe always sat in except that this patio didn't have a fountain.

The sun shone in on plush red carpet and brightened up the room. Then she saw it. A giant four-poster bed with a curtained canopy occupied almost the entire room.

A quilted purple satin bedspread covered the mattress and tasseled cushions piled against the headboard. Dina gasped in astonishment at the sight of that bed.

"Do you like it?" Renfroe asked.

"Like it!" she murmured. "It's magnificent! Where did you get it?"

"I did some research in the Senate archives on the origins of human culture. According to our records, this is the type of bed your people sometimes use. Do you think it will work?"

"Work!" she cried.

"I mean do you think you could stay in this room and sleep on this bed," he explained. "On a long-term basis, I mean."

"It's exquisite! It's like nothing I've ever slept on before. I wouldn't want to get it dirty."

"You wouldn't get it dirty," Renfroe told her. "You're going to sleep in it, not walk on it in your muddy boots."

"I only mean it's much fancier than anything I'm used to. I'm almost afraid to touch it."

"Then it won't work." He let out a deep sigh. "I'll have to think of something else." He turned back toward the door.

"No, no!" Dina called after him. "It will work just fine. I'm just surprised, that's all. It's wonderful. I'm in shock. Thank you. It's the best gift I've ever received."

He stared at her. "Then it will work? You'll be all right to sleep in here and stay in here on a long-term basis?"

"Yes!" she exclaimed. "I'll be more than all right. I'll be honored. I don't know how to thank you."

"Don't thank me. Just stay in here. That's all the thanks I need."

She moved further into the room until she stood in the middle of the floor. She turned all the way around taking in every detail of the bed, the other furnishings, and the view through the door.

Everything she saw made her catch her breath and gasp all over again. She never would have known a room like this could exist on this planet.

"I don't even want to know where you got all this," she remarked.

"Then I won't tell you." He followed her into the room, stood next to the bed, sniffed at the bedding, and curled up his nose. "I don't understand these things myself."

"What things?" she asked.

"Beds," he replied. "I've never used one, so I don't know what they're good for."

"They're only for sleeping on. They're only good for giving you somewhere to sleep other than the floor."

"The floor has always been fine for me," he growled. "The only reason I would sleep in something like this is if you were in it."

Dina blushed. "Now I understand. You want this to be our bed, not just mine."

"Of course. That should be obvious."

She lowered her eyes and stared down at the floor. "Now it is."

"Would you like to try it out?" he asked. "Don't you want to make sure it's not too soft or too hard?"

"Too hard?" She laughed. "I don't think there's any danger of that. I'm sure it will be fine."

"Why don't you lie down on it and see?"

She glanced toward the bed.

"Aren't you tired?" he asked.

"Tired?" Did her voice really come out of her mouth or did she just think it?

"You look terrible," he told her.

"Thanks a lot," she snapped.

"I only meant you look like you need some more rest to recover from your experience. I thought you might like to rest on the bed."

She stared at the bed and her whole face, ears, and neck turned bright red.

"Isn't that what a bed is for?" he asked.

"This bed is for something else," she muttered.

He swung his head away. "As you wish. I only thought you might like to rest in here instead of on the parlor floor, but if you don't, I'll go tell Belinda to bring you something to eat instead. And I'll tell her not to leave it on the floor outside the room, either."

"Where will she put it?" Dina asked.

"Why, in here, of course," he replied.

"What if....?" How should she put this? "What if we're....in here. ....together?"

He narrowed his eyes at her. "Oh, I see what you mean."

Dina giggled. "We can't exactly put up the 'Do Not Disturb' sign."

"The what?"

"Never mind," she mumbled.

"I suppose, we'll have to develop some sort of signal to her when we don't want her coming in."

"Exactly," Dina replied.

"Maybe you could hang something from the doorknob. Some piece of cloth or something."

"Perfect," Dina replied.

"That settles that, then. Now, do you want to lie down and rest or not? Because if you don't, I can go tell Belinda to bring you something to eat."

Dina chose her next words with extra care. "If I do lie down, am I going to sleep or are you going to join me?"

"Would it be so terrible if I did join you? I thought that's what the bed was for, for us to share it."

"I only want to make sure I know what to expect," she told him. "I don't want to be caught off guard."

"I won't come if you don't want me to. If you want this room and this bed to be only for you, I won't come and I won't share it with you. I won't say I won't be disappointed because I will be, but I'll keep my distance for your sake. I put this room together because I hoped we could share it."

"We will share it," she insisted. "I want to share it with you. I'm talking about right now. If I lie down in the bed, I won't be lying down to rest, will I? You'll lie down with me and we'll.....do whatever we're going to do in it."

"Oh, I see what you mean," he repeated. "Yes, I guess that was a rather backward way of putting it. I suppose you won't be resting at all, will you?" He chuckled to himself.

Dina made a face. "So, is that what this is all about? Am I lying down to rest or are we lying down together....to be together?"

Renfroe sniffed and looked her square in the eye. "If you lie down in that bed right now, I'll lie down with you—unless you don't want me to. If you let me, I will."

Dina glanced over at the bed again. It sure did look like a nice place to lie down. He was right. She would give anything to get off her feet right now......and having him at her side, wrapping her arms around him the way she used to.....that would be so nice. She'd like nothing better than to take shelter in the bulk of his massive presence right now.

"Okay," she replied. "I'll lie down." But for some reason, she still couldn't move toward that bed. It was too fancy for a.....a what? The only word that would come to her mind was, *slag*. The bed was too nice for a slag like her.

Here she was with the scars and bruises of her recent beating on her face and body. She wore the badge of shame all slags ought to wear—all slags who survived. She belonged in the cesspit with the Elite Battalion, not in this grand bedchamber with Senator Renfroe.

She looked back and found him studying her. "What's the matter, Dina? Why don't you lie down in your bed?"

She dropped her eyes back to the floor. The shame of letting him down, of throwing his tenderness and protection back in his face—it all overwhelmed her.

She didn't deserve him any more than she deserved this room. She didn't deserve to live in the Pride, not after she'd flouted all its rules and conventions. No wonder Belinda and the other helpers wouldn't be caught in her presence anymore.

"Come on, Dina," Renfroe coaxed. "Come lie down with me. It's been too long."

She stumbled to the bed without looking. She couldn't look until her hand fell on the satin bedspread. She sat down, but he didn't move to join her. He sat a few feet away from her, watching her and waiting to see what she would do.

Her head sagged and she choked for each shuddering breath. Then she felt the bed shake when Renfroe jumped up onto the bed. He stretched out on the bedspread behind her.

She turned around, but she still kept her eyes shut. She didn't want to see what was about to happen. She leaned back against the stack of pillows.

Renfroe didn't move while he waited for her to lie back on the bed. He didn't move until she stretched out full length next to him. He didn't move at all except to let out a long breath when she put her arms around his chest and buried her face in his fur.

Chapter 4

The glass doors in the bedroom wall stood black and empty to the night outside. Dina curled into Renfroe's embrace under the satin sheets of the bed.

"I'm hungry," she murmured.

"Go get something to eat," he told her.

She froze. "What do you mean?"

"What do you think I mean? Go to the kitchen and get something to eat if you're hungry."

She hesitated again. "I've never done that before. Belinda always brought me my food. She might get mad if I go digging around in her kitchen."

"It's my kitchen, not hers. I'm telling you to go. You don't have to wait for her to bring it to you. This is your home. Go get whatever you want."

She thought it over. Then she swept out of bed. "Okay. Do you want anything?"

He watched her put her clothes on and then he laid his head back down on his paws. "If you find something for me, bring it back."

"What do you like to eat?"

"You've seen me eat enough times. You know I'm not picky. Just grab anything that looks good." He shut his eyes.

Dina pulled her clothes on, slipped out of the room, and she caught herself smiling when she walked down the corridor.

This was the first time she really felt at home here. She belonged here now. This was her home. She had her own room she shared with Renfroe.

Now here she was, on her way to the kitchen for a midnight snack, just the way she would have done in any house on Earth. She found her way by feel and memory to the little door in the corridor wall leading to the kitchen.

Her smile evaporated when she pushed it open and found the room lit up by a lantern hanging from the ceiling. There was the old cook, Belinda, standing on a stool and extending her arms over her head to the top shelf of her pantry.

She scowled over her shoulder when she saw Dina enter the kitchen. "What are you doing here?"

"I only came to get something to eat. I didn't know you'd be in here. I thought you'd be asleep."

"I told you not to come in here again!" Belinda snapped. "You have no right to come in here after the way you behaved!"

"I know you don't want me in here," Dina countered. "I wouldn't have come if Renfroe hadn't told me to."

Belinda scowled at Dina, pursed her lips, and finally smacked them together in annoyance. "So what do you want? I suppose you think you're going to ransack the place until you find something that suits your fancy. Well, I'm here to tell you that isn't going to happen. You stand right there and don't set foot in this kitchen. You tell me what you want and I'll get it for you. I won't have you fouling the place when my back is turned."

"That's fine with me, Belinda. I never wanted to foul your kitchen. I'm perfectly happy to let you give me whatever you want to give me. I don't care what it is, as long as I eat. I haven't eaten anything in almost two days and Renfroe wants me to bring back something for him, too. Do you have anything suitable for him?"

"Of course I do," Belinda shot back. "I'm his cook, aren't I? What do you think this is? I wouldn't be much good to him if I didn't have anything in the house for him to eat, would I?" She turned her back on Dina and went back to whatever she was doing.

Dina looked around her. Belinda didn't make any move to fulfill Dina's request. Should she step farther into the kitchen?

Belinda had just told her not to, but Dina couldn't spend all night standing on the doorstep, either. Renfroe would wonder what happened to her and she didn't like the idea of a hungry tiger roaming the house looking for food. Anyone who happened to fall in his way could get a rude surprise.

Dina stared at the back of Belinda's head. How long should she stand here waiting?

She looked around the kitchen. Joints of meat hung from the ceiling along with cheese wrapped in cloth and strings of dried fruit. The sight of them made her mouth water, but she didn't dare to cross Belinda. Dina couldn't get those things down from the ceiling by herself anyway.

She waited a little longer and Belinda still didn't turn around. Two or three times, Dina opened her mouth to ask what she ought to do, but each time, she wound up closing it again without saying anything. Why did she have to ask for permission to get something to eat?

"Belinda?" she ventured.

Belinda whirled around. "What are you still doing here?"

"I told you. I'm supposed to bring back something for Renfroe to eat and I want something for myself, too."

Belinda stepped back from the pantry shelf and flew across the kitchen toward Dina. Dina took a step backward to get away from her, but she wound up backing up against the door instead. Was Belinda coming after her right now? Would Belinda visit her with a night of beatings and torture the way Buck visited Belinda when she let Dina escape?

Belinda startled her so badly that Dina never considered opening the door and running away. She flattened her back against the door, but Belinda didn't attack.

She crossed the kitchen in three long steps to the corner of her big worktable, bent down to a basket on the floor, tossed off the lid, and pulled out a live tree lizard by the tail.

The creature hung from her hand and swung next to Belinda's knees, let out a squawk, and twisted its head around to look at its surroundings.

Belinda shoved the lizard in Dina's face. "Here. Take that to Renfroe."

Dina didn't ask what she would do about her own hunger. In fact, in that moment, she didn't feel hungry at all. She wanted nothing more in the world than to get away from Belinda. Dina wanted to get away from that lizard, too, but she couldn't go back to Renfroe empty-handed.

She grabbed the lizard out of Belinda's hand and fled. She swung the creature by the tail exactly the way Belinda did and raced back along the corridor. The animal screeched, hissed in her hand, and contorted itself in every direction trying to see where it was and free itself from her grasp.

She burst through the bedroom door and stopped in the middle of the room. Renfroe raised his head from the pillow and examined her. "What's all this racket?"

Dina gasped for breath and struggled to pull herself together. She held up the lizard. "I brought you this."

Renfroe eyed it. "Where did you get that?"

"Belinda gave it to me.....for you."

He chuckled. "She knows what I like. It's not the same as a yearling fell deer, but it sure will hit the spot right about now." He licked his chops and hoisted himself off the bed. "Let's have it."

Dina examined the lizard and grimaced. "What do you want me to do with it? I hope you don't want me to skin it and clean it."

"Don't bother. Just set it down here."

"Where?" she asked.

"Right here."

"What?" she gasped. "On the bed?"

"Why not?" he asked.

Dina shrugged, went to the foot of the bed, and held up the lizard. Renfroe stood up on the bedspread and his eyes glittered dangerously. The lizard made eye contact with the enormous tiger and let out a piercing shriek. Dina held on tight to the animal's tail and set it down on the bed.

Renfroe tensed his muscles and waited. When the lizard felt Dina let go of its tail, it jumped onto all four feet and shot away across the bedspread, but Renfroe moved faster. He shot out one pay, pinned the lizard, and closed his jaws on its back.

A sickening crunch echoed through the room. Dina closed her eyes and looked away. Renfroe didn't notice her reaction.

He chuckled to himself, picked up the lizard, and its dead body hung out of both sides of his mouth. "Silly little things," he muttered. "They always try to get away."

He sat down on his haunches, crouched down on his belly, and clamped the dead lizard between his front paws, and licked his chops. "Hmm. Good. What are you having?"

She kept her head turned. She still found it impossible to look at him while he ate. "I already had something down in the kitchen," she lied. "You go ahead."

He didn't pay her any more attention. He chomped into his lizard, tore it apart, and spat out the parts he didn't want onto the bedspread. Dina sat down on a chair by the double door and gazed at the black squares of glass in the window.

"I don't suppose Belinda will want to come in and clean this room," she remarked. "I'll do it myself."

"What makes you say that?" he asked between mouthfuls. "Why wouldn't she clean in here?"

"She won't want to come in here."

"She has no choice. It's her job to clean the house."

Dina turned even farther away. "I don't think I'll go to the kitchen again."

"Why not? Was she rude to you? If she was, I'll have a word with her about that."

"Don't have a word with her about anything," she shot back. "Leave Belinda alone."

"What's wrong with you?" he asked. "You came all the way back here from your starship to be my special helper. That position has special benefits. You should profit from them. One of the benefits is that no other helper can be rude to you when you go the kitchen looking for food."

"I don't want special benefits. You said it yourself. I should have been killed when I came back. Belinda has a good understanding with the Pride. She's only doing what any good helper ought to do."

"You're right, but I won't have her or anyone else being rude to you. You're my helper and you're going to get all the benefits you can for that."

"Don't say anything to Belinda," Dina insisted. "She doesn't want me in the kitchen and I won't go in there again. It's the least I can do for her after the trouble she's had on my account."

"You're making a big mistake. You should take your place as the dominant helper in this house. Belinda should serve you almost as much as she serves me."

"Dominant helper?" Dina repeated. "You make it sound like we're cats ourselves. We're not. We're human. We have a different way of relating to each other."

"Maybe you do, but you're in the Pride now. You have an understanding with the Pride and that means you are the dominant helper in this house. You're still human, but I say you're dominant and Belinda serves you. That's the way the Pride works."

"I don't want to be the dominant helper."

"You are," he declared. "You are whether you want to be or not."

She turned back to the window. "Just don't make me go back to the kitchen."

"I'm not making you do anything. If you want something to eat, the kitchen is the place to get it. Belinda won't always bring it to you. You have to go get it."

She shook her head. "I'll stay away."

He raised his head and saw her cross her arms over her stomach. "You're going to get very hungry."

"I'll starve first," she muttered.

He snorted. "I'll tell Belinda to bring you your food the way she did before. You can't argue with that. Neither of you can."

Chapter 5

R enfroe licked his lips and sat up straight. He and Dina had just finished breakfast in the parlor. The bloody remains of an ox leg lay in front of him while she ate out of a bowl.

They'd settled into a routine since she came back from the village.

"By the way," he remarked, "I have some news for you about your friend, Matthew."

Dina looked up. "Matthew Geromi? What did you hear about him?"

"He isn't doing very well, you know," Renfroe told her.

"I know he isn't. Fallon ripped him to pieces. He was barely hanging on the last time I saw him."

"He's much worse now. He probably won't last more than a day or two. He can't stand any longer and he's close to death."

Dina jumped up and cried out in dismay. "What—no! He can't be! I killed Fallon in a fight! He tried to stop me from getting to my Pod and I gutted him with my poker."

"That was afterward. He had another altercation with Matthew after you ran away. Fallon accused Matthew of knowing about your plans and then Fallon left Matthew for dead before he went after you."

"How do you know all this?" Dina asked. "Who told you Matthew was close to death?"

"One of Fallon's harem females came to the Senate. She wanted to make sure you paid for what you did. She told me then."

Dina turned to leave the room. "I have to see him. If he's that close to death, I have to see him."

Renfroe didn't move off the bed. "You can't go, Dina."

"But I have to! I'm the only one of the team who can get to him. Elyse won't tell Tom about Matthew and Khalid won't let Tania out to see him. Oh, poor Tania! She's been married to Matthew for ten years and she won't even get to see him before he dies. I have to go. I'm the only one who can."

"Dina, please. Use your brain," Renfroe growled. "You're an intelligent woman, but you let your feelings run away with you. You can't go to Fallon's house. His females would tear you apart."

"You could come with me," she suggested.

Renfroe shook his head. "I couldn't defend you against them. Over fifteen adult Manx cats live in that house and that's not counting young cubs who would enjoy nothing better than sharpening their claws and teeth on you."

"But I have to!" she cried. "I can't just let Matthew die alone. Someone has to take care of him in the time he has left."

"I didn't say you had to let him die alone. I've arranged for him to come here."

"Here?!" Dina gasped. "He's coming here?!"

"I thought you might want to spend some time with him before he dies. The Manx left him lying in the mud out in the yard. I don't think they cared much about what happened to him."

She dashed across the room and threw her arms around his neck. "Thank you so much! You don't know what this means to me."

"Of course I do. That's exactly why I did it."

Dina straightened up and clasped her hands. "I'll nurse him. I'll clean up his wounds and maybe I can find some medicinal plants to heal him."

"No, Dina," Renfroe told her. "You can spend some time with Matthew, but I have to warn you. His injuries are too serious. He will never recover. He's coming here to die. Don't let yourself hope for anything else. Fallon would have killed Matthew if he hadn't heard about your escape and gone after you."

Dina's arms fell to her sides and her spirits plunged. "Is it as bad as that?"

"It really is as bad as that. You'll understand when you see him."

"When is he coming?"

"This morning," he told her, "as soon as it gets light."

He left for the Senate and Dina spent the rest of the morning pacing up and down the corridor while she clenched her hands together in anticipation of Matthew's arrival.

She still didn't even know how they would bring him. She almost hated to see him after Renfroe's dire warnings. How could Matthew be so far gone that she couldn't bring him back with proper care?

A commotion made her run to the kitchen door in time for a group of helpers she didn't know to enter from outside.

Belinda held the door open for them and they carried a makeshift stretcher into the kitchen. Dina's hand flew to her mouth when she saw Matthew. Only his head showed above the blanket covering him, but she didn't have to see anything else to know that Renfroe had been telling the truth.

The helpers moved toward the fire and stooped to set the stretcher down. "Don't put him in here!" Belinda yelled. "I won't have him in here!"

The stretcher-bearers looked around them. "Well, where else are we going to put him?"

"Not in here," Belinda shot back. "I don't care where you put him, but you won't put him in here."

"He has to go somewhere," someone mumbled.

"It's all right," Dina interrupted. "Bring him into the parlor."

Belinda scowled at her, but she didn't argue when the helpers followed Dina. They sighed with relief when they set Matthew down in front of the fire in the parlor.

"Thank you," Dina told them. "I appreciate you bringing him."

The men nodded and left the room without speaking to her. Would it always be this way? Would she ever be able to redeem herself with these people?

The old familiar silence fell over the house. The fire crackled in the fireplace and a soft drizzle of rain floated down onto the pavement out in the courtyard.

Matthew lay on the stretcher with his eyes closed. Did he even know where he was? Maybe he thought he was still in Fallon's house.

His face had turned into a grey mask of death. He looked like a corpse already. Only the tortured rising and falling of his chest under the blanket told her that he was still alive.

She took a deep breath, knelt down by the stretcher, and he opened his eyes. He struggled to focus on her face through the film covering his irises. When he realized who it was, he closed his eyes again. "Oh, it's you," he growled. "I thought it was Tania."

Dina struggled to swallow the lump in her throat. "I'm sorry I couldn't bring Tania to see you. I know she'd like to see you if she could come."

"Where is she?" he muttered. "If she wants to see me, let her come."

"I only wish she could. If she knew you were here, I'm sure she would come if she could."

"What's stopping her?" he asked.

Dina hesitated to tell him anything else. He must not be thinking clearly or he wouldn't ask about Tania. What good would it do to tell him? "She can't come."

"She must not care all that much," Matthew grumbled.

"I know she cares about you. She doesn't care about anything as much as she cares about you. I know she'll be sad when she hears about you."

"What about me?" he asked.

Didn't he even realized he was dying? "I mean when she hears you're not doing very well."

"I'm fine. There's nothing wrong with me."

Dina let that go and changed the subject. "Is there anything I can do to make you more comfortable?"

"I'm perfectly comfortable. I don't need anything. I just need to sleep."

Dina raised her hand, but she hesitated to touch him. Who was she to give comfort to another woman's husband? Tania probably wouldn't mind, though. Someone had to comfort Matthew in his dying moments and Dina was the only person here.

She let her hand rest on his chest. "Are you in any pain?"

"I told you I'm perfectly comfortable," he snapped. "I don't need anything and I don't need you hovering over me. Just leave me alone."

"I don't want to leave you alone," Dina told him. "I won't hover if you don't me to, but I wouldn't feel right leaving you—not now."

She lifted the blanket and found his hand tucked underneath it. It lay as pale and lifeless as the rest of his body, and when she picked it up, it sent a chill up her arm. She cradled it in her palm like a block of ice. He didn't react to her touch at all. He couldn't feel a thing.

"Get away from me," Matthew snarled. "I never liked you and I don't want you here now. Just let me sleep, why don't you?"

"Matthew," Dina murmured, "you're dying. I don't know what Fallon did to you, but if you fall asleep now, you won't wake up. You look half-dead already. You look more than half dead. I don't know how much longer you'll last."

At that moment, Belinda came in and set a tray on the floor near the stretcher. Dina glanced up and caught her eye. Neither woman said anything, but Dina recognized a hint of compassion in Belinda's eye. She slipped out of the parlor as silently as she came.

The delicious aroma of spicy soup wafted into Dina's nose. She lifted a cup to her nose and then held it out to Matthew. "Would you like to drink some soup? It might do you good."

She held the cup close enough to his face that he couldn't help but smell it. That smell would wake the dead, but he only turned his head away.

"Is there anything you'd like me to tell your family back on Earth?" she asked. "I don't know when I'll get back there to give them the message, but I'll make sure to give it to them when I do get back."

He didn't answer and she looked up from the tray to find him staring into her face. His black eyes burned out of his round flat face. That look shot straight to her heart from behind the waxy mask of his lifeless skin.

"Did you make it?" he asked.

"What do you mean?"

"You said you were going to try to make it back to the Pod. Did you make it?"

Dina nodded. "I made it. I made it all the way back to the *Savannah.*"

He nodded and shut his eyes. "I thought you might."

"I came back, though," she told him. "I came back to get the rest of you out."

"You'll have to get Tom and Tania out. I won't be getting out—not now."

Dina swallowed hard. Somewhere underneath it all, he knew the truth. He knew he wouldn't live to get off this planet. He would die here, just like Marcus Harte. "I only wish there was something I could do," she rasped.

"There is something you can do," he told her.

She looked up. "What? What can I do for you to make your burden lighter?"

"Get Tania out. I know it will be hard. You might not be able to get her out, either, but I'm asking you to do everything you can to help her. You're the only person who can help her now."

Dina nodded and tears swam in her eyes. "I'll do everything I can. I always have."

He blinked and swallowed. She thought he might start crying, but his eyes stayed perfectly dry. He might be too far gone to cry now. "You always did. You always took care of everyone else. You take care of everyone else even when it means putting yourself in danger. You never should have come back. You should have escaped to the *Savannah* and left us all behind."

"Maybe I should have," she admitted, "but I couldn't. I couldn't leave you all behind and I had other reasons to come back."

He turned away toward the fire, but he didn't close his eyes. "You probably won't get out of here again, either, you know. You'll probably get stuck here just like Tom and Tania."

"There are more important things in the world than getting out of here," she murmured.

"Oh? Like what?"

"Like making sure no one else has to go through what you've gone through," she told him. "Like making sure no one else gets killed down here."

"How can you stop that? What can one person do to stop what's going on here? The whole system supports it and the whole human population serves the Pride."

"Maybe there's nothing one person can do to stop it, but I couldn't just go back to my life on the *Savannah* and leave this planet the way it is. I had to do whatever I could to stop it, even if it means spending the rest of my life here."

He shook his head. "You shouldn't do this. It isn't up to you to fix this planet. It isn't worth your life."

"There are other things about this planet that I would want to stay for. It isn't all bad."

"Never mind about that. You should take better care of yourself."

"Don't worry about me. You're the one who needs taking care of right now."

He fixed his burning gaze on her face. "Listen to me, Dina. I don't have any family back on Earth. Tania is my only family and you're the only one who can communicate with her. The only message I want to give is to you."

"Me?" she shot back. "Why would you want to give a message to *me?* You just said you never liked me."

He couldn't move his body, so he just closed his eyes instead. "I never liked you--before. It's different now. *You're* different now."

"How?" she asked.

"I don't know. I can't think about it right now. I only know you aren't the same person you were when we left the *Savannah.*"

"That's strange," she muttered. "Captain Doyle said the same thing."

"You probably don't realize it, but you're the only person who can do anything about this mess of a planet. You might not be able to do anything. Maybe one person isn't enough, but you're the only one who can. You're the only person who even wants to."

"What are you saying? Are you saying I'm some kind of savior or something?" She laughed at the idea, but it didn't sound right in this room. It sounded like the cackling of a crazy person. Maybe that was what she was.

"Maybe not you," he admitted. "I know it sounds weird, but something might work through you to free these people. You never know."

She laughed again. She didn't want to think about what he was saying. "I couldn't free them. I told Captain Doyle I wanted to, but I only said that so he would let me come back. I didn't really think I'd be able to do anything. The system is too rigid and I'm stuck in this house. I can't even go outside without Renfroe protecting me. I'm a prisoner here."

Matthew blinked and swallowed. He didn't have much strength left. She shouldn't argue with him. She should just let him have his say and die in peace. He wasn't making any sense anyway. Maybe he was too far gone even to know what he was talking about.

"I know it sounds crazy, but you have something no one else has. Not even Tom has it anymore. He used to be a strong leader, but he's gone over to the other side. He won't do anything to free himself, much less anyone else."

"How do you know that? Have you seen him since you've been here? I didn't think you'd seen any of the team since you've been at Fallon's house."

"Fallon was the one who told me about Tom," Matthew told her. "Fallon told me all about what Tom gets up to with his benefactor, Elyse. Fallon told me all about the Senate hearing where Tom threw the Pride's questions about our mission back in their faces. Fallon even told me about you and your first attempt to escape. He told me about how Tom and Tania told on you the same way I did."

"Then you know they did it to protect themselves. If you know all that, you know they had no choice but to tell."

"Don't tell me Tom had no choice," Matthew countered. "I could believe Tania had no choice and that she did it in fear for her life. I'll tell you right now that that's why I did it—but Tom? No way. Not when he's living the high life with Elyse—not when he was her personal pet. She was never any threat to him. He told her to butter her up. You can't convince me otherwise."

"Okay, okay," Dina murmured. "I won't argue with you about that."

"Fallon told me enough to let me know that Tom will never break out of Prideland. He doesn't have the will anymore. You're the only one who still has it."

"But I don't plan to break out again. I came back here to stay. I don't know if I'll ever go back to the *Savannah,* but I won't run away again. I came to an understanding with the Pride and I'm here to stay with Renfroe."

"Then why did you ask me if there was any message I wanted you to take back to Earth?" he asked.

"I thought you were delirious," she admitted. "I thought that was the usual thing you say to someone who's dying."

He swallowed hard again, but now his eyes blazed with a dangerous light. "I am dying, Dina. I know that now. I don't know how much longer I'll be able to talk to you, so you have to listen to me very carefully."

"I am listening."

"You're the only one who can free these people," he breathed. "You're the only hope anyone on this wreck of a planet has left. Think about it. There are people on this planet who want to leave. You must know that."

"I know there are, but what can I do?"

"It doesn't matter what you do. Just do something. You're the only one who can. Whatever you do, don't do nothing. Don't settle in here for the long haul. You might be happy here with Renfroe, but you have to do something. That's my message. Do something and free these people."

She grinned at him. "What do you think I am? Do you think I'm Moses or something?"

His eyes drilled straight through her. "Don't joke about it. This Pride is no joke. Everyone and everything on this planet is riding on you. Don't let them down."

He closed his eyes again and let out a deep breath. Every ounce of energy in his body came out with that breath.

"But what can I do?" Dina asked again.

He didn't answer. His breath settled into a gentle, steady rhythm and he didn't open his eyes again. Dina waited for him to say something else, but he didn't.

"Matthew?" she asked.

His hand lay dead and cold on her palm. Dina held it and listened. She couldn't hear his breathing anymore over the fire crackling, but she could still see his chest rising and falling. She held his hand and waited and watched.

Chapter 6

Dina pushed open the doors between her room and the garden. Fresh air flooded the room and swept away the musty smell of bodies. She stepped out into the courtyard and turned her face up toward the sun.

Matthew's last words kept ringing in her head. She didn't really understand what they meant. She still had no plans to spoil her place with Renfroe for some far-fetched notion of freeing the people of Prideland.

From what she could see, they had no desire to be freed. Only the slags in the jungle wanted freedom badly enough to fight for it. Why should she risk everything for them? She'd done it before and she didn't like the consequences. Trying to free them would only get herself and a lot of other people killed.

The bedroom door opened and she turned around to see Renfroe coming back. "How is Matthew?" he asked.

"He's dead."

Renfroe growled deep in his chest. "Where is he?"

"He's in the parlor."

Renfroe nodded.

Another sound drew Dina's attention to the other end of the garden. The door in the garden wall opened and the ragged gang of men pushed their wheelbarrow into the garden. Renfroe tossed his head in their direction. "Oh, look. It's the Elite Battalion."

Dina spun around. "You did this, didn't you? You told them to come and get Matthew, didn't you?"

Renfroe clicked his tongue. "You should know I would never speak to the Elite Battalion. No one ever does. They're here to clean out the sand pit in the back of the garden. They always come at this time every day. Since they're here, they might as well take Matthew with them."

Dina almost retched at the thought. She turned her back on Renfroe. "I can't watch this."

"Wait, Dina," he called after her. "You have to tell them to come inside and get him."

She walked back into the bedroom. "Tell them yourself."

She threw herself face down on the bed and buried her head in the pillows. She had to block her eyes from seeing and her ears from hearing the Elite Battalion take Matthew away.

They would take the body to the old, abandoned power station and dump Matthew into the river along with everyone else who died in Prideland. Dina might be the only other person on the planet who knew the bodies of the dead floated in their drinking water.

She stayed where she was until the bed bounced underneath her. "You can get up now. They're gone."

"Good."

He put his head down on his paws and let out his breath. "Will you be all right here by yourself for a while? I have to go out again."

"I'll be fine," she replied. "Where are you going?"

"Down to the Senate building. We have a hearing later, and I have to talk to Osiris before that."

"Who's Osiris? I haven't heard that name before."

"He's one of the Senators. He's a tabby house cat. I think you saw him there when Tom addressed the Senate. Osiris was the one who questioned Tom on the Senate's behalf."

"I remember him. What's the hearing about?"

"It seems," Renfroe replied, "that the impossible has happened. We never thought we had anything to worry about, but it seems our worst nightmare has come true."

"What's that?" she asked.

"Humans have helped the cats of the Pride for centuries. I mean, they've engaged in sexual behavior with cats during that time and the two species never produced any offspring."

"They couldn't," Dina replied. "They're too far apart biologically."

"That's what we thought, but some mutation must have taken place. A few pregnancies have occurred and the Pride is in an uproar."

"Pregnancies?" Dina asked. "You mean.....between humans and cats? That's impossible!"

"Exactly. What could be more impossible than that? But that's exactly what has happened. The whole Pride is in chaos."

Dina gasped. "I had no idea."

"How could you? You've been in the house cut off from all contact ever since you got back. If you went out even as far as the market, you would see the change. This mutation has thrown over the whole relationship between cats and helpers."

Dina snorted. "I'll bet it has. The cats can't just take any helper they want whenever they want anymore without worrying about some-body winding up pregnant. It's the same old problem."

"It's not only that," Renfroe told her. "It's the Children."

"What Children?"

"The offspring."

Dina's eyes popped. "Are you telling me these pregnancies have been successful?"

"What else would I mean? Isn't that what a pregnancy does? I thought you would understand that a pregnancy leads to offspring."

"Not always. Goats and sheep aren't the same species, but when a doe goat mates with a ram, she can get pregnant. The pregnancy will slip, though. It won't develop to term and the pregnancy will naturally miscarry before it results in any offspring. When you first mentioned pregnancies, I thought you meant something like that. It's impossible enough for a woman to get pregnant from a cat or a cat to get pregnant from a man without it leading to some offspring."

"But it has led to offspring. The Pride could handle relations with helpers leading to pregnancy and even leading to offspring if those offspring were either cat or human, but they aren't. That's the problem."

"How could they be neither one nor the other?"

"Isn't it obvious? They're somewhere in between. They're part cat and part human."

"What does that mean?" Dina laughed. "Do they have fur or something?"

Renfroe studied her, but he didn't laugh. "As a matter of fact, they do. They have fur and fangs and claws and tails and pointed ears. They also have the cats' elongated pupils, so the Children should be able to see in the dark, but they have a human shape. They have human hands with five fingers and opposable thumbs."

"And do they have five toes, too?" Dina asked. "I suppose none of them has grown old enough yet to see if they walk upright."

"They haven't grown old enough yet and they aren't going to grow old enough. The Pride won't allow it."

"What can they do to stop it?" she asked. "These Children or whatever they are will grow eventually."

"No, they won't. The Pride has reduced them all so far and they'll keep reducing them as soon they're born. They won't let them grow."

"You mean they kill them?!" Dina exclaimed. "They kill these Children as soon as they're born? That's pretty harsh, isn't it?"

"It would be different if they were either cat or human. If they were cats, they would be part of the Pride like every other cat. If they were human, they would be brought up as helpers, the same way the helpers bring up their human children now, but the Children aren't either of those. They're something neither human nor cat. The Pride doesn't know what to do with them, so they reduce them. We can't have that kind of genetic mix-up tainting the Pride."

Dina stared at him in horror for a second. It took her that long to fully grasp what he just said.

Then she let out a gasp of exasperation and leapt off the bed. "You cats really know how to find the most obnoxious way of handling every situation, don't you? It's not enough that you've got every human being on this planet living in the worst kind of slavery. It's not enough that you keep your helpers in submission with sex and violence. It's not their fault they've been forced to have sex with the cats. Now you're going around killing their Children. It's pure evil."

"No one's forcing the helpers to have sex with the cats," Renfroe replied. "We've been through this a dozen times."

"No one's forcing them, are they? They only do it because the cats coerce them into it. And we can talk about it 'til the cows come home. It doesn't make it any less evil. How do you justify killing these Children? You're worried about genetic taint? That's no excuse. You're probably only worried about a generation of people arising who have the power to stand up to the cats. Humans in their original state can't defend themselves against the cats, but a person with claws and fangs and elongated pupils and opposable thumbs probably could."

"I don't make any justification for it, Dina," he replied. "I've been arguing with the Senate since the very first pregnancies came to light to let these Children live. I keep telling everyone who will listen to me that this is the next step in our evolution on this planet. I keep telling them we should incorporate these Children into the Pride along with all our other offspring, but none of the other cats will listen to me."

Dina hesitated. Then she wilted. "I'm sorry I said that. I should have known you'd stand up for what's right."

"It's not about right and wrong. What you said is true. If these Children grow up the way we think they will, they'll pose a serious threat to the Pride. We won't be able to control or contain them the way we do humans. The Children could undermine the stability of our whole society. The only way to avoid that is to make them a part of the Pride. Unfortunately, none of the other cats sees it that way. They think the way to avoid it is to reduce the Children."

Dina thought the matter over. "And what happens to the mothers? Do they get reduced, too?"

Renfroe shrugged. "That depends on who the mother is. If the mother is a cat, the Pride doesn't do anything to her."

"Except kill her babies, you mean," Dina corrected. "That's something."

Renfroe turned away. "I'm sure you know that sort of thing happens all the time, especially in lion prides. The patriarch will kill the young of any rival males to make sure only his own offspring survive to breed. It also frees the females to breed again with the patriarch."

"I know that," Dina snapped. "But that doesn't mean you have to do it here."

Renfroe sighed. "I'm not doing it here, Dina. I told you I've been arguing in the Senate that these Children be brought up in the Pride, not reduced."

Dina crossed her arms and humphed. "So what happens to the human women that get pregnant from cats? Do they get reduced, too?"

"That is at the discretion of their benefactors. I know some of the cats will reduce any human helper that gets pregnant. Others simply reduce the Children at birth and leave the helpers to their duties."

"Meaning," she countered, "leaving the helpers to breed again, just like the lions."

"As you wish." Renfroe got up and stalked across the room to the garden door. "I have to go now. I'll see you later."

Chapter 7

Renfroe didn't come back all day. Dina wandered the halls and rooms of the big old house. The biologist in her considered the matter of the Children and the mutation that made reproduction possible between cats and humans.

This had to be the only place in the whole galaxy where such a cross-breeding occurred. It might even be the only occurrence in history where it had occurred. She'd like to examine one of these Children.

Was there any way to save them from the cats? The helpers were the only people in Prideland who had sex with the cats, so all the Children would be born in the city. That would make saving them extremely difficult if not impossible. The cats controlled the city and everyone in it.

She strolled out into the garden and sat first on one bench and then under a different tree. She'd never wasted so much time in her life as she did in Prideland. She had nothing to do in this house.

She envied the cooks and gardeners like Buck and Belinda. At least they had jobs to occupy them all day long. The horrors and insults of Prideland wouldn't sting so badly if she had something else to think about.

She came to a bend in the path and spotted the door in the garden wall standing open. More trees and leafy shrubs swayed outside. The quiet, peaceful neighborhood stretched beyond the door.

She would have liked to go for a walk to the market or to Elyse's house to visit Tom. She hadn't wanted to see him after she found out that he told Elyse about her escape plans, but she felt differently now.

She understood his loyalty to Elyse and his decision to make peace with the Pride. It just took Dina a little longer and two escape attempts to come to the same conclusion.

She couldn't go out there, though. Someone might attack her in broad daylight or, if she got caught out after curfew, the sentinel cats would come after her.

She headed back toward the house and a wave of nostalgia flooded through her when she thought about Tom. If only she could go back in time to their days together on the *Savannah*.

Maybe she should have done something differently, but what could she have done? She couldn't have refused a direct order from Captain Doyle to come down to this planet. Everything after that seemed inevitable.

She could have tried harder to convince Tom to abandon their mission when they first landed and lost Marcus Hart. She shouldn't have bowed so easily to Tom's experience and leadership. She should have stuck to her guns, overrode his authority, and ordered the whole landing party back to the ship.

That was the only time she could have chosen a different course, but she couldn't have done that, either. Everyone on the landing team had outranked her. She didn't have the authority to order them anywhere and they all went along with Tom's decision.

Once they got to the village, the rest was history. Once the team got taken captive and turned over to the Pride, nothing could have brought her and Tom back together again and now nothing ever would.

Still, she'd like to see him again. Maybe if she told him how Matthew died, Tom would change his mind about the Pride. Maybe he would help her....do what? What was she really going to do? Matthew must have been delusional when he told her to free these people.

Matthew had wanted her to help Tania. Dina might actually be able to do something about Tania, but Dina couldn't visit Tania, either—not without another nasty encounter with Khalid—an encounter Dina wouldn't survive this time. Dina couldn't even find out if Tania was even still living at Khalid's house.

Thinking about all of that would only drive her crazy. She passed back into her own bedroom courtyard, but the minute she turned into it, a shadow caught her peripheral vision.

She didn't have time to turn around before three men sprang out of the bushes with clubs raised above their heads. She caught one fleeting glimpse of them before they attacked.

One of them wore the rough clothing of a village subsidiary. Another wore fine clothes she'd only seen in the city. She had time to recognize the third man's grey whiskers and dull features before his club came down on her head. It was Buck, the gardener.

They must have been waiting for her, which meant Buck must have been keeping an eye on her even here in Renfroe's house. He must have been waiting for her to step out of the house when Renfroe wasn't around to protect her. Now Buck would punish her on the Pride's behalf.

That first blow sent her staggering toward the house trying to get to the bedroom door, but she never made it. The men surrounded her with their clubs flying. Another blow would have split her skull open, but she dodged just in time and the blow cracked down on her shoulder.

She couldn't get away from all three of them attacking her at once. The minute she avoided that blow, another landed at the base of her neck from behind. Fireworks exploded in front of her eyes and her head swam and she buckled onto her knees. She only stayed conscious enough to cower under her arms before a hail of blows rained down on her.

She hit the ground and tucked her head against her chest. She managed to turn around and saw the bottom edge of the door just a few yards away. She couldn't get there with her arms over her head.

She crouched where she was and took the blows against her back. In another minute, the factors would start on her from the front, force her to uncurl, and then she would never get back inside the house alive. She had to act now if she hoped to survive this.

She gathered what little strength she had left, coiling her legs under her, and in one burst of energy, she launched herself toward the door.

She had to take her arms down to get there and the men took advantage of it. A club struck the side of her head, split her ear open, and a gush of warm blood rushed down the side of her neck. Another club landed on the other side of her head and smashed her temple.

Brilliant lights burst in her brain. She couldn't see anymore, so she had to concentrate everything on crawling as fast as she could.

She shot forward, dove onto the grass, landed stretched out on her stomach, rolled across the threshold into the bedroom, and summoned just enough energy to kick the door shut behind her.

It slammed closed. She was inside, and when she looked through the glass to the courtyard outside, she didn't see any men out there. They'd vanished into the undergrowth as quickly and as silently as they appeared.

She blinked the blood out of her eyes and caught her breath before she managed to sit up. When she did, she had to concentrate hard to focus her eyes.

Nothing moved out in the garden. Not a single person walked down the paths or worked in the flowerbeds. Buck wasn't out there, but he would be watching from somewhere. She never doubted that.

She staggered toward the bed and collapsed on it. Renfroe had been warning her about this, but she didn't think it would happen right here in his own garden.

She couldn't remember now why she didn't think that before. She thought she would be safe on Renfroe's property, but she'd obviously been mistaken about that.

Something warm landed on her hand and she looked when a drop of blood splashed on her fingers. She didn't feel the pain before now. She better do something about that.

She crossed to the washstand on the other side of the room, wetted a cloth in the basin of water, and held it against the side of her head. It came away stained with blood and now the pain really hit her.

She finished cleaning herself up and stopped the bleeding. Then left the basin of bloody water and the cloth on the floor outside the room. Belina would take it away and replace everything with fresh water and towels.

Not even the sight of blood and the pounding ache in her head and body brought her out of her daze. At least her hair would cover up the wound so Renfroe wouldn't see it.

Why didn't she want him to know about what happened? If he found out, he would get rid of Buck. Renfroe wouldn't let Buck keep working in the house after he attacked Dina.

Maybe that was why she didn't want Renfroe to know. Better to have Buck nearby where she knew who was watching her. If Renfroe got rid of Buck, someone unknown would take his place. The danger wouldn't go away. She just wouldn't know who was after her.

She lay down on the bed. Her head throbbed and it weighed a ton. She let it fall onto the pillow and she lost consciousness instantly.

She woke up with the evening sun slanting through the windows. She rolled over and gazed out at the leaves moving in the trees. Even blinking hurt. She didn't dare touch her ear and she couldn't lie down on that side.

The fountain in the distance offered a quiet reminder that Renfroe wasn't here. He'd been gone all day and hadn't come back yet. If Buck and his men hadn't attacked her, she might have ventured out to see if Belinda had brought her any food, but Dina didn't want to leave the room. She didn't even want to leave this bed.

Was she going to spend the rest of her life in this room with only Renfroe for company? Is this what she came back to Prideland for?

So much for freeing the captives. She was more a prisoner here than any other helper. She couldn't set foot out of the house without risking her life.

She sighed and sat up just as the door opened and Renfroe came in. He nudged the door to close it behind him and jumped up on the bed next to her, but he didn't look at her or say anything. He flopped down on his stomach and closed his eyes.

"Where have you been?" she asked. "I thought you'd be back hours ago."

He kept his eyes closed. "Don't talk to me."

She stared at him for a second trying to decide what to say, but she couldn't say anything to someone who just said, *Don't talk to me.*

She waited, but he didn't open his eyes. She didn't really want to talk, either, so she lay down next to him and put her arm over his shoulders. She moved right up next to him, rested her cheek against his fur, and closed her eyes, too.

Chapter 8

The door opened without a sound and Belinda tiptoed in. She set a tray of food on the table in the corner of the room along with a bloody carcass next to the tray.

Renfroe sniffed, opened his eyes, and raised his head. "Ah," he rumbled. "Just what the doctor ordered."

Dina sat up, too. "Are you feeling better now?"

"I will be after I finish this. I haven't eaten all day."

He dragged the carcass off the table. It flopped onto the ground and he started tearing it apart.

Dina got her tray and sat down in the chair to eat her own food. She'd been living with him in this room for so long that his eating no longer bothered her the way it did when she first came to live with him. She ate alongside him the way she would eat with any other person.

"How did the Senate hearing go?" she asked.

"The Senate hearing," he growled between mouthfuls, "went exactly the way all the Senate hearings go. A lot of cats said one thing and a lot of other cats said the opposite and they argued about it. They would have ripped each other to shreds if Lord Helion and I hadn't thrown our weight around and threatened to rip *them* to shreds if they did. Then we parted ways more divided than ever. That's the way all Senate hearings go and today was no exception."

"What was the hearing about?" she asked.

"Just what I told you before," he told her. "It was about these Children and what we ought to do about them."

"At least the Pride is considering accepting them. That's better than just killing them outright."

"The Pride will never accept them. I was the only one arguing for that, but I've given up trying to convince them."

"Then what is there to discuss?" she asked.

"Some of the cats want to completely eliminate any human female that gets pregnant with one of these Children. The cats think they can eliminate the mutation and keep the species separate if they do."

Dina choked on her soup. "But that would mean killing almost every human female helper in the city. As long as cats and people are engaged in sexual activity, the possibility will always remain that the mutation will come back. That's how biological evolution works."

"You don't have to convince me. The only logical conclusion to that argument is reducing every helper in the city, male and female, young and old, and keeping only subsidiaries in the villages who won't help the cats."

"You mean," she corrected, "who won't have sex with the cats."

"You know what I mean. We're talking about wiping out more than half the human population of the planet, but it will never happen. The cats are too attached to their human helpers to ever get rid of them. We enjoy their service too much. We wouldn't want to give up the brushing and scratching and cleaning and helping. We're almost as dependent on it now as the helpers are on the cats. It's a mutually obligatory relationship."

Dina snorted. "I'll bet it is."

"It's bad enough that we can't take these Children into the Pride. They would only strengthen us."

"How many of them have been born so far?" Dina asked.

Renfroe put his head on one side. "I would say about five hundred."

She gasped out loud. "What?! How can it be so many?"

"Don't you know? Think about how many people in this city alone are helping their cat benefactors. It must be in the thousands and this is just one city. Multiply that by all the other cities in Prideland and you have an idea of how many of these Children have been born so far."

"They've been born.....and they've been killed. That's a lot of dead babies. What is the Pride going to do—continuing killing them all for the rest of eternity?"

He shrugged. "It's not up to me. None of them will listen to me anymore."

"At least you're not the one killing them."

"Yes, I am. I have to."

Her bowl fell out of her hands and the soup spilled all over the floor, but she didn't even notice. "You're....killing them? I thought you were against it!"

"I have to. I told you before. I used up all the goodwill I ever had by saving your life. Now I have no choice but to go along with the others."

"But you don't have to kill them!" she cried. "You're a tiger. Why can't you just go off alone? Why do you have to go along with the Pride? You're not even supposed to be in a Pride at all!"

He sighed and went back to swallowing chunks of meat. "I'm a part of this Pride whether I want to be or not. If I left now, I would leave you completely unguarded. You wouldn't last five minutes. I'm Chairman of the Senate. I have to go along with the majority. As long as they're killing Children, I have to go along with it. I'd be dead at the next hearing if I didn't. The Children are protected."

"Protected!!" she shrieked.

"You know what I mean," he muttered. "You know what protected means."

"I know what protected means," she snapped. "It means forbidden. It doesn't mean protected at all."

"Dina," he grumbled, "I thought we were past all this. You know I can't do anything about the Children if they're protected."

Dina collapsed into her chair and buckled under the strain. Images came back to her from her worst nightmare.

Her voice faltered when she tried to speak. "Tell me you didn't do this. Please tell me you didn't go out killing helpless Children. They're just babies."

He didn't look up. "I have to. That's all there is to it. I have to choose between my own life and the lives of these Children. Unfortunately, I choose myself. They're babies like you say. They're dying before they really start living. Maybe in time the Pride will come to see them in a different light. For now, though, the Pride has no place for them. It's just such a colossal waste!"

Dina struggled to breathe, but she wound up choking instead. Why, oh why, did it have to be this way? Why did everything the Pride did have to be such an atrocity against human decency?

She stood up feeling sick. She didn't see the tray fall out of her lap onto the floor. She walked over to the bed and threw herself face down on it, but she couldn't stop seeing people being torn apart by cats. Would she ever stop seeing all those horrors?

Her body shook all over. They were only Children. They weren't even Children. They were babies—kittens, even. Why did they have to die?

Renfroe put his carcass down and flopped down on the bed next to her. *They're only Children,* kept repeating in her head. *They're only Children.*

If anyone in all Prideland deserved to be freed from this terrible slavery, they deserved it. They deserved it even more than the children of the helpers and subsidiaries.

What could she do about it, though? Not even Renfroe, Chairman of the Senate and a full-grown tiger, could stop it.

He had to help the other cats kill these Children. He had to do it just to save his own life. If Dina tried to save the Children, she would die, too. If she got caught undermining the Pride again in any way, nothing on this planet or off of it could save her. Then she wouldn't be any good to anyone.

"Dina," he murmured, "you can't allow such things to affect you so much. This is the way we live in this Pride. You have to make peace with it once and for all. You won't be able to stand it if you don't. You need to come to an understanding with the Pride or you and I can never live together the way we want to."

"I don't want to go through all this again," she mumbled into the pillow. "You can't expect me to just accept this sort of thing with no reaction at all. I can have a reaction to it and still have an understanding with the Pride. You and I can still be together."

He nuzzled the back of her head and took a deep sniff of her hair. His whiskers tickled the back of her neck. "Having an understanding with the Pride is not the same as having an understanding with me. You can't continue to contradict everything the Pride does. The other cats won't stand for it."

Dina rolled onto her side to face him. "They can't do anything to me that they aren't already doing. I can't leave the house without someone trying to kill me. I'm completely cut off from everyone on this planet except you. No one is hearing my contradictions but you."

"Even that is too much. If anyone found out....."

"Even you disagree with what they're doing," she pointed out.

"That's different. I'm a cat of this Pride, and I'm Chairman of the Senate. You're a helper."

"Isn't there something we can do for these Children?" she asked.

"I'm afraid not. Believe me, I've tried everything. If anyone could stop them being reduced outright, it's me. If I couldn't convince the Pride to let them live, no one can."

"At least you of all people realize how wrong this is. You can't just go around killing innocent little babies. It's barbaric."

"It's not wrong," he argued, "not in the way you think it is, but these are members of our Pride. These are our sons and our daughters. They should be brought up in the Pride along with our other cubs and kittens. It only makes sense."

Dina closed her eyes and turned away. "It doesn't matter. Like you said, there's nothing we can do."

He scooted across the mattress and rubbed his cheeks and chin along the top of her thigh. "I missed you today."

She sulked just a little longer before she rolled back toward him and faced him. "I wish you didn't have to stay away so long. You're the only company I have."

"Maybe we could change that," he replied.

"How?"

"I don't know. Maybe some other helpers could come into the house sometimes."

"You mean just to keep me company? That doesn't make sense. You said Buck and Belinda were the only helpers you had before I came."

"They were, but if you're lonely, we should do something to change that."

Dina shook her head. "Not just for me. There's no reason for that. I'm sure as time goes on, I'll make peace with the Pride enough that I'll be able to go out again. This isolation can't last forever."

He licked her hand and she turned her palm up toward his mouth. He licked up her arm, and the breath rasping in and out of his nose turned to a subtle growl. The low vibrations of his voice penetrated her body and then her soul. She could lose herself in him.

He let out a loud growl and rolled on top of her. She gasped for breath, closed her eyes, and let her head fall backward. The old power of passionate excitement ran through her veins, he bore down on her with all his weight, and crushed her into the bed.

Chapter 9

Dina woke to the sound of the bedroom door closing. Renfroe was gone again. He'd let himself out and slipped away leaving her alone in bed.

She gazed up at the ceiling for a while and then stared at the garden outside the window. Nothing had changed in the weeks since she came back to Prideland. She still spent all her time alone except for the few hours she spent with Renfroe.

She couldn't really count the hours they spent asleep together. They spent at most an hour or two together each morning before he went to the Senate building. Then they spent another two hours in the evenings when he got back.

He never told her anymore what he did in the meantime. She didn't need to know. In a way, that was her understanding with the Pride. She didn't want to know and she didn't find out.

At least she got some time with him. Even then, they didn't spend much of that time talking. They had better things to do. They had to catch up on their first weeks together when she hadn't been able to stand Prideland.

Now that they understood each other and she understood the Pride. Now they could finally enjoy each other's company the way they wanted.

He didn't spend all night next to her in bed, either. She woke up in the middle of the night sometimes to find him gone.

Then he would wake her up when he came back in with his paws and coat wet with dew or rain. She didn't ask what he had been doing. He could only be out hunting. Any cat would be at that time of night. It wasn't natural for him to be doing anything else.

Only Dina herself had changed. She thought less and she didn't think about Prideland at all.

She didn't think about all these people being slaves and she definitely didn't think about the plan she proposed to Captain Doyle to incite a domestic rebellion to overthrow the Pride. That was the last thing she would think about. Buck and his men had cured her of that.

She never went outside the house except for the few times when she and Renfroe wandered the garden together. He never again mentioned bringing in other helpers to keep her company.

She spent most of her time staring into space thinking about nothing more important than her next meal.

Belinda brought her trays of food at set times of the day. Belinda brought them without being asked so Dina never had to speak to her.

Belinda brought Dina's food along with Renfroe's in the morning and evening. In the middle of the day, Dina went for a walk around the house by herself and found a tray waiting for her when she came back.

Dina didn't think about the matter enough to notice the change in herself. She only noticed the peace she felt in her situation. She no longer fought against it or tried to change it. She didn't question Renfroe about the Children of the Pride being born out there somewhere. She didn't ask if he still took part in hunting them down and reducing them.

She had her own insulated world here a thousand miles from the Pride's politics. The Senate and the Pride were his business. The Pride was his people. She didn't need to understand why or how he did what he did. She trusted him to do the best he could with what he had.

She tossed back the bedspread, got out of bed, and stood naked in front of the glass doors to examine some scratches on her legs. Renfroe had given them to her last night in the heat of passion. He had a habit of forgetting his own strength at those times.

She pulled on her clothes. She wore clothing made in Prideland now with the helper's long tunic over her leggings. If she ever dared to venture away from Renfroe's house, no one would ever know she hadn't been born and raised in the Pride just like all the other people in this city.

All the other people in this city—except for Tom Sharples and Tania Barnes. Dina never wondered how they were doing with their own benefactors. She didn't plan how to go visit them. She wouldn't visit them even if she got out of the house. They'd come to their own understandings with the Pride and they had their own paths to follow. What they did and how they managed it had nothing to do with her.

She wandered out into the corridor toward the portico leading into the private courtyard with the fountain. She always sat there for a while each morning. That was the only place besides her bedroom courtyard where she could go outside without risking another attack from the factors.

The beauty of the garden and the peaceful music of falling water told her everything she needed to know about her world. She buried herself in beauty and let everything else vanish from her mind.

She had no idea how long she sat there. One hour disappeared into another with no beginning and no end. One day blurred into the next, year after year.

She had no way of knowing when she got up to move on. Not even the sun moving across the sky gave her any clue how much of the day had already passed or even how long she'd been living in this house. She didn't think about it.

Even the curiosity she once experienced to see and examine one of these half-breed Children no longer bothered her. She would probably never see one—definitely not alive. What was the point of thinking about it?

She wandered back to her own courtyard, and in the distance, she saw the Elite Battalion cleaning out Renfroe's sand pit. Their presence no longer bothered her. She barely saw them when they came and went.

She sat down on another bench in her courtyard and drifted into another dozy dream. She looked away when the Elite Battalion trundled by with their wheelbarrow and let themselves out through the door in the garden wall. The squeak of the wheelbarrow's wheels faded away into the neighborhood beyond the wall.

Some other little noise caught her ear. If she hadn't been sitting on that bench, in exactly the same place every single day, she probably wouldn't have noticed it at all. She knew every sound in this garden. Her ear picked up something out of place right away.

She shouldn't have paid it any attention. Some random sound couldn't mean anything to her. It was probably just something or someone outside the wall. In that case, it definitely didn't concern her.

She got up to go back inside, but just before she got to the door, a frail figure appeared out of the bushes near the wall.

Dina stopped on the spot and Dina gasped. "Tania! What are you doing here? Don't you know you could get into big trouble for coming here? No one's supposed to talk to me. I'm protected."

Tania glanced right and left even though the courtyard and even the garden beyond was completely empty. Just for a second, Dina wondered how Tania got inside the wall, but Dina already knew.

Tania must have come in while the men from the Elite Battalion were doing their work. They would have left the door in the garden wall open.

If Buck and the other factors were still out there watching, they would only be watching for Dina. They might not have thought someone else coming in was anything unusual or they might have assumed Tania was here on some business for the house and let her through.

Tania's eyes darted around the garden, searching for anything. "I couldn't get into any trouble worse than I'm already in."

"What's the matter?" Dina asked. "I thought you'd made up your mind to come to an understanding with Khalid and the Pride."

"I did. I made up my mind to become a helper to Khalid. That was the last time I saw you."

"And did you become a helper to Khalid?" Dina asked.

Tania looked down at the ground.

"You don't have to worry about telling me, Tania," Dina told her. "I'm a helper to Renfroe now, so I have no reason to judge you if that's what you're worried about. You did what you had to do and I understand why you did it. It's no more or less than any of the rest of us did. Even Tom is a helper to Elyse now. It's the normal thing to do here."

Tania raised her head just enough to catch Dina's eye. "I really appreciate you saying that. I just hope Matthew understands."

Dina froze. Should she tell Tania that Matthew was dead? Was now the right time to do it?

Before she could make up her mind, another thought pushed the question out of the way and she broke into a smile. She took Tania's hand. "I'm so glad to see you, even if you aren't supposed to be here. I'd forgotten how good it is to talk to someone. I just don't want you don't get visited for coming here."

"I won't get visited. I'm not going back."

"What do you mean?"

Tania's face dissolved into a mask of terror and her eyes skipped around the garden again. "You don't know how bad it is, Dina! I don't know what I'm going to do. I can't go back. If I get caught, I won't get visited. I'll get reduced. You have to help me, Dina! You're my last hope."

"What can I do? I'm a prisoner here myself. I can't even go outside without someone trying to reduce me. I can't even help myself, much less anyone else."

Tania didn't hear her. "You have to help me, Dina! Don't you understand? If I go back to Khalid's, he'll reduce me the second I walk through the door."

"I thought you were Khalid's helper. You said you wanted to make yourself his helper to get some protection from him. How can you be in danger of being reduced?"

"Don't you understand?! It's *because* I'm his helper that I'm in danger!"

Dina frowned even deeper. "I don't understand. Didn't you get any protection from being his helper?"

"Being Khalid's helper only gave me protection as long as he could make use of me. He can't have anything to do with me now, and the next time he sees me, he'll reduce me—if his other helpers don't beat him to it."

"What happened?" Dina asked. "Why did his protection come to an end?"

"Do I really have to explain it? Haven't you heard by now? Renfroe's a Senator. He should have explained it to you. I'm pregnant."

Chapter 10

Dina stared at Tania with her mouth open. "Are you sure it's... ...?"

Tania nodded. "It has to be. I had my last period right after I came to Khalid's house. I haven't been with anyone else besides him."

Dina did a quick mental calculation. Her eyes scanned Tania up and down. "Then, this baby, it's......"

Tania nodded again. "It's one of the Children. If anyone finds out, the cats will do anything to get rid of it, even if it means killing me to end the pregnancy."

Dina shut her mouth with a click. "What can we do? What can *I* do?"

Tania went wild and tears poured down her cheeks. "You have to help me, Dina! I don't know what you can do and I don't care. I can't go back to Khalid. He kills anyone who gets in his way and he kills one of his helpers almost every week. He does it out of pure boredom. Do you remember Maddy? He killed her just because she laughed too loudly in front of him once."

Dina nodded. She remembered Maddy. How could she forget?

"Khalid went hunting some slags in the jungle," Tania went on. "One of them injured his leg so now he limps when he walks. Ever since he came back with his leg damaged, he's ten times as vicious toward his helpers as he was before. He kills them for no reason. He kills them just to show he still can. He's a sadist."

Dina flushed. She definitely wouldn't take this opportunity to explain to Tania that she, Dina, had been the slag who injured Khalid's leg. "Do you know for certain that he'll kill any helper that gets pregnant with one of the Children?"

"He told us all he would. He told us any helper carrying one of the Children would be reduced on the spot. He's been using his influence to pressure the Senate ever since the Children mutation came out to wipe them all out. If you ask me, he wants to wipe out all the helpers, too."

"But I'm just a helper just like you are," Dina pointed out. "There's nothing I can do. I mean, where would you stay?" She waved her hand around the courtyard and the house. "It's not like you could stay here. It isn't even safe for me here."

Tania dissolved into a fresh fit of sobs. "You're my only hope, Dina! If you don't help me, I'm as good as dead. You can't send me back to Khalid. He can smell when one of his helpers is pregnant and he knows I didn't do it with anyone but him. He already killed one of his other female helpers who got pregnant and she wasn't even carrying one of the Children. She got pregnant from a male helper, but Khalid doesn't care. If any of his helper finds out where I am or that I tried to get away, they'll come after me." She glanced over her shoulder toward the garden. "If I leave here, I'm dead."

Dina followed her glance and shuddered. Dina already knew what leaving the garden meant. If Tania go back to Khalid's house soon, the factors standing guard over Dina would figure out that Tania was hiding from Khalid. Then Tania would be just as trapped in this house as Dina was.

And then there was Renfroe. He had killed Children because the Pride demanded it. If he found out Dina was hiding Tania in the house, he might feel obligated to kill both women to satisfy Khalid and the Pride. He wouldn't risk himself to save Tania and he couldn't risk himself to save Dina.

Dina thought fast and wound up studying in a new light. What did Dina ever see in this fragile, helpless creature?

Tania had been so tough on the *Savannah*. She'd been everything Dina had wished she could be, but Tania wasn't that anymore. She'd lost her whole identity, now that she didn't have the Armada's influence to stabilize her.

Was this what Matthew meant? Maybe everyone on the team changed, including Tania. She had become the exact opposite of everything she had been.

Tania couldn't take care of herself. Tania would never have worked up the courage or summoned the mental resource to escape from this planet.

She'd never even considered escaping on her own the way Dina did. When Dina thought about it, she shook her head in amazement that Tania took the drastic step of coming here for help. That was the furthest she was capable of going to save her own life. It never once crossed Tania's mind to run away completely. She couldn't even fathom doing it on her own.

Now Tania's life rested in Dina's hands. Tania made the first move toward getting away. That was a sight more than Tom had ever done.

Now it was up to Dina to take Tania the rest of the way. She didn't know how she would do it, but she had to help Tania. Dina couldn't throw Tania back out there to certain death.

She grabbed Tania by the hand. "Come with me." She pulled her across the courtyard and through the glass doors into her own bedroom.

Tania gasped when she saw the bed and the other furnishings. "What is this place?"

"Don't worry. You're not staying here. This is my room."

"Your room!" Tania exclaimed. "Don't tell me you're staying here with Renfroe. This is like some kind of palace."

Dina winced. "Don't worry. I'm just as much a slave and a prisoner here as I would be in Khalid's house and you're in just as much danger here as anywhere else. We have to hide you, and if any other helpers find out you're here, Renfroe will have to kill you himself. He'd probably have to kill me, too, for hiding you. Now stay here and keep quiet. I'll just check the corridor and make sure it's clear."

Dina held her finger to her lips. Tania's eyes widened and she nodded her agreement. Dina tiptoed to the door and eased it open. If anyone saw her, they would get suspicious if they saw her sneaking around, so she pulled the door the rest of the way open and strode out into the hall the way she normally did.

It was deserted. Buck and Belinda stayed away from her now. They stayed away from this end of the house entirely if they could.

Dina took a few more steps down the corridor and ducked back to her own room, grabbed Tania's hand again, and led her out into the corridor. Dina hurried halfway down it to another closed door, pushed Tania inside, and closed the door behind them before they looked around.

A plain woolen blanket covered a divan against the far wall under the window. The sun reflected off the dust floating in the air. "What is this place?" Tania whispered.

"This is my old room. I stayed here when I first came to live with Renfroe, before he made me....." She jerked her head toward the door. "Before he made me that other room. You can stay in here. No one uses this room anymore. You just have to keep absolutely quiet....and stay away from the window."

Tania nodded. "You don't have to worry about me."

"I don't know how long you'll have to stay here before we can get you out, but it's the best we can do for now." Dina headed back toward the door. "I'll have to go to the kitchen and get you some food and water. I don't know how I'll do that, either, because Belinda watches every move I make and I'm not supposed to go to the kitchen at all. I'll have to think about that."

Tania's eyes brimmed up with tears and she squeezed Dina's hand. "You don't know how much this means to me, Dina. I don't know how to thank you."

"I do know how much it means to you and you don't have to thank me. This could cost us both our lives before it's all said and done. So please, just keep quiet and still. I'll see what I can do about the rest of it later."

She went toward the door, but when her hand touched the doorknob, she stopped. She glanced back over her shoulder at Tania and saw the tall, blonde woman gazing back at her. Dina couldn't leave this room without telling Tania the truth.

Dina turned around, went back to her, and took Tania's hand again. "I have to tell you something."

Tania's eyes flew wide open again. "What is it?"

"Matthew died."

Tania opened her mouth, but no sound came out. Then her chin fell onto her chest and tears trickled down her cheeks. "When? What happened to him?"

"He died about three weeks ago," Dina murmured. "His benefactor, Fallon, never liked him and Matthew didn't help matters by
trying to escape a bunch of times and getting caught. I don't know
exactly what happened. Every time he tried to escape—and even when
he didn't—Fallon beat him and mauled him and tore him to pieces. I
don't have to tell you all the gory details. Anyway, I guess Fallon got
tired of him after a while. Fallon was in the middle of killing Matthew
when he got called away to hunt down...." Dina hesitated. "To hunt
down the same slags that injured Khalid. Fallon left Matthew for
dead."

"Did he kill him in the end?" Tania whispered.

Dina shook her head. "The slag that injured Khalid killed Fallon,
but not before Fallon hurt Matthew too much. He couldn't survive
his injuries. Renfroe heard about him and arranged to bring Matthew
here. He spent his last hours here, in this house."

Tania brightened up. "You saw him? You spoke to him?"

Dina nodded. "I spoke to him in his last hours alive."

Tania opened her mouth again in wordless wonder.

"He talked about you," Dina went on. "That's what I wanted to tell
you. He talked about you with his dying words."

"What did he say?"

"He told me to help you. He told me I was the only one who could
help you and he put you in my care."

Tania stared with her mouth open. Then she lowered her head and
nodded. "I see."

Dina gave her hand one more squeeze. "So I'll do whatever I can to
help you. I don't think I'll be able to do much. We're probably both
goners, anyway, but I'll do what I can."

Tania nodded again, but she didn't look up. "Thank you."

Chapter 11

Dina stood in the empty corridor and strained every nerve to listen. No one moved in either end of the house.

Her mind raced through all the dangers and possibilities of hiding Tania in her old room. Dina didn't like keeping the secret from Renfroe, but he would never go along with it if he found out.

He presented a problem all on his own. He could smell whenever Dina was lying to him. How could she go about her normal life of sleeping, eating, and spending hours a day with him without him finding out she had something to hide? He might be able to smell Tania the minute he set foot in the house.

And then there were all the other logistical details of keeping Tania alive in that room. Dina had to find a way to bring her food and water every day, not to mention some sort of chamber pot.

Dina used a chamber pot of her own in her bedroom. Belinda emptied it when she cleaned out the room. Dina would have to find something Tania could use and then Dina would have to empty it into her own chamber pot so no one realized there was another person staying in the house.

She wandered on down the corridor toward the kitchen. The first order of business was getting around Belinda. If Dina couldn't do that,

Tania would starve in that room and Dina could give up the project of hiding her right now.

To Dina's surprise, she found the kitchen door standing open. Dina saw Belinda at work ladling stew into several dozen small bowls laid out on the kitchen table. Belinda was getting ready to hand out charity to the children of the village subsidiaries who brought animals and food to the market.

Dina took another step toward the doorway. The outer kitchen door also stood open with a view of the path leading out to the street.

Belinda's eyes shot up and she scowled at Dina, but Belinda didn't stop what she was doing. She filled the bowls one after the other and set the pot back on the hearth just as a bunch of boys came around the corner. They stopped outside the outer kitchen door.

Dina recognized the wary, reserved expressions on their faces. The village children never laughed or ran around in play the way normal children did. They never talked to strangers or joked among themselves.

They saw her standing outside the kitchen and she and the boys stared back at each other. Were these children loyal to the Pride? Had they gotten old enough and seen enough of Prideland's horrors to tell on someone for breaking the rules?

Belinda hardly looked at them. "Come in and get your meal," she called over her shoulder. "I have to go to the shed and get a load of firewood. Come on. Don't hang around the door all day. Your food is waiting for you. Get in here and eat. I have a lot of work to do today, so I want you in and out before I get back."

The boys flooded into the kitchen and surrounded the table. The moment they cleared the door, Belinda bustled through it and disappeared around the other side of the house. The boys fell on their bowls of stew and wolfed the food down in seconds.

Dina stepped the rest of the way into the kitchen. She didn't want to deal with these children any more than she wanted to deal with Belinda, but she would never get another chance like this to get some food for Tania.

She approached the table where one bowl of stew sat near the corner untouched. A spoon stuck out of the side of it. Dina picked it up and brought it to her nose in a pantomime of getting ready to eat it herself.

None of the boys paid any attention. They were all too hungry and too in a hurry to leave for home.

Dina took the bowl to the fire, scooped another ladle full of food into it, set the ladle back down, and went back to the house door.

She looked back over her shoulder, but she couldn't see anything other than the tops of the boys' heads. She didn't hear anything other than the shoveling of their food into their mouths. None of them noticed anything out of the ordinary in her actions—at least, she hoped they didn't.

She slipped out of the kitchen into the corridor, but just before she left, she grabbed a wide-mouthed jar from the shelf behind the door. It wasn't a perfect chamber pot, but it would have to work.

She raced down to Tania's room and found her lying on the divan with the blanket over her. "How are you doing?"

Tania sighed. "I'm exhausted. This is the first moment's peace I've had since we landed on this horrid planet and I'm wiped out. All I want to do is sleep."

Dina set the bowl down next to her head. "You're pregnant. You're likely to be tired a lot. Here. Eat this. You need to keep your strength up."

"I don't feel like eating," Tania muttered.

"Maybe you don't, but your baby does."

"I don't care what my baby wants," Tania grumbled.

Dina compressed her lips together. "Eat it. I'm running a big risk getting this for you and I don't know when I'll be able to get you anymore. I'll bring you some water later....and use this as a chamber pot."

Tania opened her eyes and raised her eyebrows. "A chamber pot?"

"You know.....to go to the bathroom."

"How will you empty it?" Tania asked.

"Leave that to me. Renfroe will be home soon, so I won't be able to come see you very much. You'll be spending a lot of time alone in this room until we decide where to move you."

"I don't care," Tania replied. "All I want right now is to be alone."

Dina left her there and went back to her own room. She sat on the edge of the bed and thought things over. She'd seen several pitchers in Belinda's kitchen that would work to take water to Tania. Dina only had to get into the kitchen when Belinda wasn't around—and when Renfroe wasn't around.

Now that Dina had a moment to turn the problem over in her mind, she thought of all kinds of possibilities. She couldn't keep Tania hidden in that room forever or even for very long. Someone was bound to put the pieces together. If that someone turned out to be Renfroe, he might put the pieces together sooner rather than later. Dina had to move Tania somewhere else, somewhere safe, before that happened. But how....and where?

The late afternoon sun hit the glass door and warmed up the room. A flush of heat washed over Dina's face and body and her head reeled. She had to get out of this oppressive room.

She pushed herself up off the bed and opened the doors. The cooler air outside breezed into her face and she stepped outside to refresh herself before Renfroe came home. They spent their time in the bedroom, so she better get out now while she had the chance.

She strolled around the courtyard and passed the spot where Tania had been hiding. Dina's life sure had changed in only a few short hours. Just this morning she'd been floating in a mindless dream and letting Prideland look after its own business outside this garden.

Now she carried another human life in her hands and courted death herself for Tania's sake. Why not just let Tania stand or fall on her own? Why should Dina risk herself here to meddle in someone else's affairs?

Dina already knew the answer to all those questions. She couldn't let Tania fall to the Pride, not when Dina had it in her power to save Tania.

Dina had only let Prideland look after its own business because she told herself she couldn't do anything to stop it.

She couldn't save the Children from slaughter. She couldn't free the slaves from captivity, but she could save Tania. If Tania was the only person Dina ever saved, that would have to be enough.

Dina lifted her face into the last sunshine of the day and took a deep breath. She didn't want to go back into that house or that bedroom. The stuffy air made her sick sometimes, but she couldn't leave Renfroe waiting for her.

He would want her there in their room when he came home. She took one last deep breath of fresh air and turned around when she saw Renfroe entering the courtyard to meet her.

She smiled at him, but right then, something strange happened to her eyes. An overpowering wave of heat surged upward through her body from the bottom of her stomach all the way to the top of her head. It hit her with unstoppable force and knocked her clean off her feet.

She didn't feel the impact of her body hitting the ground, and when she opened her eyes, the sky overhead looked different. Rainbows of electric lights twinkled around the edges of her vision. Flashes of color shot into her field of view and explosions pounded her eardrums.

All of a sudden, the noise and flashing light vanished. Dina went completely blind and deaf, and her head fell backward into a bottomless gulf. Would she fall through it into nothingness?

She came back to her senses and found herself watching herself from a distance. She lay on her back on the ground, but she wasn't in Renfroe's garden anymore.

She lay in the middle of a golden autumn meadow somewhere outside the village where the landing team made first contact with the planet's human population. She saw the roofs of houses not far away.

The sky rose clear and high above her all the way up to the clouds, but the Dina lying on the ground didn't see that. She couldn't tell from where she stood whether the Dina on the ground even had her eyes open.

She stared down at herself. Why didn't she get up? Was she asleep there in the grass?

Then, while she watched, the body on the ground split down the middle like a pea pod. That Dina didn't react at all. Was she dead? She tried to call out to the person lying on the ground, but no sound came out of her mouth.

She watched herself in amazement as the split traveled from her sternum all the way down to her hips. It yawned open and the two sides of her body fell apart.

A green shoot sprouted from the opening and stretched its tender tip toward the sun. It twisted and wriggled out of the split in her body, cleared the two sides of the pod, and delicate emerald leaves sprang out from the shoot.

She watched the shoot grow and side branches burst outward from the main trunk. They spilled and grew all over the body on the ground and eventually covered it with green leaves.

In another minute, she couldn't see the body at all. Only a stout trunk with a thick tree growing out of it stood in the middle of the meadow where a lifeless body had been lying a minute before.

The next second, fireworks shot out of the tree's branches. Those rockets launched into the sky and fell in a rain of bombs onto the landscape. Dina raised her hand to protect her eyes from the explosions as sparks and burning gunpowder catapulted down on the meadow and fields.

The fireworks crashed through the house roofs, and before long, the whole village caught fire and burned to the ground before her eyes. The fireworks shooting out of the branches of that tree—the tree that sprouted from her own body—they spread wider and wider across the landscape until they destroyed all of Prideland.

All at once, her vision cleared and she found herself lying on the paving stones in the courtyard with Renfroe leaning over her. "Are you all right, Dina?"

She blinked and a tear ran out of the corner of her eye into her hair. "I'm pregnant."

Chapter 12

Dina lay back on her pile of cushions on her bed. Renfroe rested the side of his head against her belly and they breathed together in the stillness of the house. They lay there like that, together, for hours until she finally asked, "What are we going to do?"

Renfroe sighed. "*We* aren't going to do anything. I can't do anything. If anyone does something it has to be you."

"What can I do?"

"I don't know," he replied.

"How could this happen?"

"It happened the same way it's happened to all the others. We're no different than the rest of them. We did it together and you got pregnant. That's the way it happens."

"But we can't let this baby die!" she exclaimed. "I won't let it."

"What are you going to do about it? You can't keep it hidden all its life. Even if you did, what's going to happen when it realizes it's different from everyone else on the planet—even in the whole galaxy? It won't work."

"I won't let this baby die," she told him. "This could be the only child I have in my life. You should at least try to help me. This is your own child. Are you just going to stand by while the cats kill it? You wouldn't do that, would you?"

Renfroe sighed again, raised his head, and fixed Dina with a piercing stare. "If anyone found out you were pregnant from me, I would have no choice but to kill the Child myself. You know that as well as I do. This Child has no chance of survival. That's just the way it is. If you want another child—a human child—then perhaps we can arrange something with one of the other helpers."

Dina shot upright off the pillow. "What?! What are you talking about?! You aren't actually suggesting bringing in some kind of stud to get me pregnant so I can have a human child! Not even you could be so crass as to suggest that."

"I'm only saying that, if you want a child, you can have a human child. Lots of helpers do it."

She turned her head away. "I don't believe I'm hearing this."

"You can't keep this Child, Dina," he went on. "You might as well kill yourself right now rather than try to save this Child from the Pride. They've made up their minds to kill these Children and that's what they're going to do. Save yourself the heartache of getting attached to this Child and get used to the idea right now that you have to give it up. We can find a way for you to have another child—a human child."

"I don't want another child," she shot back. "I want this Child. I want a Child that's half you and half me. Isn't that what having a child is supposed to be? Isn't that the whole point of having a child with someone you love—so you can see the child's other parent in them? Why would I want to have a child with someone else?"

"So the child could live and you could keep it. That's why." He sat up. "Don't give yourself false hope. If you have a child with one of the helpers, it will still be half you. That's the best you can hope for. What about your friend, Tom, your old mate? Would you want to have a child with him?"

Dina threw herself back down on the cushion and crossed her arms over her stomach in a hopeless effort to protect this Child from reality. "Don't talk about Tom. I'm not having a child with Tom. I'm having one with you."

"You're not having a Child with me—at least not one that will survive more than a day or two. Believe me, Dina. I don't like this any more than you do. I don't want any of these Children to be killed, especially not one of my own, but there's nothing I can do about it."

"I won't let you or anyone else kill this Child," Dina shot back. "I'll protect this Child with my life. You'll have to kill me, too, if you're going to kill it, and if you cared at all about me or this Child, you would do the same thing. You would find a way to help me protect this Child from the Pride."

He stared at her and held her motionless with his eyes, but she wouldn't back down. The more she thought about this Child growing inside her, the more determined she became to keep it.

She might not be able to protect any other Children from this madness, but she would protect this one if it was the last thing she ever did. This insanity had to stop somewhere and it would stop right here, with her.

In the end, he turned away. "The only way you could possibly keep this Child is if you ran off to the jungle and raised it among the slags."

Dina's head whipped around and she gasped out loud. "What are you saying? Are you saying the slags would take us in? Would we be safe out there?"

"I don't know about safe, but you'd be a lot safer out there than you would be in this city. You might die out there just as quickly as you would die here, but at least you'd have a chance. At least the Child would have a chance."

The fog clouding Dina's mind broke apart and started to lift. Her rusty brain kicked into gear and her thoughts cleared. "But would the slags accept us? They don't take too kindly to any cat of the Pride."

"The Children are not cats of the Pride," Renfroe pointed out. "They're enemies of the Pride. All the cats say so and an enemy of the Pride is a friend of the slags. As a matter of fact, a few helpers who've gotten pregnant with Children have run away to the jungle and I hear they're living in the cantons. Some cats in one of the other cities went out to clear an infestation of slags and they found human mothers with their Children among the slags they reduced."

Dina grimaced in disgust at his language, but she didn't argue. Only one thing he said made any sense to her. She had a chance to save her Child. She would go out to the cantons the way she did the first time she escaped from Prideland. She knew what the cantons were like.

One more thing stuck out in her mind. She would take Tania with her. They would both find shelter in the cantons and Renfroe would never know Tania had ever been in his house.

"The question is," she remarked, "how am I going to get out there?"

Renfroe shrugged. "That shouldn't be too difficult. You've done it twice before. You should be able to do it again."

Dina lowered her eyes. She'd done it alone last time. She'd run away during a lightning storm the first time to avoid the sentinel cats. The second time, she fought the sentinel cats off and floated down the river in an empty barrel.

She wouldn't be doing either of those things with Tania in tow. Dina wasn't sure she could do them pregnant anyway, but she didn't tell Renfroe that.

Renfroe broke in on her thoughts. "I should tell you, since you're thinking about it, that the slags have reoccupied the canton where I found you last time. It's not far from the last village on the road out of the city, so you shouldn't have any trouble getting there. Once you get there, I'm sure the slags will help you settle in."

Dina looked down at her hands as memories from her time in that canton came rushing back. "I didn't know they'd moved back into it."

"You should warn them, when you get there, to clear out of it as soon as they can. That's the first place the cats will come looking for you when they find out you're gone."

Dina's thoughts swirled so fast she couldn't keep track of them all. If she got out of this city with Tania, if they made it all the way out to the jungle and took refuge among the slags, Dina would make sure they didn't suffer another massacre by the cats.

"There's just one more thing, Dina," he went on.

She glanced up at him. "What is it?"

"Whatever you do to get out of the city and get out to the canton, you'll have to do it on your own. Don't even tell me what your plans are. You have to escape from his house and this city exactly the same way you did last time—with no one knowing what you plan to do—not even me. Do you understand? If anyone, cat or human, finds out that I knew your plans, I'm finished. I would have to hunt you down and kill you or I would be killed myself. Not even I can stand up to the Pride. So make your plans and carry them out, but don't tell me what you plan to do. Keep it a secret."

Dina nodded. She wouldn't have told him her plans anyway. She wouldn't tell him about Tania for all the tea in China.

Her mind revolved around all the possibilities. She only came back to the present moment when Renfroe put his head down in her lap.

Her eyes focused on the shaggy hair on either side of his ears. She studied them from a million miles away. Her brain no longer functioned the same way. Then, automatically, her fingers burrowed into that hair and she rubbed at the base of his ears.

Renfroe purred. "I'll be sorry to lose you, but I suppose it's the only way."

Dina hardly heard him. She couldn't stop thinking about her time in the canton. She would be back there soon, among free people, and she would live the rest of her life and bring up her Child there.

She wouldn't have to worry about her Child getting the House of Man or being passed off as a helper to some cat to spend his or her life in slavery. Would she be sorry to leave Renfroe in exchange for all that?

"Why don't you come with me?" Even as she said the words, she knew it was impossible. Maybe that was why she said it. She had to play along with their make-believe romance so he would let her go in peace, but he wouldn't come.

"You know I can't come," he replied. "It would never work. For one thing, the slags would never take you in if we were together. They wouldn't let me come within a hundred miles of their canton without trying to kill me......and the Pride would kill me if I tried to leave."

"What?!" she gasped. "Do you mean to tell me that not even the cats are allowed to leave? It's one thing to keep the people prisoners, but the cats, too?"

Renfroe nodded. "It's true. We're prisoners of our own dominance. We've taken power over all the people on this planet and thrown the slags out on their own resources. Now not even a cat can leave the Pride. Where would I go? I can't go to the village without being revered as a savior and I can't go to the jungle without fighting the slags to the death. In a way, a cat who disagrees with the Pride and wants to part ways is even more a captive than a person. A person can run away to the cantons. I don't even have that."

"So what will you do? How will you live with yourself?"

"I'll just have to keep going. I'll keep chairing the Senate and I'll keep arguing to let the Children live and it will keep not making any difference. Pretty soon, no one will listen to me at all anymore and then someone else will take over the Senate."

"And that's what you wanted all along, isn't it? You've been talking for a while about stepping down."

He nodded. "It will happen eventually, but not any time soon. I'll have to make a good show of getting along with everyone."

"And that means going along with the killing," she added.

He nodded.

They fell into silence and leaned against each other the way they always did. Night fell and they drifted into each other's arms.

For the first time in weeks, she saw her future play out in front of her eyes. She saw a future where before she saw nothing, not even the present.

Now the pulse of life beat in her veins and called her back from her dream world. Her heart beat faster and she bent her mind to the problem of escaping from Prideland one more time. Only this time, she had a reason to do it.....and she had Tania to think about, too.

Chapter 13

Dina opened her eyes in the morning with her arms still wrapped around Renfroe's body. She turned her head without waking him and she stared out the windows the way she always did.

Everything had changed. Thoughts came into her head with crystal clarity and she knew exactly what she had to do.

She would do anything for this Child. She no longer clung to Renfroe as her cornerstone. If anything, he was the biggest obstacle she faced in getting away from here. She had to put him behind her so she could get to her new life.

Even if she died trying to get out, she wouldn't let this Child grow up in Prideland. Even if the Pride hadn't intended to wipe out the Children at birth, even if the Pride had accepted them, she would have to get away.

She had to raise her Child in freedom. She owed it nothing less. What was a mother for if not to protect the Child from danger and give it the best possible life? Surely even the cats could understand that.

How could the female cats of the Pride who got pregnant from their human male helpers allow the Pride to kill their babies? Where was their animal sense?

Had they fallen so far from their natural state? Could it be that they no longer felt the same motherly instinct to protect their young?

Maybe Renfroe was right and the cats of the Pride were as much victims of their own mind control as their human slaves. Cats couldn't express disagreement with the Pride any more than humans could.

Dina lay perfectly still, but her mind churned in the same ferment of excitement as it had the night she escaped. She had to find some way to get out of here. She would find a way. Something would show itself. She knew that now. She'd escaped twice before. She would do it again. Prideland wasn't as secure as people liked to think.

The noise of the door opening roused Renfroe. He growled and shook his head. Then he and Dina sat up when Belinda brought in their food. Renfroe muttered something that Dina didn't catch and he hopped off the bed. He lapped at the water basin in the corner and they met back up at the table.

He pulled his leg of deer meat onto the floor and started eating it without a thought. Dina took her usual chair and glanced at the tray. A pile of fried lizard feet sat on the plate. Their toenails still stuck out of the end of the crispy skin at the end of each toe.

Dina swallowed hard and turned away. "I can't eat this."

Renfroe stole a glance at her. "What's the matter?"

"I feel sick. I can't eat."

He didn't stop eating his own food. "Maybe you'll feel better later."

She didn't answer. A surge of nausea rose up from somewhere deep inside her and threatened to spew out of her mouth right there on the beautiful clean carpet.

She went to the glass door and pushed it open. The fresh air hit her in the face and her stomach settled down, but she couldn't go back into that room. She heard Renfroe behind her gulping down his meat while she stood in the courtyard and gazed up at the sun.

The world looked so different now. How could she let herself fall under Prideland's spell? How could she ever have been happy here and plan to spend the rest of her life here? Why did she ever come back from the *Savannah?*

Now she had this Child to think about. That alone was worth coming back for. She wouldn't have had it on the *Savannah.* She and Tom would have worked away at their careers for another ten years or so before they considered having a family.

Maybe she and Tom would never have had a family. Maybe they would have put the Armada before everything and remained childless all their lives. What a waste of their lives that would have been.

She had this Child now and she wouldn't turn back from her responsibility to it. She looked forward to the day ahead. She could search the house for some opportunity to get away. There had to be some way, somewhere. She only had to find it.

Renfroe's eating noises changed and he growled again when he gnawed on the leftover bone. "Dina," he called.

"I'm right here. I just needed some fresh air."

"I have to leave for the Senate building soon," he told her.

She came back to the doorway, but the instant she put her head inside, the smell of the room made her stomach heave. She pulled back. "I'll be here when you come back."

"Are you sure?"

"I'm sure. I won't be able to find a way out that fast. I have no idea how I'm going to do it."

He cocked his head to one side and then humphed, nodded, and walked toward the door. "If you don't eat this, what will you eat? You can't go hungry with a baby to feed."

"I don't know. I'll have to figure that out, too."

"Go down to the kitchen and get yourself something. Oh, I know you don't want to go there and face Belinda. Well, come along with me. We'll go down there together and I'll tell Belinda you're to have free run of the kitchen whenever you want to. You should be able to go in and get whatever you want to eat."

Dina opened her mouth to argue, but then she realized that having free run of the kitchen would solve most of her problems in one stroke.

She followed Renfroe out of the room and down to the kitchen. They found Belinda puffing and sweating at her daily chores.

She stopped dead in her tracks when she saw Renfroe in the doorway. Dina observed Belinda's face from behind him and almost pitied her. He never came into the kitchen and she feared him to death. She would suffer any torture not to have to deal with him at all.

"Belinda," he boomed and she almost fell over in terror. "I want you to make room for Dina in this kitchen. From now on, she's to have free run of the kitchen and she's going to come in and get her own food whenever she wants to. You'll keep bringing her meals the way you always have, but she's going to be coming into the kitchen to get other food, too. Is that clear?"

Belinda nodded in mute shock.

Renfroe humphed under his breath again and turned away. "There. That's settled. Now, then, Dina dear, walk me to the door because it's time for me to leave."

They strolled to the front door of the house and Dina rested her hand on his shoulder the way she always did when they walked side by side.

Renfroe stopped on the threshold. "Don't leave just yet. I want to spend a little more time with you before you go, so don't make it a complete surprise. I want to have a chance to say goodbye to you, at least."

"Don't worry. I'll be here tonight."

"Good." He nudged the door open and disappeared.

Dina wandered back to her room and stayed there just long enough to give Renfroe time to leave the neighborhood. Then she grabbed the plate of lizard feet, did her best not to look at it, and scurried down the corridor to her old room.

She found Tania in exactly the same position on the divan with the blanket over her. Dina set the plate down on the floor and sat down by Tania's head.

Tania opened her eyes when Dina came in, but when Dina sat down, Tania closed her eyes again.

"How are you doing?" Dina asked.

Tania nodded. "I'm okay. I'm just sleeping a lot. I'm exhausted."

"I brought you something to eat."

Tania glanced at the plate. "You don't expect me to eat that, do you?"

"You should eat it. I know it doesn't look all that nice, but you have to eat something. You can't expect to stay healthy without food."

Tania tucked her head back down into the blanket and pulled it up under her chin. "I don't want it. You have it."

Dina didn't even dare to look at the plate. How did she expect to stay healthy without food? She had a baby to grow, too. "Listen, Tania. We're going to get out of here. I don't know when and I don't know how we're going to do it, but we're going to leave here. We're going to leave Prideland."

Tania's eyes popped open. "What? How?"

"I don't know yet, but I'll figure out a way. It will probably be soon, so be ready to travel. It's a long walk out of the city and past the village, so you need to eat some food and drink plenty of water. You're going to need your strength."

"Where will we go?" Tania asked. "The Pride controls the whole planet. Khalid told me so."

"They don't control the *whole* planet. Some people live out in the jungle. The Pride doesn't control them."

Tania stared at her. "You're talking about the slags. You want us to leave here and go live with the slags? They're animals! They live in the mud and let their children starve in the wintertime."

"That's a lie," Dina snapped. "It's all lies. The slags are the most civilized people on this planet."

"How do you know?"

"I know because I've been there. I stayed with them in their cantons. I've seen the way they live and what they eat. I've seen the way they treat their children and I can tell you it's a sight better than the way the helpers and the subsidiaries live. The slags are kind, brave, intelligent people and I would rather live with them than anyone else on this side of the galaxy. I'm going back out there and you're coming with me."

Tania hesitated. "I don't know about this."

"Would you rather stay here and take your chances with Khalid?" Tania shut her mouth with a click. "That's what I thought, So you need to get up, get something to eat, and get ready to leave. I don't know when we'll go, but it will be soon. It will be just as soon as I figure out how to do it."

Tania sat up with the blanket still wrapped around her. She glanced again at the plate of lizard feet, but she didn't make any move to eat it. "It must be almost impossible. The Pride would never let its helpers escape."

"It's not the easiest task in the world. I admit that. If we go at night, the sentinel cats will be after us."

"Who are the sentinel cats?" Tania asked.

"They patrol the city streets after curfew. They're only small cats, but there are so many of them they could easily bring down a person with sheer numbers. I wouldn't want to fight them, not after......" She trailed off.

"After what?" Tania asked.

"Never mind.....and then there are the helpers. They'll be watching out for us during the day. You've been gone long enough for Khalid to notice and someone will have told him by now that you were last seen coming here to see me."

"Who would have told him that?" Tania asked. "No one saw me come here."

"Oh, come on, Tania. You know better than that. All the helpers keep track of all the other helpers. If a helper didn't see you come here, the Elite Battalion sure did. No one is supposed to talk to them, but they must have some way of reporting what they see to the Pride. I'm sure they know you're here."

"But that's impossible!" Tania exclaimed.

"Nothing is impossible here. No atrocity is too horrible to happen here and escape isn't impossible here, either. That's how I know we can make it out. I just have to keep my eyes open for an opportunity and you need to be ready to go at a moment's notice. One of these days I'll be coming in here saying, 'Let's go,' and you need to be ready to get up and go. Do you understand?"

Tania nodded at her with wide, round eyes. "How will you stop Renfroe from knowing you're planning to leave? He'll be watching you, too."

"I don't have to stop him from knowing. He knows I'm planning to leave and he's letting me go."

"He's letting you go?!" Tania repeated. "Why?"

Dina paused. "I'm pregnant."

Tania sucked in her breath and her hand flew to her mouth. "Dina! No!"

Dina nodded. She couldn't help but smile.

"Are you sure it's Renfroe's? It couldn't be Tom's, could it?"

"I'm sure it's Renfroe's. I had my last night with Tom on board the *Savannah* and I had my last period just before we left. Renfroe's the only one I've been with since then. This is one of the Children. That's why he's letting me go. He doesn't want to be part of reducing his own Child."

Tania stared at her. Then she dropped her eyes and shook her head. "He's so different from Khalid."

"He doesn't want any of these Children reduced. He thinks they should be brought into the Pride and they could strengthen the Pride. I begged him to let me keep this Child and he said the only way it could survive is if I went out to the jungle to live with the slags. He said some other female helpers who have gotten pregnant have already gone out and the slags take them in."

"If that's the way he feels, why doesn't he help us get out of the city? We could walk right past the helpers and the sentinel cats with him protecting us."

Dina shook her head. "He can't. For one thing, he doesn't know about you, and for another, not even he can help us escape from the Pride. If he tried, he could get reduced himself. He even told me to keep my plans secret from him. He doesn't want to know when I'm leaving or how I plan to do it. He would have to reduce me himself if he knew."

Tania shook her head in blank astonishment. "But how are we going to do it, then?"

Dina stood up. "I don't know. I'll let you know as soon as I figure it out."

Chapter 14

Dina hid Tania's chamber pot under her tunic and went back down the corridor to her bedroom to empty it. She only made it a few steps before she heard Belinda moving around in the house behind her.

That sound set Dina's nerves on end. She couldn't let Belinda find out what she was doing.

Dina sprinted to her room, shut the door, and emptied the chamber pot into her own container under the bed. Then she washed it out in her room and took it back to Tania's room.

Tania still hadn't touched the lizard feet, but Dina didn't have time to argue about that. Tania would get hungry enough to eat them soon enough, but what about Dina? What would she do when she got hungry?

She still couldn't face Belinda. In spite of what Renfroe had said, Dina still couldn't bring herself to intrude on Belinda's territory and Dina couldn't even think about eating now anyway.

She went out into the courtyard to get some fresh air, but this time, unlike all the other times she'd come out here, she examined every brick in the wall for any sign of a way out.

She even went to the edge of the courtyard and looked out into the garden itself. This was the first time since the factors' attack that she'd dared to come out this far.

She couldn't go through the garden doorway with Buck and his friends waiting for her out there. Dina had fought the sentinel cats before, but she'd only won because she surprised them.

They weren't used to humans running away, much less ones who stood up to them and fought back, but every cat in the Pride knew about her now. The sentinel cats would know how to deal with her if she tried to fight them again.

Dina also didn't count on Tania helping her fight off anyone who tried to stop them. Tania had become so passive and weak-minded in the last few weeks.

Tania was afraid of her own shadow now. Dina didn't trust Tania not to crumble at the first sign of danger, especially if it came from a cat threatening her.

Dina wouldn't be able to protect herself and Tania. Dina didn't know if she could fight at all when she was pregnant. She'd been getting bouts of weakness, nausea, and hot flashes ever since she realized she was pregnant.

Tania had been complaining about the same thing and Dina hadn't seen Tania eating nearly enough. The journey from the city to the jungle would be hard enough. Tania might not even make it.

Dina could drive herself to the point of collapse, but Tania? She might have a nervous breakdown on the way from plain old fear. Then what was Dina supposed to do—leave her behind?

Dina might have to leave Tania behind to save her own life. Dina's own Child came first. She couldn't let herself get captured or killed for Tania or anyone else.

She circled the courtyard and searched the garden more than once, but she had to admit to herself that there was no way out through either of those places.

She couldn't climb the wall, and even if she could, she still had the problems of the sentinel cats and the helpers to think about. Whatever she did, she had to get around all of them. Between the two, they had both day and night covered.

She searched the whole house for any resource she could use, but by the end of the day, she'd come up empty-handed and she couldn't ignore her hunger anymore. She started toward the kitchen when the front door opened and Renfroe came in.

"So you are still here," he remarked.

"I told you I would be. Did you think I would lie about that?"

"It's happened before."

She ignored that. "How was your day?"

"Surprisingly average." He turned down the corridor and she fell in at his side. "By the way, I meant to tell you. There's a helpers' festival tomorrow at Helion House. You'll be going, along with everyone else."

She froze. "Is that wise? The last time I tried to leave the house...." She stopped.

"All the helpers have to go. I'm sure you'll be fine."

"They won't show their enthusiasm for the Pride by smashing my head in, will they?" she asked.

"What makes you say that? Why would they smash your head in?"

"It's happened before," she muttered.

He pretended not to hear. "Come up to the bedroom. I want us to spend the night together."

"Don't we always spend the night together? What makes you think tonight will be any different?"

"I won't know when it might be our last night together. I want to enjoy your company while I have the chance."

They walked down the corridor side by side and Dina's fingers trailed through his fur. She wanted to enjoy the time she still had with him, too, but the whole time, her mind buzzed in excitement.

Tomorrow was a Festival. All the helpers would be there. That meant Belinda would be out of the house and Buck and his men would leave the garden door unguarded. Tania and Dina could walk away from the city. They could walk right down the street without being seen by a single helper.

Dina mentally traced the route from Renfroe's house to the main road out of the city and then to the village. If she stuck to the back streets through quiet neighborhoods like Renfroe's, she and Tania might not see any cats, either.

They wouldn't see Khalid. He lived on the other side of the city. They wouldn't see Renfroe. He would spend the day down at the Senate.

She and Tania wouldn't see any cat they knew. No one would recognize the two women. If they acted naturally, they could get away without tipping anyone off that they were doing something they shouldn't be doing.

Renfroe paused outside their bedroom door and looked up at her. "Is anything wrong, Dina?"

Could he hear her heart pounding? Did he smell her anxiety through her sweat?

She would leave tomorrow morning. She had to get away from him sometime tonight. She had to get to the kitchen to get food for the journey and any other supplies they might need.

Could she take some kind of fire-making supplies without making Belinda suspicious? Dina also had to get to her old room to warn Tania of her plans.

How would she get away from Renfroe? He wanted at least one last night of romance with her before she left and she wanted to give it to him. She had to show him how much she appreciated him for letting her go. The project would have been impossible if he hadn't.

She smiled down at him. "I'm fine. I'm just hungry. I haven't eaten all day."

He narrowed his eyes at her. "I told you to go down to the kitchen and get something. I even told Belinda to let you take whatever you wanted. What did I do that for if you're going to starve yourself all day?"

"I was just on my way there when you came home, but you're here now and I want to spend the time with you. Belinda will bring our dinner into the bedroom soon. I can eat then."

He grumbled under his breath and pushed the door open.

They actually found Dina's tray and Renfroe's usual meat waiting for them on the table. They both sat down to eat right away, so they didn't say much. Only after she'd cleared her plate and Renfroe licked the juice off his paws did he turn to her.

"Have you thought any more about how you'll get out of the city?" he asked.

"Yes, but I won't tell you about it. I don't want to compromise you."

He nodded, jumped onto the bed, and stretched out on his side. "Come up here with me."

She went to him and laid down next to him on the bed. She knew her place. She draped her arm over his body, rested her head on the pillow, and he gazed down at her from above.

"You've been happy here, haven't you, Dina?" he asked. "You wouldn't leave if it was just you and me, would you?"

She stared up into his bright golden eyes. She didn't have to lie to him about this. "You know I've been happy. I would never even have thought about leaving if I hadn't gotten pregnant. I came to an understanding with the Pride and I would have stayed here with you forever if this hadn't happened, but it did happen. That's the only reason I'm leaving."

In her mind, she thanked her lucky stars that she did get pregnant. She might never have snapped out of her trance otherwise. Now at least she had a chance to live her life in freedom—her and her Child.

Renfroe sighed and put his big, shaggy head down across her hips. He rested his ear against her belly and listened. "I know it's true. You've acted differently these last few weeks. You didn't fight against the Pride the way you did when you first got here. You settled in. I thought you were happy."

She hadn't been happy. She'd been asleep. She put herself to sleep so she could tolerate being a slave, but maybe that was what coming to an understanding with the Pride really was. "I was happy. I am happy. You know that. You don't have to ask."

He lifted his head again and his eyes drilled into her soul for a long moment. She felt no fear at all when she looked back deep into his eyes.

"You smell different now," he told her. "I don't recognize your scent anymore."

She took a moment to understand what he meant. Did he detect a lie? Did he realize she was already gone? "Maybe it's because I'm pregnant now," she suggested.

He nodded and put his head down on her belly again. "It must be that. You're a different person now. I don't know you anymore."

"I haven't changed. I don't think a person could change that much, that fast." But even she knew it was true. The simple knowledge that she had a Child to look after made all the difference in the world.

She wasn't the same person. She was a mother now. She didn't belong to him anymore. She belonged to her Child.

He didn't answer. He lay with the side of his head pressed against her abdomen, listening. What did he hear in there? Finally, she asked, "What are you doing?"

He raised his head. "By the way, you're carrying twins."

Her eyes flew open. "How do you know?"

"I can hear them in there. I can hear two sets of fluids circulating. It's common among larger carnivores, although not so much with tigers, but I'm not surprised."

"I am. I was expecting one. That's what's normal for humans."

"This isn't a human child—or rather, I should say *these* aren't human children. These are Children of the Pride and they're different from both cats and humans."

"Have you seen many of them? Tell me what they're like."

"I haven't seen many and the ones I have seen were tiny babies. I couldn't tell you much."

"You've seen more than I have. Are they more like cats or more like people?"

He tilted his head to one side. "Sort of half and half. It's hard to explain. I wonder sometimes what they'll look like when they get older. I wonder what they'll be capable of."

"Maybe by the time these Children grow up, the Pride will be ready to accept them. You might be able to see them when they grow up."

He shook his head. "I don't think, but I might see them before that. I hope I don't, but I might."

"Why do you say that? Why do you say you hope you won't see them? You're their father."

"If I do see them, it will be because the Pride will go into the jungle to hunt them down. Remember this, Dina. You won't be safe even if you make it to the cantons. The Pride will never let these Children reach adulthood. The cats will strike deep into the jungle to find them and reduce them. They will hunt these Children much more ferociously than they ever did the slags and I will have no choice but to come with them."

"But you wouldn't!" Dina cried. "You wouldn't hunt your own Children, would you? Not even you could do that."

"I might have to," he told her. "I will hold out as long as I can, but eventually I'll have to come, too. I'm Chairman of the Senate. I'll have to prove my loyalty to the Pride. They won't allow me to do otherwise."

She closed her eyes against the image and shuddered as she relived those awful moments when she watched the cats exterminate the jungle people in the cantons. Could she stand to watch him coming after her Children? Could she stand to face him hunting her down and killing his own Children—her Children?

His voice rumbled into her soul and brought her back to the present. "There's one more thing, Dina."

"What?" she whispered. What more could there be after that? Wasn't that enough?

"I want you to promise me something. I'm letting you go. You would never be able to go if I didn't let you and I want you to do something for me in return."

She opened her mouth to say, *What?* again, but no sound came out.

"You can go to the jungle to have these Children and bring them up," he told her. "I'll do everything in my power to make sure you're left in peace. I won't be able to do much, but what I can do, I will do."

"Thank you for that," she choked. She couldn't stop shaking in anticipation of what was coming.

"Don't thank me," he snapped. "I'm letting you go on one condition. Once these Children have grown old enough to take care of themselves, when they no longer need you, I want you to come back to me for good. That's the condition. No more escapes. No more arguments. I want you to come back to me the way you've been these last few weeks. I want all of you all to myself."

"But that could take years, maybe even decades It could be fifteen to twenty years from now if these Children develop the way human children do."

"I understand that. I want you to give me your word that you'll come back. Once the Children are old enough to protect themselves from the cats, I want you to come back. If you don't promise me that you will come back, I won't let you go."

"But how....?" she began.

His eyes glittered in the dying rays of the sun coming through the window. "If you don't promise, I'll make sure you never leave here and I'll make sure these Children never reach adulthood."

She stared into his eyes one last time. Then she let her chin fall onto her chest. "I promise."

Chapter 15

Renfroe rolled off Dina and uncoiled his long body across the bed. He stretched his legs out behind him, put his head on the pillow, and closed his eyes. His breathing relaxed and lengthened.

Dina pulled the blanket over her bare chest and sat up. "I'm going down to the kitchen to get something to eat."

His whiskers twitched and one of his eyelids flicked open. "But we just ate."

"That was before. I'm hungry again. My appetite is all over the place. One minute I can't stand the sight of food and the next minute I could eat a whole ox."

She climbed out of bed and picked up her clothes. Renfroe didn't open his eyes again. "Be back soon," he growled. "I haven't finished with you yet."

She smiled over her shoulder at him and pulled her tunic over her head. "Do you want me to bring you anything?"

"Fill up the water basin, will you?"

"I'll do that when I get back. I'll have to take it out to the fountain and I'll have my hands full from the kitchen."

He grunted under his breath. He was already half asleep. Dina drew her leggings the rest of the way on and slipped out the door.

Moonlight peeked through the windows and lit up the corridor, so she didn't have any trouble finding her way to the kitchen. Dina heard Belinda crashing around in there even before Dina put her hand on the doorknob.

The cook whipped around when Dina opened the door. Belinda gave Dina a scorching frown, but Belinda didn't demand to know what Dina was here for.

Belinda didn't say anything to her at all. She had her orders straight from Renfroe. She spun back the other way just as fast and turned her back on Dina. Belinda went back to whatever she was doing in the corner by the fireplace.

Dina went to the pantry. Joints of meat, rounds of cheese, bundles of herbs, and braids of vegetables hung from the ceiling in here the same way they did out in the kitchen. Packets of unidentified food lined the shelves. The food had all been wrapped in paper and dried leaves and tied up with dried grass twisted into twine.

Dina studied everything while she tried to decide what to take for the journey. What could she take that wouldn't arouse Belinda's suspicions? She wouldn't be able to carry much and she couldn't count on Tania carrying anything.

She didn't realize that Belinda's presence would bother her so much, so Dina gave up. She would decide tomorrow when they actually left the house. She couldn't take anything now, anyway, not with Belinda standing right there in the kitchen.

She turned around to go back to her room when a loud knock banged on the outside kitchen door. Belinda opened it and exchanged a few words with someone on the threshold.

A female voice echoed into the kitchen. "Where is she?"

"Who?" Belinda asked.

"The helper," the visitor replied. "Renfroe's helper. Where is she?"

Dina stepped out of the pantry. "I'm right here. Who are you and what do you want from me?"

In the lamplight, Dina found herself face to face with a middle-aged with a frank, practical expression. She wore a dark dress unlike Dina had ever seen any other helpers wearing. The woman kept her dark black hair tied up in a bun.

"You're the one I'm looking for," she announced. "You're the only one who can do anything."

"Who are you?" Dina asked. "I don't know you."

"I'm Fan Tiko. I'm helper to Aurora Helion. Do you know who that is?"

Dina shook her head. "I guess it's one of the Helion family."

"Not just one of them," Fan replied. "She's the mate of Kaido Helion, the oldest of Lord Helion's sons. Kaido is in line to inherit the patriarchy when his father dies. Your benefactor, Senator Renfroe, is grooming Kaido to take over the Chairman's position in the Senate."

Dina nodded. "Renfroe mentioned that he had one of the Helions picked out for the job, but he didn't say which one. So what do you want with me?"

"I've come from Aurora. She sent me to find you. She says you're the only one who can do anything."

"About what?" Dina asked.

Fan stepped into the kitchen and pulled out a bundle from under her tunic. She held it out to Dina and lifted back the corner of the bundle, which turned out to be a blanket tied into an envelope.

Dina peeked inside and her heart stopped when she saw six tiny creatures curled up inside. They looked like kittens only a little bigger, but their faces looked too much like human faces for them to be cats.

Beautiful golden hair covered their bodies and swirled inward from the edges of their faces. They kept their eyes shut tight and they squirmed around in their nest.

Dina raised her hand, but she didn't dare to touch the little creatures. She opened her mouth, but she couldn't say anything.

"These are Aurora's cubs," Fan told her. "She told me to give them to you."

"But...." Dina stared down at the tiny things. "What am I supposed to do with them?"

Fan shifted in a way that made Dina look up at her. Their eyes locked and Dina knew the answer before Fan said it. "Do you know what these kittens are? My benefactor, Aurora, had a helper—a man. He....helped her. You know what I mean. Kaido doesn't know about it. He thinks Aurora got pregnant from him. If he found out about this, he would do a lot more than reduce the cubs. He would reduce Aurora, too. She has to get rid of them. You're the only one who can do it."

"But why me?" Dina asked. "I can't do anything. I can barely keep myself alive, much less these kittens."

"Aurora remembers that you came from a starship. I don't know what you're supposed to do with them, but it's certain that no other helper can do anything, either. If you don't take them, I'll go drown them in the river before I go back to Helion House."

Dina snatched the bundle out of her hands. "Give them to me."

"What will you do?" Fan asked.

"I don't know, but I won't drown them in the river."

Fan nodded. "Thank you. Thank you from my benefactor."

"Thank her for me. I'll do my best and I'll make sure no one ever finds out that they came from her."

Fan turned away, and in an instant, she was gone.

Dina stared down at the wriggling creatures inside the blanket. She couldn't call them kittens or cubs. These were Children.

She had wanted to examine them from a biological point of view, not have a brood of them thrust into her care, but here they were. They would be dead if she didn't take care of them.

She glanced up and saw Belinda scowling at her. Dina blushed. The bundle moved in her arms. "Belinda...." She trailed off.

Belinda compressed her lips. "I hope you understand what will happen if Renfroe finds out about this."

"You won't tell him, will you, Belinda? Please don't tell him. They're helpless babies. You wouldn't do anything that could get them reduced, would you?"

Belinda set her fists on her hips. "You're taking a mighty big risk. They're the enemies of the Pride."

"They aren't! They can't be. How could they be enemies of the Pride? They're newborn babies. Look at them. They're totally defenseless." She held up the bundle for Belinda to see.

Belinda recoiled and held up her hand to block her own view of the creatures. "Get them away from me! I don't want to see them. I should report this to Buck right away. He'll know how to deal with this."

"No, please don't!" Dina exclaimed. "Please, Belinda, you have to help me. Please don't tell Buck or Renfroe or anyone else about this."

"Don't you know you could get all of us reduced for this? It's bad enough that you and I and these.....things could all be reduced if anyone found out, but Renfroe could be reduced, too. If anyone thought he knowingly harbored these Children in his house, he would be reduced right along with the rest of us."

"I know," Dina whispered. "Believe me, I know the risk as well as you do. Just please, Belinda, please don't tell anyone. I can't let these babies die. I have to do something to give them a chance."

"And you expect me to do the same thing, I suppose," Belinda shot back. "You expect me to take the same risk because you can't let them die. Let them die, I say! I would rather they die than to die myself."

Dina lowered her eyes, and once she did, she couldn't take her eyes off the babies. They were absolutely beautiful. "Please, Belinda. I'll do anything. Please don't tell anyone."

Belinda hesitated. "What are you going to do with them?"

"I don't know, but I swear to you, Belinda, if you keep this quiet for just one day, I'll get them out of this house so you never have to worry about it again. Please, just give me one day and they'll be gone."

Belinda narrowed her eyes at Dina. "All right. I'll give you one day. That's all. If they aren't gone by then, I'm telling Buck."

"Oh, thank you, Belinda! I don't know what I can do to thank you."

"You can drown them in the river, but you aren't going to do that, so get them out of my kitchen. I don't want to have anything to do with them."

Dina hurried across the kitchen, but when she got to the house door, she stopped and looked back over her shoulder. "Belinda?"

"What do you want now?" Belinda snapped. "Why can't you just leave me in peace?"

"They'll get hungry in the night. If they start making noise, Renfroe will hear them. I need something to feed them."

Belinda let out a gasp of exasperation, stormed across the kitchen to the pantry, and snatched down a leather pouch from the wall where she kept milk. A wooden plug in the neck stopped the milk from splashing out at the top.

The pouch sloshed in her hand when she shoved it at Dina. "Here. Now get out of here before I change my mind."

Dina gathered the bundle into one arm, the milk pouch in the other, and fled out of the kitchen as fast as she could. The kitchen door slammed behind her as she tore down the corridor to her old room and ducked inside.

Tania raised her head from the divan. "What are you doing here at this time of night? Isn't Renfroe in the house?"

Dina caught her breath and sat down next to her on the divan. "Listen, Tania. We're leaving here in the morning. I've got it all worked out. Make sure you get a good night's sleep tonight because you're going to need to do some hard traveling in the morning. Do you hear me?"

Tania nodded and looked down at the bundle. "What's that?"

Dina peeled back the corner. "Look."

Tania peered into the little nest and sucked her breath in through her teeth. "What are they?"

"Can't you tell? They're Children. Their mother is a lioness and their father is a human man. They aren't cat and they aren't human. They're something in between. They've just been born."

Tania stiffened. "What are they doing here?"

"Their mother's mate is heir apparent to Lord Helion. If her mate finds out, he'd kill the mother along with the babies. She sent them to me. I don't know why. She heard that I was from a starship and she thought I was the only one who could do anything. To tell you the truth, I don't think she was so much concerned about the Children surviving as keeping them a secret from her mate."

"Well, you can't keep them here," Tania countered. "If anyone finds out about them, we could all be dead."

Dina fought down rising anger. "We couldn't all be dead. We will all be dead—no questions—no explanations—and that's why you're going to make sure no one finds out about them. You're going to keep them quiet until we can leave tomorrow. That's your job."

"And how exactly am I supposed to get a good night's sleep if I have these....these Children to take care of all night long?"

"I don't know, but you better take care of them and you better take care of them well. If they make one tiny peep, Renfroe will hear. He's right down the hall and he could hear my babies moving around inside my body. That's how strong his hearing is. So whenever they make a sound, you better feed them. It's your job to keep them happy and settled and fed until we can get out of here. Do you understand that?"

Tania made a face and turned away. "I'm not having anything to do with those things. They're hideous. They're an abomination. They should be reduced right here and now."

Dina stared at her and all of Dina's compassion for Tania evaporated. Dina would have liked to drown Tania in the river at that moment.

Instead, Dina lowered her voice to a snarl. "These Children are the same as the one you're carrying right now. You better learn to like them because you're going to have your own to take of pretty soon."

"No, I won't. I won't touch them."

"If you don't take care of them tonight," Dina snapped, "I'll leave you behind tomorrow. I'll turn you over to Khalid and you can take your chances."

Tania's head whipped around. "You wouldn't dare."

Dina stood up. "Take care of these Children tonight. It's only for one night. Once we leave here, I'll take care of them myself. Here's the milk. Make sure they're fed and don't make any noise. I'll see you in the morning."

Chapter 16

Dina gazed at the darkened windows of her garden door. Moonlight brightened the tops of the trees outside, and the leaves waved against a background of stars.

She didn't feel Renfroe moving on top of her anymore. She repeated the sequence of events she planned to follow tomorrow when she left the house with Tania and the Children. She saw herself walking out the kitchen door, down the street, and away from Prideland.

She didn't allow herself to think about the promise she'd made to Renfroe to come back to him. She'd be raising her Children for the next several years. Anything might happen between now and then.

Something might happen that would prevent her from keeping her promise. If these Children took as long to mature as human children, Renfroe might be dead by then......or Dina might be.

Was she willing to break her promise in exchange for her freedom? She *was* willing to break her word to Renfroe for her Children's sake. She would do anything for them.

She went through the motions of passionate love-making, but the whole time, she kept retracing the road to the jungle again and again. She rehearsed it in her mind all night long.

So much for getting a good night's sleep. She wouldn't get a good night's sleep on the road, either. She might not get a good night's sleep until she made it to the canton. Then again, she was having twins. She might never get a good night's sleep again.

Her heartbeat quickened when the first dawn light peeked through the window. She had to stop herself from jumping up, grabbing Tania, and leaving right now.

She also wanted to see how well Tania had taken care of the Children during the night. After the comments she'd made about reducing them, Dina didn't trust Tania to take care of any Children, not even her own.

Dina forced herself to lie still until Renfroe got up. She had to stay calm.

He got a drink of water and they sat down to share their breakfast the way they usually did. The same wave of nausea made her sick, but she forced herself to sit down and eat a bowl of hot stew. She couldn't walk all day and into the night on an empty stomach.

"Would you like to go to the festival with Belinda?" Renfroe asked. "If you're worried about the other helpers reacting to you, I could tell her to take you with her. They might leave you alone then."

"I'd rather go by myself. Belinda will probably want to go and come back as quickly as she can. She has a lot of work to do and I want to see if I can find Tom."

Renfroe eyed her. "I'm sure he'll be there, but most helpers don't hang around socializing afterward. They leave as soon as the festival is over. They have their own work to do."

"I know." She cocked her head and eyed him. "How do you know that? Have you ever been to the festivals?"

"Of course not," he snapped. "Cats don't go to the festivals. I only know the helpers don't hang around afterward because I've been in the neighborhood of Helion House when the festival ends. I've seen the helpers when they come out of the building. They go straight home afterward. Sometimes they go to the market if they have shopping to do, but they don't socialize."

"I know," Dina replied. "I only wanted to talk to Tom for a minute. I haven't seen him for weeks and I don't know when I'll have another chance to see him. You can't blame me for that."

"I don't blame you, but you might be disappointed. The last time we talked about Tom, you didn't want to see him again."

"I feel differently now. Maybe it's because I'm pregnant from you and I always thought it would be him."

He glanced up. "You don't regret anything, do you?"

"Not at all. Maybe I'm just remembering the past when I was with him. That's what makes me want to see him again."

"He might not want to see you," Renfroe pointed out.

"He might not. He doesn't seem to have made much of an effort to see me."

"What makes you say that?" Renfroe asked.

"I think you would have told me if he had asked to see me....and I think Elyse would have let him if he'd told her he wanted to see me. If he wanted to, he could have. There's nothing stopping him, but you haven't said anything and he hasn't come."

Renfroe shrugged. "That doesn't mean he doesn't want to see you. Things don't always work that way in Prideland."

"How exactly do they work?" Dina heard the old bite in her voice.

Renfroe heard it, too. "I only mean, Dina, that there may be other things standing in the way of Tom seeing you and talking to you. He may be too busy with his new life at Elyse's house to get away."

"I'll bet he is," Dina muttered.

Renfroe's head shot up. "What's wrong with you? You haven't acted this way since you came back from your ship. What happened? I thought you were past all that."

Dina turned away. "Never mind. It doesn't matter now. I'm going to the festival, and if I see Tom there, I'll talk to him. I'll find out how he's doing over at Elyse's house."

Renfroe said something more, but Dina didn't hear it. She ate the rest of her meal and walked him to the door before he left.

"Will you be in the neighborhood of Helion House today?" she asked. "Will you be watching the helpers leave the festival?"

"No," he replied. "Lord Helion and I plan to go over to a house on the other side of the city. One of the helpers just gave birth to two Children and we're going to reduce them."

Dina spun away from him with her hand over her mouth. "Why do you have to tell me that?"

"You asked," he shot back. "I don't want to go. It isn't my idea of a fun morning at the park. Lord Helion wanted me to go do it by myself, but he can't trust me to do it at all anymore. He has to go along with me to make sure I do it."

Dina shook her head and looked down at the ground. "I didn't realize it had gone as far as that."

Renfroe started toward the door. "I wouldn't say it if it hadn't gone as far as that. Now, I have to go. I can't be late. I'll see you later."

He didn't look back as he sauntered out into the sunshine and down the street. Dina would have liked to run after him, throw her arms around his neck, and breathe her goodbye into his fur.

She couldn't even say, *See you later,* back to him. He wanted her to leave him without warning and that's what she would do. She wouldn't see him later. She couldn't even be sure she would ever see him alive again.

She turned away and headed down the corridor toward her old room when a clattering noise from the kitchen made her stop in her tracks. She'd forgotten about Belinda.

Belinda had definitely not forgotten about Dina, though. Belinda came to the kitchen door, stopped there, and narrowed her eyes. "You're going to the festival, aren't you?"

Dina nodded. "When are you leaving?"

Belinda studied her. She knew a lot more than she let on. She must know that Dina had something planned, especially after Fan had brought her those kittens last night.

Dina swore she would take the kittens out of the house today. When else could she do it but during the festival? Belinda wasn't stupid. She would put two and two together.

Belinda didn't do or say anything, though. She'd always said that, to do her duty to the Pride, she ought to grab Dina by the hair and lock her up until Buck could deal with her. That was what a loyal helper to the Pride would do with a slag like Dina, but Belinda never did it.

She didn't do it when Fan brought those kittens to Renfroe's house. Belinda could have let the kittens starve by keeping back the milk they needed to drink on their first night alive, but she didn't keep it back.

She hadn't turned Dina over to the Pride before and she wouldn't do it now, not even when she knew for certain that Dina had some scheme up her sleeve to undermine the Pride.

She scowled at Dina a little longer before Belinda turned on her heel and vanished back into the kitchen.

Dina raced down the hall toward her old room and found Tania sitting on the floor leaning over the bundle of babies. Dina relaxed when she saw them and she smiled in spite of herself.

"How are they?" she whispered.

"They're just fine. They didn't drink as much milk as I thought they would. As soon as they got some milk in their stomachs, they curled up together and went to sleep. They only woke up a little while ago.

I fed them again and now they're asleep again. Almost all the milk is still in that pouch. They hardly drank any of it."

Dina let out a long, slow breath, but she made sure to do it quietly in case even her breathing woke them up. She put her hand into the pouch and touched their sleek, shining fur. "Thank you, Tania. I really appreciate this. job. Look at them! Aren't they beautiful?"

Tania pulled away and made a sour face. "I don't want to have anything to do with them. You take care of them from now on. I don't even want to look at them. They're disgusting."

"They're newborn babies," Dina countered. "They're innocent and harmless. They deserve the same care any baby deserves."

"Then you take care of them. I won't touch them again."

Dina gathered the bundle into her arms. "I will."

"Can we get out of here now?" Tania asked.

Dina didn't look up. The babies enchanted her. Would her own Children look like this?

These Children didn't look like kittens or cubs at all. They looked like human babies except that they had fur all over their faces and bodies. They didn't wake up when she touched them.

Their facial features looked a little more catlike than most human newborns, but these Children had the same captivating beauty as human newborns. Dina couldn't look at them without wanting to stroke them and care for them. She wanted to protect them and keep them comfortable and warm.

"We can't leave yet, but we will soon," Dina murmured. "We have to wait for Belinda to leave. She's Renfroe's cook, but she'll be going soon. Then we can go."

"How long will that take?"

"I don't know. It will take as long as it takes. We can't rush if we want to get out without getting caught."

Tania threw herself down on the divan. "How will you know when she's gone?"

Dina still did look up at her. She couldn't wipe the smile off her face. "There's no hurry. We can't go anywhere until all the helpers leave for the festival. Some might leave late. We can't let any of them see us leaving. Just sit tight. We'll be gone soon."

"Not soon enough," Tania grumbled.

Chapter 17

D ina slid the door open and listened. She didn't hear anything, so she ventured out into the corridor. Tania almost bumped into her from behind when Dina stopped again to listen. No sound came from either end of the house.

She tiptoed the rest of the way to the kitchen and paused again when she found the door standing open. The kitchen was empty which meant Belinda wasn't around.

Dina glanced up the corridor one last time and then waved Tania forward to join her. Tania checked through the outer door leading into the neighborhood. "It's clear. Let's go."

"Not so fast," Dina murmured. "We need to take a few things."

"Like what?"

Dina went over to the pantry and studied the food hanging from the ceiling. She needed to take some of it with them, but she couldn't carry it with the bundle of babies in her arms.

Tania already carried the milk pouch over one shoulder. How much could they really carry? They would have a long walk to the jungle. This slapdash escape was messy enough without going empty-handed.

She set her bundle down on the table and lifted down a haunch of cured meat and a mid-sized round of cheese. She set them on the table next to the blanket and she looked around again for some way to carry everything.

She searched the kitchen and found the net bags Belinda used for carrying goods home from the market. They hung on hooks behind the kitchen door along with a stout leather rucksack.

Dina put the food in the rucksack. Then she wrapped the babies in their blanket and tucked the whole bundle into a pouch bag that hung over her shoulder.

She hung the rucksack across her back and nodded to Tania. "Let's go."

Tania pointed toward the fire. "Should we take something to start a fire with? We might need it."

"I don't think so. We'll need to stay hidden and unseen. We won't be able to light a fire, but there is one more other thing we will need."

She crossed the kitchen to the big wooden table where several knives of different sizes stuck out of the surface in the corner. Which of them should she take? She would have liked to take all of them.

She yanked out the big meat cleaver, weighed it in her hand, and gave it a few trial swings before she stuck it into her waistband.

Then she pulled out a long, narrow fleshing knife. She would be much better prepared this time than she had been during her previous two escapes. She stuck the knife into her belt on the left side where she could grab it at a moment's notice.

She planned to take one more, but which one? She put her hand on three different handles before she decided on a short, strong paring knife. It fit perfectly in the palm of her hand and she tucked that one into the top of her sock.

Finally, she took out a light, strong fillet knife and handed it to Tania. "Take it."

Tania waved her hand and backed away. "I couldn't. You keep it."

Dina held it out again. "You'll need this. Just take it. Trust me. You'll be glad you did."

Tania shook her head. "I don't want it. If you don't want it, then put it back."

Dina changed her tone. "Take it now," she ordered. "I'm not asking you. If you don't take it now and keep it handy for the rest of the trip, I'll leave you here."

Tania tried to scowl back, but she finally took the knife and found a place for it in her belt. Tania gripped the handle and tried the angle she would need to use to draw the knife in a hurry. Dina relaxed a little when she saw that. Maybe Tania wouldn't be as useless as Dina had expected.

The next minute, all thought of relaxing vanished from her mind when she eased over to the outside door. She paused on the threshold and stole a glance to the right and left. The street extended away in both directions without a single person or cat to be seen.

Dina slipped outside and down the street with Tania right behind her. The farther they got from Renfroe's house, the faster Dina walked until Tania almost had to run to keep up.

Dina hurried away for ten blocks before she dared to slow down to a more manageable pace. She and Tania wouldn't make it very far if they didn't keep their speed comfortable.

Tania stayed right behind her and Dina kept moving through the back streets of residential neighborhoods toward the main road out of the city. Dina couldn't stop herself from checking every side street and garden. Would the cats come out to stop the two women from escaping? It was only a matter of time before they encountered someone who would try to stop them.

Who would come? What would happen when Renfroe came home and found her gone? He might have to report her escape to the rest of the Pride. Then Lord Helion might force Renfroe to come after her.

What would she do then? Would she have to fight him? Could she fight him? She didn't know if she could bring herself to kill him the way she'd killed Fallon.

Dina pushed those thoughts out of her head and forced herself to walk faster. She had to put as much distance between herself and the Pride as possible.

She made up her mind that she would fight anyone who came after her Children and that meant Renfroe, too. He might be caring and compassionate, but he was still a cat of the Pride. He would never be anything but that.

He might care about her and their Children, but in the end, he still went out and killed Children the same way all the other cats did. She couldn't think of him as being any different from the rest.

Her heart soared when she came to the last buildings and she and Tania left the city for open farmland. They hadn't seen a living soul on the way. It couldn't be this easy.

Tania kept up well enough. She wasn't turning out to be as much of a burden as Dina expected.

She pushed on toward the village. The sun crossed the sky and the day slipped away toward evening, but Dina still didn't see any cats or people. Should she be worried about that?

Her hopes drained away when she turned the next corner and froze when she saw a cat sitting in the middle of the road. He was just a normal-sized tabby house cat and he sat all alone blinking in the sunshine like he had been waiting for them.

Dina stopped in her tracks, but she couldn't exactly run away from him. What was the point? He had caught her red-handed trying to escape from Prideland—again.

She should have trembled in fear that he would bring the rest of the Pride down on her head. He could kill her, Tania, and the Children with one word, but she couldn't tremble before him or any other cat anymore and she wouldn't back down from one little tom cat alone.

She cocked her head to study him. "Senator Osiris?" she asked.

He swiveled his ears toward her. "Aren't you helpers supposed to be at Helion House? There's a festival on, you know."

"I know." Dina scanned the surrounding terrain. Should she try to fight him right here and now? If she did, the Pride would find out sooner than if she and Tania tried to get away from him. She had hoped they could make a more subtle exit with no one the wiser, but it sure looked like that possibility had flown out the window.

She could try to lie her way out of this. Maybe she could convince Osiris that she had a reason to miss the festival and leave the city. He might not mention to anyone that he caught them on the road when they shouldn't have been here at all, but she couldn't count on that.

"I have permission from my benefactor to travel out to the village," she told him. That part, at least, was true.

He kept inclining his head from one side to the other while he examined her. "Is that so? All the helpers go to the festivals. There are no exceptions. You better come back with me. I'll take you to Helion House. While you two attend the festival the way you're supposed to, I'll discuss this situation with your benefactor. I'll get to the bottom of this. I'll find out for myself what was so important that you had to leave the city instead of going to the festival. Something tells me this situation isn't quite as straightforward as you make it out to be."

Dina looked around again. "And what will you do if I say I'm not going to go back to Helion House? You can't force me to go back. You're one cat. You can't make me do anything."

Osiris sniffed and turned his head away. "You can make this as difficult as you want. It's nothing to me."

He stood up and walked away to return to the city. It wasn't that far behind them. He could get there, report this to the rest of the Pride, and come back with his bigger friends long before the two women could outrun any cat who pursued them.

Dina made up her mind. She couldn't let him leave. If he left now, she and Tania would get caught and reduced before they ever made it to the village, let alone the jungle. She had to stop him here and now.

The instant Osiris turned his back on her, she lunged for him. Dina attacking him was probably the last thing in the world he ever expected. Every cat Dina had ever fought reacted this way. They expected people to cower and obey, not stand and fight, and certainly never to attack.

Every cat Dina had ever fought reacted first by cringing in surprise that a human was coming at them to attack. Osiris was no different. He didn't think twice about turning his back on two women. He didn't see her pull her knife from her belt and charge him.

By the time he spotted her, she was almost on top of him. She stretched out her other hand to grab him by the scruff of the neck. He only had time to spring aside and avoid her.

He landed on his feet a few feet away and that was the end of her surprise. He must have heard from someone about Dina fighting Fallon and Khalid. Osiris didn't hesitate an instant before he leapt at her, and this time, he caught *her* by surprise.

Dina couldn't move fast with the rucksack and the bag of Children hanging off her. She spun around to face him, but not fast enough. He might be a small cat alone, but he still outmatched her.

He launched himself off the ground without flexing his legs and hit Dina in the face slashing his claws and gnashing his teeth. His attack surprised her so much that she had to drop her knife to protect her face.

She shut her eyes to protect them and pushed him away, but his claws stuck in her hair and scalp. The harder she pushed, the more he tore at her skin. He hissed and spat in her face, and she staggered backward, stumbled, and fell.

She toppled onto her rucksack and tried to get hold of the little knife in her sock, but she couldn't take her hands off the cat. She had to struggle with all her might just to stop him from tearing her apart.

Osiris redoubled his efforts once he got her down on the ground. He clawed at her eyes and brought his fangs down on her face. The points of his teeth dug into the sides of her eye and she panicked. "Tania!" she screamed. "Help me! Get him off me! Help me!"

No one answered her. Dina managed to crack one eye open and peek out from under Osiris.

Tania stood stock still in the middle of the road and stared at Osiris attacking Dina, but Tania didn't move a muscle. She didn't even seem to hear Dina screaming, "Tania! Tania, help me!"

Tania glanced around for some other Tania that Dina might be calling. Tania's eyes darted in every direction, but she didn't move her hand toward her knife or take one step to help Dina.

Osiris glanced over to see if Tania answered Dina's call for help. If Tania thought about stepping out of place to help Dina, one look from Osiris's eyes kept Tania frozen where she was.

Dina finally got it through her head that Tania wouldn't come to help her. That realization gave Dina the strength to rip Osiris's claws out of her skin and his teeth away from her face. She hurled him away, rolled sideways, and jumped to her feet.

Osiris hit the ground and bounced right back up, but he didn't come after Dina again. He went after the weakest target—Tania. He flew through the air and hit her in the face the same way he hit Dina.

Tania didn't even try to fight back. She crumpled under him with a scream and folded over into a ball on the ground while he shredded her face and head. He pushed her over onto her back to get to her neck, but she barely resisted at all.

She flailed her arms, but never effectively enough to knock him out of position. Dina grabbed the knife from her sock, lunged for the cat, grabbed him by the scruff of the neck, and stabbed down at his body.

The instant he felt her hand on him, he twisted in her hand and contorted all the way around to face her. She couldn't keep a grip on him and she brought the blade down just as he twisted out of her grip. The knife point tore the skin of his shoulder as he fell out of her hand and landed on the ground at her feet.

Dina spun around to face him, but Osiris sprang away a second time and didn't stop until put enough distance between them so she couldn't get to him again. He paused there and regarded her with his steady, blinking eyes. Blood trickled down his shoulder and matted into his fur.

He shook his head and sniffed. "You've won this round, but you can't get away. I'll be back in an hour with the Helions. They'll bring you in. You have nowhere to run and nowhere to hide." He turned his back on her the way he did before. "Enjoy your last few minutes of freedom while you can."

Dina watched him walk away. She couldn't go after him again even knowing he would bring the Helions to track her down.

Her hand clutching her knife trembled. She'd lost a lot of strength in the last few weeks. Fighting one cat drained her in ways it never had before. She couldn't stand up to the Helions.

Chapter 18

D ina let out a shaking breath and her knife hand dropped to her side before she turned back toward Tania.

Tania crouched on the ground with her head tucked under her arms. She didn't look up until Dina put her hand on Tania's shoulder. "Come on, Tania. We can't stay here. We have to find a place to hide."

Tania didn't uncurl herself from her ball. Her whole body shook with silent sobs.

Dina tugged at her arm. "Come on, Tania. We have to get off the road before he comes back with the Helions."

Tania broke down in loud sobs. "I can't, Dina! I can't go on! Leave me here. I can't handle this! You go on without me."

Her sobs only made Dina mad. "What are you going to do? You can't go back to the Pride. Khalid will kill you the minute he lays eyes on you."

"I don't care!" Tania moaned. "At least I won't have to worry about anything after that. Let him kill me. It's better than dying out here on the road."

"We aren't going to die on the road," Dina snapped. "We're going to find a place to hide. The Helions will be here in a little while, but once it gets dark, we can get past the village and out into the jungle.

We'll be okay there, but you have to get up so we can keep moving. We can't just sit here and wait for them."

"I'm not cut out for this!" Tania wailed. "I'll only slow you down and maybe get you caught and killed, too. You have a much better chance of getting free without me. Go on. I want you to. Leave me here and take care of yourself instead."

Dina gasped in annoyance. "What is wrong with you? You've been trained in combat in the Armada. Get up and pull yourself together. That's an order. You can't fall apart now. We have a long way to go before we can stop and rest. Now get up. Get up right now."

Dina didn't wait for a response. She dragged Tania to her feet, locked her hand around Tania's wrist, and hauled her down the road by force.

Dina walked a lot faster now than she did before. She didn't care anymore if Tania could keep up with her. If Tania hesitated for an instant, Dina yanked her forward by the wrist.

Dina couldn't think about Tania anymore. She had to find a place to hide. Within a few minutes, the first rooftops of the village houses came into view.

She'd decided a long time ago not to try to pass through the village in daylight or even in at dawn or dusk. She knew better than to take the chance of getting recaptured by the factors. She would try it once night fell and all the subsidiaries shut themselves up in their houses.

First she had to find a place to hide—somewhere the Helions wouldn't find her. Her friend Frank Mathus once hid from the cats in a cow shed. The smell of cattle masked his scent so the cats couldn't find him. She needed to find someplace like that.

She stopped at the top of a rise in the road. The village spread out in front of her. Only a few people still stood at their doors and called to their neighbors or children. Their voices carried on the evening air and smoke curled out of every chimney.

Dina cringed at the sight. She was back here again and this village set her nerves on edge. Nothing good ever happened to her in this village and she didn't hold out any hope of this time being different.

Going around the village would take too long. The road going straight through it offered too great a temptation to just keep on going into the jungle, but the Helions would catch up with her if she did that.

She scanned the village for any possible hiding place and spotted a few men putting their oxen into a shed behind Alexander Mathus's house. She and Tania could hide there. It would mask their scent until the cats gave up searching. Then the two women could make their escape before sunrise.

Full dark had fallen over the village by the time she and Tania got to the bottom of the hill. No one stood in their doorways anymore. The only light came from the roof holes and only muffled sounds drifted through the sod walls.

Dina tiptoed past the houses to the shed and paused there to listen for any sound. She didn't have a chance to think twice before one of the house doors swung open. A square of yellow light fell on the ground nearby. Dina pushed Tania into the shed and closed the door after them.

Dina pulled Tania into an empty stall and tugged Tania into a squat next to her. The shed smelled powerfully of livestock. Rakes, hoes, and axes stood in the corners and left no room to sit down.

"Now what?" Tania whispered.

"Now we wait," Dina replied. "Wait and pray. The Helions will start searching the village soon. We can only hope we get lucky."

Tania fell silent and Dina settled in for a long wait. Hours passed and the night air chilled Dina's bones. She should have brought some more protective clothing, but it was too late now.

All of a sudden, she grasped Tania's arm and held her breath as voices called across the village and footsteps rang out on the road outside.

A man stopped right outside the shed door shed and called to someone out of earshot. Dina and Tania froze in place. Dina strained to hear any sound over her blood pounding in her ears.

The voices faded and didn't come back. Dina was just relaxing into another long wait when more footsteps approached the shed from the opposite side. She didn't have time to move before a hand pulled the shed door open.

Lantern flooded the shed and some of the oxen stamped. The lantern wavered against the sod walls and Dina froze when it stopped right in front of the stall.

A female voice cried out at the sight of them and Tania started to stand up, but Dina pulled her back down.

The woman with the lantern jumped back in alarm. "Who's there?" she demanded.

Dina's heart leapt when she recognized that voice. "Darcy! Darcy Mathus!" She jumped to her feet. "It's me. It's Dina Dyer. I stayed with you when your daughter Sonya got the House of Man. Do you remember?"

Darcy held the lantern in front of Dina's face. "Of course! I know who you are. Come out of there quick!"

"We can't come out. We're hiding from the Helions. We're....."

"I know why you're here!" Darcy interrupted. "The Helions are all over the village looking for you."

Dina glanced toward the door. "They are?"

"Come quick!" Darcy took Dina's hand and dragged her out of the shed. "I know all about it. The Helions are all down at the other end of the village. They're organizing the village factors to search the village and find you."

Dina and Tania stepped out into the cold night air. Darcy held onto Dina's hand and Dina held onto Tania. "I thought the Helions would track us by our scent. That's why we had to find somewhere they couldn't smell us."

"They can't track you by your scent in the village. There are too many other human smells. That's why they need the factors to help them. Come on. We don't have much time. They'll be out looking for you any minute now."

"But where will we go?" Dina asked.

"Come into my house. Alexander is out with the other factors. Our house is the last place in the world they'll think to look for you."

She led the two fugitives to the nearest house and shut the door behind them. Dina suffered another flood of memories when she walked inside.

Four children sat around the fire pit in the middle of the floor and they all turned around to stare at Darcy when she came through the door. The youngest girl even smiled at the sight of her mother, but that smile evaporated when Dina and Tania walked in behind her.

"Quick!" Darcy murmured. "Get under the bed. I don't know when Alexander will come back, so you might have to stay under there for a while—at least until the Helions leave."

Darcy led the way to the platform against the back wall of the house, bent down, and flipped the blanket on the bed back to reveal the space underneath.

Dina didn't wait to be told twice. She pushed her rucksack under the bed first, scooted in after it, and flipped over onto her stomach so she could peer out. The children stared at her from across the room, but they didn't make a sound, not even to ask who Dina and Tania were.

Tania squeezed in after her, and when they lay side by side on their bellies on the hard dirt floor, Darcy flipped the blanket down in front of their faces. They couldn't see out into the room and no one could see them hiding under the bed, either.

They got into their hiding place only just in time. The minute the blanket covered their faces, the door of the house flew open. A man's voice filled the room and Dina recognized Alexander Mathus.

Chapter 19

"Y ou're back!" Darcy exclaimed. "I thought you'd be out all night."

Footsteps pounded into the house beyond the blanket covering Dina's face. Those steps stopped right in front of the bed where she and Tania lay hidden. They both held their breath in fear of being discovered.

"We searched the whole village," Alexander replied. "We didn't find anything. Osiris thinks they might have hidden closer to the spot where he saw them last. We're going with Kaido and two of his brothers to search along the road between here and the city."

"When do you think you'll be back?" Darcy asked.

"It won't be any time soon," Alexander replied. "I'm taking Christian with me."

"He's just a boy!" Darcy countered. "He can't spend all night out in the open searching for some escaped slags."

"He's my son," Alexander replied. "He'll be factor after me. The sooner he learns the job, the better for him. He's not too young for some hard training. He's had it too soft up until now anyway."

"Oh, Alex," Darcy breathed. "Treat him a little more gently. He hasn't had an easy time here, you know."

Alexander moved away toward the door. "You treat him too gently. That's the problem. The sooner he gets out with the other village men, the sooner he'll toughen up and things will get easier for him. He'll be a man himself soon and he needs to know the ways of men. He won't get that by being treated gently by women all his life."

He didn't wait for her answer before he walked out of the house and closed the door behind him.

No one moved in the room or even breathed. A log snapped in the fire. Dina waited along with everyone else in the room for any sound of Alexander coming back.

After an eternity of waiting, someone crossed the room and stopped in front of the bed. The blanket flew back and Darcy leaned down. "You can come out now. He's gone."

Dina scanned the children's faces. They stared at her and Tania with huge eyes. "Are you sure it's safe?"

"He won't be back tonight. You heard him. They're going to search farther up the road. Come on out and sit by the fire. You can have something to eat and drink and maybe get some sleep before you move on."

Dina climbed out from under the bed and brushed the dust off her clothes. "I can't thank you enough for hiding us like this, but we can't stay. We'll have something to eat and then we have to get into the jungle. As long as the men are gone, we can get out of the village without getting caught. We'll never have a better chance to get free."

The children made room for the two women by the fire and Darcy put bowls of steaming soup in their hands. Then she sat down opposite Dina. "So you're going out to the canton again? You're running a big risk. If they catch you, they'll kill you."

"That's what I thought last time, but I'm still here. The Pride isn't as all-powerful as people think." Dina eyed Darcy. "You should come with us. You don't have to stay here."

Darcy stared into the fire. "That's what Frank said. He told me you came to his canton and stayed with him. He told me you planned to evacuate the slags to your starship. What happened to that idea?"

Dina looked down at the bowl in her lap. "It didn't work out that way."

"Are you going back out to his canton now? Is he waiting for you out there somewhere?"

Dina's head shot up. "Frank's dead. The cats attacked the canton the same night he came back from visiting you. They reduced everyone in the canton—except me. My benefactor, Senator Renfroe, protected me. I was the only person left alive."

Darcy stared at her. Then her eyes welled up with tears. "I should have known something like that would happen to Frank. He took a lot of risks to help other people."

"This had nothing to do with Frank," Dina shot back. "He did everything he could to protect the people of the canton from the cats, but the cats came after me. That's the only reason they went after that canton at all. If I hadn't been there, those people would still be alive."

Darcy laid her hand on Dina's arm. "Don't tell yourself that. It isn't true. The Pride hunts slags in the jungle all the time and they clear cantons all the time, too. If your benefactor wanted you taken back alive, that was unusual, but the Pride would have gone after that canton eventually whether you were there or not. You weren't responsible for those people getting killed."

Dina twiddled with the spoon sticking out of her food. "Maybe."

Darcy squeezed her arm. "It's true. So Frank is dead. I always knew it would happen sooner or later. I'll always be grateful for everything he did for us, but it was bound to happen. So your plan to evacuate the cantons is off, I suppose."

"Not necessarily. I made it back to my starship and I came back here to finish what Frank and I started. If you or any of the other subsidiaries still want to leave, I'll find a way to get you out."

Darcy glanced back and forth between Dina and Tania. "Is that why you're going out to the jungle now? Are you preparing to evacuate now?"

Dina shifted in her seat. "Not exactly—now now—not yet, anyway."

"What are you going for, then? What other reason could you have for going back and forth between the jungle and the city? You're taking your lives in your hands every time you do it. You said you had friends in the city that you wanted to get out. Did you make contact with them?"

"That's not the reason, either."

"What then?" Darcy asked.

Dina paused. Then she pulled open the top of her pouch. "This is why."

Darcy peeked into the opening and her hand flew to her mouth. "What's this?"

"Don't you know? They're the Children of the Pride. Their lives are in danger in the city. The Pride kills any Children it can find as soon as they're born. That and......" She stopped and glanced at Tania.

"And...?" Darcy prompted.

"And we're both pregnant with our own Children. My friend Tania here is a—or was—a helper to Khalid. You know what kind of benefactor he is. He swore to kill any helper who got pregnant with any Children, so Tania can't go back to the Pride at all. My benefactor wouldn't kill me, but his position in the Senate would force him to kill our Children. The jungle is our only chance to bring up our Children in peace."

Darcy's mouth hung open. When Dina stopped speaking, Darcy shook her head in amazement. "I never thought......I mean, I've heard about these Children, but I never thought how it must be for their mothers. I didn't think the mothers would do anything to protect them, especially not something as dangerous as going out to the jungle to live with the slags. That's taking a little too far, don't you think? Why not just stay in the city where it's safe?"

"It's not safe in the city. That's exactly what I'm telling you," Dina countered. "It's much safer in the cantons. You should see them for yourself before you decide it's not worth the risk of going there. There are mothers in the world who would do anything including risk their own lives and even die to protect their children. Maybe you wouldn't, but others would."

Darcy shut her mouth and lowered her eyes to her hands in her lap. "You're right. I deserved that."

Now it was Dina's turn to squeeze Darcy's arm. "Come with us. If you really want to get out of here, the cantons are your best option. They aren't like the factors and the Pride tell you they are. The cantons are really nice there and you'll feel a lot safer and more comfortable there than here. I promise you that."

Darcy smiled and her eyes misted over with tears. "That's exactly what Frank said the last time he came here."

"What did you say?"

"I said I'd think about it," Darcy replied.

Dina nodded and stood up. "Right. You think about it. We have to get going. Thank you again for hiding us. I won't forget this. We'll let you know when we're ready to do something about getting you out of here, but it might be a while before we have some other option for you besides going to the canton."

She went to the door and Darcy followed her. Dina was just about to step out into the night when the older of the two girls jumped up from her place by the fire and ran toward her. "Wait!"

Dina faced her.

"I remember you," the girl told her. "Do you remember me?"

Dina nodded. "You're Sonya, aren't you?"

For just an instant, the girl's face broke into a smile. Then it disappeared again. Sonya looked like she'd aged several years since Dina saw her last.

When Dina saw Sonya receive the House of Man, Sonya had only seemed about eight years old. Now she looked more like eleven or twelve even though it had only been a few months.

What could Dina say to this girl? Dina hadn't been able to protect her then and Dina was just as unable to save Sonya now.

Dina settled on something bland and meaningless. "I'm glad you're doing better now."

"I'm not doing better!" Sonya shot back. "I'll never be better after that. That's what I'm saying. I want to come with you. I want to get out of here. Let me come with you."

Dina glanced over at Darcy. "It's fine with me as long as...."

"No," Darcy snapped. "You can't go. You're just a girl. Your place is here with your parents and your brothers and your sister."

Sonya turned on her mother with a vicious snarl. "I wasn't just a girl when you gave me the House of Man. If I'm old enough for that, I'm old enough to go out to the jungle. I don't want to stay here anymore and I don't want to come to an understanding with the Pride. I don't want to have anything to do with the Pride and I don't want to have anything to do with anyone else who has an understanding with the Pride, either."

Dina suppressed a smile. At last, someone in this madhouse was talking sense. "I'm more than happy to take you or anyone else who wants to go, but I can't take you against your mother's wishes. I'm sorry. I really wish I could."

Sonya's face hardened into stony mask. "I understand. I hear the same thing from everyone. Just promise me you'll take me when I'm old enough. Promise me that, when I'm old enough to make my own decision, you'll come back for me and get me out of here."

Dina let her smile break out across her face. "I promise I'll come back for you. I wish I could have helped you before and I'll do anything I can to help you now, but you can do more here. Once we figure find a way to get everybody out, we'll need someone here to communicate with everyone else who wants to go. That could be you."

Sonya brightened up at the thought. "Could I really help you by staying here? I could find out who in the village wants to leave. Once you find a way to get us out, we'll be ready." She waved her hand at the young boy at her side. "My brother Jared wants to go, too. He doesn't want to get the House of Man. He could help you, too."

"Don't you even think about getting any of my children involved in this!" Darcy snapped. "Don't you know how dangerous this is? If you get caught, you'll all get visited and your father will strike back twice as hard to make sure none of his children winds up in the cantons."

Dina started to answer, but she didn't get a chance before Sonya turned on her mother with more venom than before. "When I get old enough to make my own decisions, you won't be able to stop me from doing what I want. You can't stop me from talking to my friends now. You won't do anything to step out of line, even though you know it's the right thing to do. So just sit back and keep quiet while the rest of us plan how to save your life."

Darcy pulled her head down between her shoulders. "I'm only worried about your safety. I don't want to see you get hurt."

"If that was true, you would have protected me from getting the House of Man," Sonya fired back, "and what about Christian? If you didn't want to see him get hurt, you would do something now to make sure he doesn't get the House of Man, either."

"But I can't...." Darcy began.

"You mean you won't," Sonya interrupted, "but I will. I'll make sure Alva and Jared don't get it. You sit around here and pat Papa and Christian on their backs and leave the important decisions in life to the rest of us."

Dina listened to her own thoughts coming out of Sonya's mouth and Dina started to envision how she could get these people out from under the influence of the Pride and its followers. The old fire woke up after all these weeks of walking in her sleep at Renfroe's house.

She never imagined anyone in the village—or anywhere else in Prideland—would work to break the Pride's grip on their lives. Maybe Dina could dare to hope for some better future for these people after all.

Dina smiled at Sonya. Darcy looked the other way. "I might not be able to stop you once you get older," she told her daughter, "but until then, I won't have you running off to the cantons with the slags."

Dina nodded. "All right. We'll wait. Don't worry, Sonya. You'll hear from me soon. Don't forget what we talked about."

"I won't forget," Sonya replied.

Dina stepped out into the night and Tania followed at her heels. The door closed behind them and shut off all light that might show them the way. Dina hesitated outside to let their eyes get used to the dark.

"Are you sure this is a good idea?" Tania whispered.

"All the village factors are up the road along with everyone else who would be looking for us." Dina turned back toward the road. "We'll be fine as long as we keep quiet. It's not that far to the jungle, and once we're there, we can talk more."

Tania didn't answer and they headed off into the dark. Dina rested her hand on her pouch bag. She should have fed the babies at Darcy's house, but Dina didn't want to get comfortable there.

She only hoped she could get out into the thick of the jungle before they started crying, but she didn't dare to stop on the open road—not with the Pride out looking for her.

She had no idea what time it was, but it must be getting close to dawn. They had to make it as far as the jungle before daylight. With any luck, they would be inside the canton's protective fence before the sun got too high. She would feed the babies then.

Chapter 20

Dina listened to Tania's footfalls behind her for any sign that Tania might be succumbing to fatigue. To Dina's surprise, Tania didn't falter. She kept up without a word of complaint. She stayed right behind Dina all the way to the place where the footpath left the road and struck out into the jungle.

"How much farther is it?" Tania whispered.

"We're almost there," Dina replied. "We can talk normally now. We're a long way from any village. There won't be anyone around unless the cats come looking for us here. We have a few more miles to go before we get to the canton. Then we can rest."

"You told that woman the canton was nicer and safer than the village or the city."

"That's right. It's the nicest, safest place on the planet. You'll see."

"How do you know?" Tania asked. "You sound like you've been there before."

Dina took a deep breath. Here it came. "I have been there before."

"When?" Tania asked.

"A few months ago."

"How did you get there?" Tania asked.

"I walked there, just like we're doing now."

"Didn't you get visited? The cantons are protected, you know."

Dina turned to face her. "The first thing you need to learn about the cantons is how to speak without all that Prideland double-talk. I used those words in Prideland so people would know what I was talking about, but out in the cantons, you can call things by their real names. You can ask me if I didn't get beaten black and blue for running away from the Pride and you can say the cantons are forbidden. They're not protected. The word 'protected' doesn't mean 'forbidden'. Use the right words for the right things....and you can say a person or even a whole village got murdered and wiped out. They didn't get reduced or cleared or any other code word."

Tania fell silent for a while. "You really have been out there, haven't you?"

"Yes, I have. I ran away and I came out to that village. Alexander Mathus caught me on the road and he took me back to his house while he and the other factors decided what to do with me. That's when I saw them giving Sonya the House of Man. Have you ever seen anyone getting it?"

Tania shook her head.

"You're lucky. It's horrific and they give it to them when they're helpless children. Their parents hold them down while the cats scratch those scars into the children's bodies. You heard Sonya. She's going to do everything she can to make sure her brothers and sister don't get it, either. That's the reason I came back."

"Back from the canton?"

Dina took another deep breath. How could she explain anything to someone like Tania? "No, from the *Savannah*."

"The *Savannah!*" Tania gasped. "When did you go back to the *Savannah?*"

Dina sighed. "It's a long story. Maybe I'll tell you sometime."

"Tell me now. From what I can tell, we've got all the time in the world. Tell me exactly how you wound up back on the *Savannah* without taking me and Tom and Matthew with you."

Dina stopped walking and faced her. This conversation had been a long time coming. Dina had better get it over with now.

"All right," she began. "You want to know? I'll tell you. I went to each of you before I left and told you that I planned to escape. You said you didn't dare to run away from Khalid. You said you planned to offer yourself to him as a helper so you wouldn't have to be so scared of him all the time. You said that was the only chance we had to live in safety here. Do you remember that?"

Tania crossed her arms over her chest and turned away.

"I also went to see Matthew. He said he'd tried to escape so many times that he wasn't willing to do it again. He said I was too stupid to escape on my own and to go away and leave him alone. Then I went to see Tom. He said he wouldn't turn his back on our mission and he wouldn't run away from his benefactor—I mean, his mistress. She was too nice to him and he thought he owed it to her to stay."

"But that doesn't explain....."

Dina held up her hand and cut her off. "Do you know what I found out? After the Pride tracked me down, the cats wiped out everyone in the canton, even women and children and little babies. I was the only one left alive and only because Renfroe wanted me back. The cats brought all the bodies back to Helion House and ate them. I saw it all with my own eyes—and do you know what I found out afterward? Renfroe told me that all three of you—you and Matthew and Tom—you all told your benefactors—your masters—that I planned to escape. The Pride found out I was gone because you told them."

She stared at Tania while she waited for Tania to say something—anything to justify selling Dina out to the Pride. The two women faced off against each other for a long time, but of course Tania didn't say anything.

"After I got back to Renfroe's house, I escaped a second time," Dina went on. "When he told me the three of you had given away my plans, I decided I had to go alone if I was going to have any chance at all. I only had two days left before the Pod's power packs ran down. I got out. I didn't go through the village that time and I made it to the Pod."

"How did you make it to the Pod without going through the village?" Tania asked.

"Never mind. The fact is that I made it to the Pod and I got back to the *Savannah*. I told Captain Doyle everything that was going on down here and I decided to come back. I decided to come back for the same reason Sonya decided to stay in the village. I wanted to do anything I could to get these people away from the Pride and I wanted to make sure no more children got the House of Man."

"So how are you going to do that?" Tania asked. "It looks impossible to me."

"You think so? And yet, here we are, you and me and these babies. We've made it all the way to the jungle without getting caught. This is the third time I've left Prideland. It's not as impossible as it seems. My friend Frank—you didn't know about him, did you?"

"I heard what you said to Darcy about him."

"Here's what you don't know. He was Frank Mathus, Chancellor Mathus's other son. Alexander is his older son and they were both on that shuttle when it crashed. The Chancellor sent us here to rescue Alexander and not Frank."

"But that's impossible!" Tania argued. "If word of that got out in the Coalition....."

Dina nodded. "I know and now Frank is dead. He died defending the canton against the Pride and the Chancellor is responsible for his death. When I mentioned it to him at a briefing in the captain's office, he blamed Frank for being foolhardy. Anyway, when the people in the canton found out we came here to rescue Alexander and his family, they all wanted to leave, too. They wanted me to evacuate everyone. Frank went to give the news to two other cantons and they want to leave, too. I think there could be several thousand people in the jungle alone who want to leave."

"That doesn't get you any closer to actually getting them out," Tania pointed out. "Wanting to leave is different from actually leaving. The Pride will do everything it can to stop you."

"These aren't helpers and subsidiaries. These are free people. They have no understanding with the Pride. They can't fight back against the Pride because they don't have any weapons strong enough, but these people will fight. All they need is someone to organize them and a reason to do it. They'll fight for a chance at freedom. They're the best people on this planet."

"Even with all the slags fighting, they still won't be able to defeat the Pride. Human beings can't fight against cats. They would be wiped out."

Dina lowered her eyes. "I know. There would have to be some other factor to tip the scales. Otherwise, there won't be no sense in even trying."

"So what are you going to do?"

Dina turned back down the path. "I have no idea."

She headed deeper into the thickest jungle just as the first light of dawn spread across the sky. Tania fell in behind Dina and, thankfully, Tania didn't ask any more questions so Dina had a chance to think the situation over.

Did she still really think there was some way to overthrow the Pride? She sure didn't want to fight against the cats. Fighting small cats like Osiris or the sentinel cats was one thing.

The memory of taking on even a moderately sized cat like Fallon still gave Dina the chills. She never wanted to face a cat the size of Khalid as long as she lived, let alone a lion like the Helions or a tiger like Renfroe. She would wilt in fear if she ever had to do that.

She couldn't blame Darcy or Tania for not wanting to fight. Dina didn't want to fight, either.

That was what she loved so much about Frank. He offered her a chance to evacuate the cantons and even some of the village subsidiaries without any confrontation with the cats.

Now that chance was gone along with him. If anyone was going to get off this planet, they would have to find a way to defeat the Pride in open combat. The Pride sent that message loud and clear when it wiped out Frank's canton. The Pride would never tolerate anyone escaping, not even slags.

Dina cringed even more at the thought of violence now that she was about to become a mother. She would rather hide in the jungle for the rest of her life—or at least until her Children grew up—rather than face the Pride.

Maybe, just maybe, she could raise her Children in the peace and quiet of the canton and then leave them to rejoin Renfroe when they got old enough. Maybe they would keep living in peace and harmony out here and she wouldn't have to worry about the Pride coming after them.

She dangled that daydream in front of her own eyes, but she already knew it would never come true. The Pride would come after these Children more forcefully than it would come after anyone who tried to escape. It would never let these Children live in peace—ever.

Chapter 21

The rising sun struck the forest canopy and made all the leaves glow emerald-green up there. Dina didn't wonder anymore what time it was.

Her thoughts stretched out in front of her to the canton ahead. Would it welcome her with open arms the way it did before? Would she ever feel at home there without reliving the nightmare of the massacre she'd witnessed?

She would have rather run to a different canton, but she didn't know the way and this one was the closest.

Renfroe's warning kept ringing in her head. The Pride would come after her and Tania sooner rather than later. This canton would be the very first place the cats came looking. They knew her history with this canton.

She tried more than once to shake those thoughts out of her head, but it became increasingly difficult the closer she got. Familiar landmarks she'd seen on her last visit brought all the memories back.

She had to go there, though, at least to warn the canton's current residents of the danger. They would leave the canton and take her and Tania deeper into the jungle. Then Dina wouldn't have to stay here and keep remembering the sight of her friends getting slaughtered.

She didn't realize she'd slowed down until Tania bumped into her from behind. "Dina? Are you all right?"

Dina shook herself awake. "I'm fine. I'm just thinking."

"Maybe we should stop for a while," Tania suggested. "We've been walking for almost twenty-four hours straight. I'm exhausted."

"We can't stop yet. We're almost to the canton. We'll stop there."

Then she heard something over the tree lizards squawking in the canopy overhead. She bent her head and heard the babies squeaking in her pouch. She peeked inside. They were awake again and they waved their little arms and legs around trying to swim over each other in their nest.

"I forgot about them," Dina remarked. "They need to stop, too."

She sat down under a tree and handed her rucksack of food to Tania. Tania handed her the milk container and Dina drip-fed it into the babies' wide-open mouths.

One of them nipped her finger with its tiny needle teeth and made her giggle. She used her finger to rub the little creature under the chin and then stroked down its back. Its golden fur gleamed in the morning sun.

"They're so beautiful!" she breathed. "It's hard to imagine them growing up into....well, I don't know what they'll look like when they grow up."

Tania made a face, groaned, and turned away. "I don't know how you can touch those things or even look at them. They're disgusting."

"They're just babies. Whatever Khalid or any other cat of the Pride has done, these babies are totally innocent."

Tania grunted under her breath. "Ugh! They're monsters."

"You better get used to it. You're going to have some of these monsters yourself one of these days and you're the only mother they'll ever have. You better get ready to be that for them or they might wind up just like Khalid."

Tania made another face and turned even farther away. She refused to look at Dina at all.

Dina glared at the back of Tania's head. Dina was really starting to resent Tania's attitude toward the Children. It wasn't their fault they looked so similar to the cats.

The Children were as much enemies of the Pride as Dina, Tania, and the rest of the slags were. The Children were more enemies of the Pride than anyone else on the planet.

Dina's mission to Prideland had become a constant search for anyone who might be as against the Pride as she was. She thought she'd found those people in the free people living in the cantons.

Then the Children came along. If anyone was going to stand against the Pride, it would be these Children. They would have to stand against the Pride just to save their own lives.

Anyone who threatened the Children would become Dina's enemy, too. She just didn't expect it to be Tania. Dina had always considered Tania a friend, but Dina couldn't do that if Tania put herself against the Children.

Dina went back to dripping milk into any little mouth that opened itself to her. She smiled at the Children even though they still had their eyes closed. She found each of them impossibly charming.

They made her laugh more than once. As soon as they filled their bellies and settled down to sleep again, she took all the time she wanted to admire their glossy coats and stroke their curious bodies. She couldn't imagine what they would grow into.

Each one had five flexible human fingers with an opposable thumb, but each finger ended with a razor-sharp claw that dug into Dina's hand when they tried to grab hold of her. Four prominent needle-sharp fangs stuck out of the corners of their mouths and they had a very cat-like way of climbing around inside their pouch.

More than one of them hooked their claws into the fabric and tried to climb out before Dina pulled them off and put them back toward the bottom. As soon as they opened their eyes, they would become predators with all the cats' skill and agility.

They fascinated her, not just for their unique physiology, but for all the implications of their very existence. Nothing on this planet would ever be the same, now that these little creatures had been born.

Something else caught her attention. She didn't know what it was because she didn't hear or see anything. A prickle went up her scalp and she glanced sideways into the undergrowth.

Movement startled her into jerking around the other way. She realized half a second later that it was only a tree lizard, but that instant of alarm made her sit up and close her pouch. "We needed to get out of here. Come on."

She hung the pouch and rucksack over her shoulder and set off deeper into the jungle, but more and more noises startled her the farther she went. She was getting perilously close to the canton.

Maybe it was too dangerous and she shouldn't go there at all, but where could she go instead? She pressed on through the morning and the foliage blocked more and more of the sunlight. The heat faded, but the shadows also made her more nervous.

She jumped at the slightest sound and jerked right and left in search of any cats who might be creeping up on her. Her behavior infected Tania. She crowded closer and glanced up and down and in every direction, too.

The sun migrated across the sky until midday. Dina's nerves threatened to snap when another tree lizard squawked in the branches overhead.

Dina's head swung up. She expected to see birds and lizards up there minding her own business. She froze when she saw a cat lurking in the very highest branches. She didn't recognize it. It didn't even belong to any breed or species she recognized, but the sight electrified her to high alert.

She grabbed the cleaver out of her belt ....and then she saw more and more cats prowling through in the canopy overhead. Did they just appear out of nowhere or had they been following her and Tania all this time?

Dina glanced behind her. She couldn't see the canton through the trees. She and Tania were still too far away.

Tania moved closer to Dina's side and followed her gaze to the high branches. Dina's eye skipped from one cat to another.

They were too high up for the branches to support the larger cats. Most of these prowlers looked like smaller breeds of house cat with a few ocelots and maybe lynxes. Dina hadn't seen them in the cities. Did they only live out here?

They slunk along the branches and cocked their heads to peer down at Dina and Tania. The cats twitched their ears and noses and crouched on their branches to inspect the pair from directly above.

Those cats could drop on Dina and Tania without warning. These cats had been hunting the two women. There was no question in Dina's mind about that.

"What are we going to do?" Tania whispered. "There are too many of them. We couldn't fight them all."

"Come on!" Dina husked. "We gotta run for it!"

She didn't wait for Tania to reply. Dina spun away and took off running in the direction of the only place that offered any shelter.

Tania raced up behind her. "What will we do when we get there?! We can't defend the canton alone!"

"We won't have to! There are people there!" Dina yelled over her shoulder. "Come on! Faster!"

She crashed through the undergrowth, batted leaves out of the way, and used her cleaver to smash her way through the undergrowth. She dared to look up once and spotted cats streaking through the branches to keep up with the two women.

"You better be right about this canton!" Tania yelled from behind. "If you aren't, we're screwed!"

Dina didn't reply. Her eyes traced the terrain ahead searching for any landmark to guide her way. The canton was her only hope. She only wished she wasn't showing up on the residents' doorstep bringing a whole flock of cats with her.

She would have liked to warn the canton ahead of time, but that wasn't possible now. She only had to look up once to see more cats gliding out of the undergrowth. They'd descended to the understory where they could get closer to the two women.

Dina prepared to stop running and make her last stand when she spotted the canton's fortified walls ahead. The house roofs rose above the outer stockade fence.

She burst through the last veil of leaves and skidded to a halt when she saw the front gate standing wide open. No one moved around inside the canton. No one manned the gate or stood guard on the walls.

She looked straight through the gate to houses with their doors hanging off. Some of their ladders had fallen down and lay on the ground between the stilts that held the houses off the ground. There was no one here. The canton lay as lifeless and deserted as the last time Dina saw it.

"Now what do we do?" Tania panted in her ear.

Dina cast a glance behind her. Half the cats still prowled the branches behind and above her. The others had descended to the ground, and as she watched, more dropped down and padded closer to surround the two women.

The cats paced back and forth getting nearer by the second. They would be within pouncing range any minute now.

Dina whirled away. "Come on! We can get into one of the houses and pull up the ladder! Hurry!"

She sprinted for the gate. She wouldn't have time to shut it before the cats caught up with her.

She scanned the canton as quickly as possible on the run, spotted a house with the ladder still in place, and wheeled in that direction. The babies squeaked in her pouch when it bounced against her hip and she held it steady to protect them.

Tania yelled something, and when Dina glanced back to check on her, Dina's stomach dropped into her shoes as five cats broke cover. They shoot across the open ground to catch up with the two women.

One of the cats looked like a massive version of a tabby. Dina had never seen anything like it. Another looked more like a Manx, but it also had a tortoise-shell pattern to its skin.

Her biologist's brain tried to understand what she was seeing, but she didn't have time to think about that before the tabby coiled his legs under him and launched himself at her.

She floundered for a second between turning around and facing him down, but at the last second, she dodged to take shelter behind the canton fence. He would have sailed right past her, but at that moment, a man stepped out from behind the fence right on the spot where Dina had been planning to hide.

She was running too fast to stop and she wound up running straight past him, but he didn't try to stop her. He pivoted into the gate opening, raised a homemade longbow, and released an arrow at the cat pouncing on Dina.

The whole thing happened so fast that Dina didn't realize anything until the arrow struck the cat in the upper front chest area of his shoulder.

He let out a hair-raising screech, staggered, and landed the wrong way. His chest and face plowed into the dirt and snapped off the arrow.

Dina spun around to defend herself, but at exactly the same moment, a bunch of other people in homemade clothing came out of nowhere. They aimed and fired bows and arrows at the cats, too.

Dina realized a second later that these people didn't come out of nowhere. Some had been hiding behind the fence. Others had been hiding in the undergrowth around the canton's exterior.

They stalked into the open threatening the cats with their bows and arrows, and in some cases, firing at any cats that didn't back off.

The jungle people hit a few cats and sent them shrieking into the undergrowth. Five or six cats retreated to the branches and kept skimming back and forth up there. They eyed the jungle people with venomous eyes, but the jungle people didn't retreat.

Five of them advanced still aiming their arrows at the cats. The two sides faced off against each other for a while with neither backing down or leaving.

Dina stared at these people while she caught her breath. None of them so much as glanced at her and Tania. The jungle people all kept their backs to the two women while the defenders kept the cats in sight at all times.

Chapter 22

A tall, sturdy man with very broad shoulders backstepped toward the gate and barked over his shoulder at the strangers nearest him. "Get inside and shut the gate. We need to get into one of the houses before they come back."

Everyone did exactly as he said. He must be the man in charge of the group who saved Dina and Tania from the cats.

He and four other men stayed by the gate with their bows aimed out at the undergrowth. The rest of their party got busy hustling inside the canton, taking hold of the gate, and sliding it shut.

The four guards backed over the threshold. They didn't lower their bows at all until their comrades shut the gate and lashed it closed with ropes.

The big guy finally relaxed, eased the tension off his bowstring, and turned around to scowl at Dina. His dark brown curly hair hung over his forehead and framed sparkling hazel eyes.

His jaw and cheekbones had a heavy, powerful quality that extended to every part of him. He was one of the biggest men Dina had ever seen and his back and shoulders flexed when he drew or released his bowstring.

The others had a much thinner, more athletic quality as though they were used to moving lightly through the jungle, hunting, and hiding from the cats.

"Are you all right?" the guy asked. "They didn't attack you, did they?"

"No....but they were about to. Thank you!" she gasped. "I thought this place was deserted."

"It is. Our patrol just came over to scout the place out to see if we could move some of our people here. This place has been deserted for a while."

"I know, but you can't bring anyone here," Dina exclaimed. "It isn't safe. The cats are already threatening this canton and they know all about it....from last time."

The guy furrowed his brow even deeper. "You know about that?"

Dina gulped and nodded. "I was.....I was here.....when it happened."

"How did you survive?" another man in their group asked.

Dina lowered her eyes to the ground. She didn't want to talk about that, but she supposed she had to. These people all obviously knew about the massacre. They might even have been friends with the victims.

"My benefactor wanted me back, so he convinced the Pride to spare me," she husked. "I didn't want to go back. I was trying to escape from this planet when it happened."

"We got word that these people were planning to evacuate everyone off the planet," the big guy went on. "Our friend came over to our canton and told us to get ready to leave.....and then *this* happened."

Dina gasped out loud. "Frank?! You knew Frank? I was the one....! I was the one who was going to evacuate everybody! He was just waiting for word from the other cantons and then...."

She broke off when she became aware of the whole group staring at her. A chill fell over her when she realized what she was saying.

These were the people she'd been on the brink of saving when the cats wiped out this canton. She glanced over her shoulder at the deserted houses. All those ghosts still haunted this place.

The big guy cleared his throat. "We should get inside for the night. We won't stay here, now that we know the cats are keeping this place under surveillance. Thank you for warning us. We would have moved mothers and Children in here and then the same thing might have happened all over again." He held out his hand. "I'm Link Randall."

Dina shook his hand. "I'm Dina Dyer and this is Tania Barnes. We're carrying a litter of the Children out of Prideland....and we're both pregnant. I don't know if you have room for us, but...."

"We never turn away mothers with Children," Link told her and then went around the circle pointing out his companions. "Come on. We'll get inside and pull up the ladder. Then we can talk."

He led the way to the nearest house and his bulky body didn't slow him down at all when he climbed up into the building.

Dina and Tania followed him and four of his comrades came with them. The rest of the patrol spread out through the canton gathering broken pieces of wood that had fallen away from the houses during the last attack.

Link put his bow on the floor in the corner and unslung his quiver of arrows while he surveyed the room. Only enough light came through the door to illuminate the main room downstairs. "This is Frank's house," Link remarked.

"I know. I stayed here before the massacre. I escaped from Prideland and he was the first person I met when I got here. Our team came from the Coalition to find him and his brother Alexander after their shuttle crashed."

Link shot her a grin when he wiped dust and lichen off the kitchen table. "I see you know more about it than I do. I can't remember how many times I sat around this table with him and Elana and the kids. It doesn't seem possible that they're gone."

Dina took a chance and asked the question that had been bothering her ever since he mentioned not turning away mothers and Children. "Do you have a lot of mothers and Children out here?"

"Hundreds of them." He broke off when the rest of his companions returned.

They set armloads of wood against the living room wall and then pulled up the ladder before they shut the house door. Link called two of his men to stand the first watch. The patrol went through the house and Link posted the other two men at strategic windows where they could keep an eye on the rest of the canton.

The house fell into darkness as the sun set. Barely any light came through the spaces between the logs that made up the walls.

"Now the place is as secure as it's going to be," Link went on. "We'll keep watch just in case any cats come over the walls during the night."

"What are you going to do?" Tania asked and glanced around the room. "There's nowhere to sleep here."

"There are bedrooms upstairs," Dina told her.

"You two can take those. We'll stay down here." Link squatted down in the middle of the living room and started to arrange the firewood into a log-cabin shape.

"You're.....you're just going to build a fire right here on the floor?" Dina asked. "Won't it burn a hole through the wood?"

He shot her a grin and laughed. "I wouldn't do that! What do you take me for?"

Right then, one of the men brought over a sheet of metal from somewhere. Dina didn't see where he got it from. He laid it on the floor next to Link and Link moved his log cabin onto the sheet.

"It looks like you don't know all this place's secrets," the other remarked and stuck out his hand to Dina. "I'm Troy—Troy Engel."

He was taller than Link, but Troy had long, straight dark hair drawn back into a ponytail behind his neck. He had a very long, angular face and small eyes that gave him a bookish look. He didn't look like the kind of person that was used to fighting, but the rest of him had become wiry, muscular, and tense from long exercise and hardship.

Dina shook his hand. "Good to meet you. Like I said, I only stayed here for a few days."

"You said you brought some Children out of Prideland," he went on. "Are they yours?"

"No, someone gave them to me to take out when I escaped." She opened her pouch and found the little ones struggling to climb around again. "It looks like they're hungry again. Man, they really eat a lot!"

Link laughed. "This is nothing. Wait until they get older."

"How do you know?" Dina put her pouch on the floor just as he set the firewood alight. She didn't see how he did it.

"We all have Children," Troy replied. "They grow up a lot faster than human children."

Dina looked up at him. "You do? I mean....are they.....?"

"Go ahead and ask," Link interrupted. "There are no stupid questions when it comes to the Children."

Dina bowed her head over the pouch so she wouldn't have to make eye contact with either of these men. "I'm sorry. I guess I don't really know anything about anything."

"I have five of them," Troy began.

Dina's head shot back up just as fast. "Five! Wow!"

"My benefactor let me sneak them out." He squatted down by the fire as the light widened to fill the house. It shone on his high cheekbones and glistened in his eyes. "They would have been dead otherwise."

Dina found herself staring at him. The darkness of his eyes gave him a haunted look and she didn't ask all the questions his statement raised.

He must have been in a sexual relationship with a female cat benefactor back in Prideland. She must have been one of those cats with at least a shred of compassion if she let him take his Children to safety to save their lives.

"There aren't many of us that don't have Children," a tall woman with long, straight black hair added. "The jungle people who lived in the cantons before the Children mutation are in the minority now. Nearly everyone living out here now has escaped to save their Children....and themselves." She stuck out her hand. "I'm Meredith Fellows.....and this is Cook, Lucy Callaghan, Harmony Leach, Fitch, Salman Kramer, Nicholas Lockerby....."

She went around the circle as all the other newcomers gathered nearer to the fire. Meredith introduced everyone else in the patrol, but Dina lost track of who everyone was. She would just have to catch up on that later.

Fitch had a very long, wiry body, too, but he lacked Troy's bookish quality. Fitch's lighter coloring gave him a hard, determined, almost brutal look like he'd seen the absolute worst that Prideland could dish out and still survived to overcome it.

Cook was a big, portly man with short-clipped hair and a badly shaven bristly black beard covering his face. He looked like he could have been a cook on a pirate ship or something, but he had a cheery, childlike smile and laughing, twinkling black eyes.

Salman was the shortest of their group and watched everything in silence. Lucy was also much shorter than the others with a dainty figure, curly blonde hair, and a petite, angelic face. She didn't look tough enough to be on this patrol, but she held her own with the others and she had been right there with them in threatening the cats away from the canton.

Dina's eyes skated from one person to the next. "So.....so you all have Children?"

"Not all of us are parents," Link corrected. "Some of us just left to save other people's Children....like you."

"That's amazing." The babies distracted Dina again. "I have a lot to learn about these little angels."

Link laughed. He had dimples and an infectious, impish laugh that lit up his cheeks and eyes. "You're one of the few that thinks of them as that."

Dina made a conscious decision not to look at Tania. She'd remained silent through the whole conversation.

"Whose Children are they if they aren't yours?" Troy asked.

"Their mother is Aurora Helion," Dina replied. "I don't know who their father is."

"You're braver than most—bringing them out like this," Meredith remarked. "Most people won't touch them, much less try to save them."

"I couldn't let them die!" Dina exclaimed. "Anyway, I had to leave myself, so it was just as easy to bring them with me." She laughed again when one of them bit her finger. "Take it easy, champ! That isn't part of the meal."

The others laughed. "They can pack a punch when they bite," Link replied. "Just wait until they get older."

"How old are yours?" Dina asked.

"Not even a year old, but like Troy said, they grow up fast. Mine are already climbing all over the place."

"You can't get them to sit still," Troy added. "They're all over the place."

Dina glanced from one person to the next. "Wow. I can't wait to see them."

"Be careful what you wish for," Link countered. "Once they start moving around, no one can control them. They're a law unto themselves." He nodded toward the pouch. "You'll see."

"Wow," she breathed again and traced her finger down one of the babies' furry spine. "It's hard to imagine them any other way."

"You're a mother, too," Meredith went on. "You'll be having some of your own pretty soon."

Dina grinned at her. "Yeah. I guess I will."

"Who's your benefactor?" Troy asked.

"Senator Renfroe," Dina replied. "He let me leave, too."

"I don't think it's all that uncommon," Link interjected. "The cats have a natural inclination to protect their young. None of them wants to see their own Children get killed."

Dina didn't tell them about Renfroe helping the Senate kill Children. These people didn't need to hear that, so she changed the subject. "Who are your benefactors? I might know them."

"None of us is from here," Troy told her. "We all come from different cities. That's why we're here—to get as far away from familiar territory as we can."

"I don't know anything about the other cities," Dina replied.

"They're the same as this one," Link told her. "The Pride doesn't change from place to place."

"And the people don't change, either," Meredith added. "No one wants to fix what isn't broken."

Dina made a face. "It might not be broken for them, but it is for some of us."

Troy started to say, "That's why we're here," when Fitch called over from the window. "They're coming in! They're coming over the walls!"

Everyone scrambled up and Link and the others grabbed their weapons. Dina looped her pouch over her shoulder to join them. She and Link went over to Fitch's window.

Everyone looked out to see cats clambering over the walls, but they didn't invade by the dozen the way they did when the Pride wiped out this canton. Smallish cats pranced along the tops of the fence posts, touched noses with each other, and passed each other going somewhere else.

They strutted back and forth with the moonlight shining on their fur. "It doesn't look like they brought any bigger cats with them," Dina pointed out. "I don't see anyone bigger than a Manx."

"They're coming inside," Link murmured as the first cats hopped down inside the fence. They skimmed over the ground on silent paws, slithered through the shadows under the house stilts, and kept on going.

"None of them are climbing up," Salman remarked.

"Keep an eye on them." Link nodded down at Dina. "You and your friend should get some sleep. This could go on all night and we'll have plenty of warning if they try to get into the house."

"I don't think I could sleep right now for anything." Her hand instinctively flew to the pouch, but the babies inside made no noise. She didn't feel them crawling around, either. They'd gone back to sleep. "You might as well put me on watch, too. I want to be ready if they decide to come in."

He nodded. "That's the way it is when they come around to attack us."

"Do they attack a lot?" she asked.

"Too often for my taste. We're always having to either defend ourselves or move from one canton to another to keep out of their way. The Pride is always sending out gangs of cats to kill the Children."

"That's terrible!"

"You're in the middle of it, now that you're carrying *them* around." He nodded at her pouch and then squinted out into the darkness. "You might as well get used to standing your turn on watch. Sleepless nights are par for the course when you're a parent."

She studied the side of his face in the shadows. He kept clenching his jaw while he scanned the canton through narrowed eyes. His knuckles whitened when he clamped his hand on his bow.

These people were the first she'd met in Prideland who went to such lengths to protect themselves and their loved ones from the cats. Not even Frank had been as well armed and well prepared to fight the cats if necessary.

Would the massacre have happened at all if Frank and his people had been armed and ready to defend themselves? Link and his patrol were the first people she'd seen who carried weapons specifically for fighting cats.

Dina's whole idea about Prideland flipped on its head, now that she met some people who actually planned to fight the cats. She'd always thought these people didn't have the weapons to put up any meaningful resistance. She must have been wrong about that.

Link noticed her watching him and then shot a fierce scowl at Tania. She'd stayed by the fire when the rest of the group got up to observe the cats. "What's wrong with her?" Link growled.

"I'm not sure," Dina murmured. "She's been like this since we landed here."

"She better toughen up. No one lasts very long around here without knowing how to defend themselves."

"That's the thing. She *does* know how to defend herself." Dina shook her head and turned back to the window. "I don't know what's wrong with her. Prideland did something to her head and now she's too scared to do anything."

"That isn't good."

"I know, but what am I supposed to do? She won't even fight to defend her Children. I don't think she even wants to acknowledge that she's going to have any Children."

Link grimaced in Tania's direction again. Dina had been more inclined to excuse Tania's behavior when the two of them had been alone together on their journey. Now these people made Dina realize how far Tania had gone over the edge.

Link humphed under his breath and refused to look at Tania again. "She better learn real quick. We've all been fighting for months to protect our Children. If she doesn't pony up and do the same thing, she won't have any place with us. We don't tolerate anyone mistreating Children, not even their own parents—especially not their own parents. We didn't come out here to stand around and watch our Children get mistreated. They have enough to worry about from the Pride. If someone doesn't grow a spine and help them, then they aren't welcome with us."

Chapter 23

Dina woke up to see daylight streaming through the open door. She took a second to remember where she was and how she got here.

She sat up. She'd fallen asleep on the leather couch in the living room of Frank's old house in the canton. The fire had completely burned down, but someone had laid a blanket over her. Deer hide with the fur still on it had been stitched to one side of the blanket to make it extra warm.

She ran her hand over the soft fur remembering the evening she'd spent with Frank, Elana, and their children. Dina would give anything to see them again, now that she'd escaped from Prideland for the third time.

She would never see them again, but she forgot about them when she took another look around the room. Tania sat on the floor in exactly the same position Dina remembered her sitting last night.

Tania stared at the dead embers and didn't look up, not even to greet Dina. Had Tania been sitting there like that all night? It sure looked like it.

Link stood at one window looking out at the canton. Troy and Meredith stood guard at the other window. All three held their weapons ready just in case.

Someone had opened the main house door to let in light and fresh air, but the ladder still lay on the floor where the other patrollers had left it. No one had gone down to the ground yet.

Dina went over to Link. "Why didn't you wake me up to stand watch? I told you I wanted to take my turn."

He smiled down at her and his eyes twinkled. "You need your rest if you're gonna grow some babies. Besides, you looked like you needed it after your journey out of Prideland."

"I want to do my share," she told him. "I don't want you treating me any differently."

He smiled even more broadly and then his cheeks colored when she made eye contact with him. "That's exactly why I didn't wake you up."

Her stomach turned a somersault when she realized he was looking at her in some kind of infatuated bliss. She didn't want any man looking at her like that, but it still made her heart skip a beat.

No one had looked at her like that since she first got together with Tom and they'd been together for so long that he hadn't looked at her like that in a long time, either.

She forced herself to look away, and when she did, she caught another glimpse of Tania sitting in exactly the same place.

Link read her mind and lowered his voice to a deadly snarl. "She better start taking better care of herself. Her Children need her to sleep even if she doesn't want to."

"What should I do about her?" Dina asked. "I risked a lot to get her out of Prideland. I can't leave her behind, and even if I wanted to, I couldn't do that to her Children."

"We'll take her back to the canton. If she still doesn't take care of her Children, the Council will take them away from her and give them to someone who *will* take care of them."

Dina's head snapped around at those words and found herself staring deeply into his eyes. She could no longer deny that he definitely was feeling something toward her and communicating it with his eyes and his body language.

His words stopped her in her tracks, though. So these people had a Council that made these decisions on behalf of the community.

Dina had never known that the free people had any kind of government or social structure. Frank never mentioned consulting anyone when he planned to evacuate multiple cantons off the planet.

Maybe they didn't have a social structure when Frank was alive. Maybe this had all developed recently. Maybe the Children mutation changed that, too.

Link frowned when he saw her reaction. "Don't tell me you'd let her harm her Children. I'd never believe that about you. You care about them too much."

"No, of course not. I guess I just never figured...." She trailed off and cast another glance at Tania.

Dina had never considered what she would do about Tania's negative attitude toward her own Children. Dina didn't think she could do anything, but now that Link mentioned it, taking the Children away seemed like the most logical course.

Dina didn't think Tania would put up too much of a protest. Tania wanted nothing to do with her Children.

Dina felt a surge of maternal protective rage toward Tania on her Children's behalf. Dina agreed with Link. No one better harm these Children.

Tania being their mother didn't mean a thing. Dina would identify the Children's enemies by their behavior and nothing else. Someone who threatened or harmed the Children was an enemy no matter who they happened to be related to.

Link brought her back to her senses. "Do you want to feed your Children before we leave?"

Dina's hand flew instinctively to her pouch again. "I should, but....I don't have any food left. I used up all the milk last night. I don't know what I would give them."

"Can't you nurse them?" he asked.

Dina's eyes flew open. "Nurse them! You mean...."

"You're pregnant, aren't you? Are you lactating yet?"

Dina's jaw dropped and she stared at him with her eyes hanging out of their sockets. He said it so casually—like this was the most normal subject in the world to be having with a total stranger he'd only met yesterday.

"What's wrong?" he asked. "Most of the mothers start lactating within a few days of getting pregnant."

Dina gulped. "I just....never....um.....no, I haven't. I didn't think ....."

"Don't worry about it. You can take some of my food." He cast one last piercing glare through the window, strode across the room, and then glared at Tania's hunched form when he picked up his own rucksack.

He gritted his teeth and his eyes flashed dangerously until he got away from her. He held out the bag to Dina. "Take it. They need it more than I do. They shouldn't be eating solid food this early, but it's better than nothing."

"Um.....thank you," she replied. "I really appreciate it."

"We'll be back in the canton tomorrow and you should start lactating soon. Then you won't have to worry about feeding them solid food when it isn't available."

He pushed the bag into her hand and turned back to the window like that was the most normal thing in the world, too.

He gave her a quizzical look when he saw her staring at him with her eyes wide open. "What?" he asked.

She shut her mouth with difficulty and turned away. She could only mumble, "Thanks," while she sat down crosslegged on the floor, opened the pouch, and then opened his rucksack.

He had some dried meat in there that was way too hard for these babies' tiny teeth, but he also had some softer, more freshly cooked meat wrapped in a piece of clean, tanned hide.

She pulled the meat apart and fed tiny scraps of it into the Children's hungry mouths. "They're a lot more active now than they were just a few days ago," she remarked. "They seem to be a lot more aware, too. They're coming straight toward the food like they can smell it. OW!!"

He laughed and she glanced up to find him looking down at her from above. He had that shiny twinkle in his eyes again. She looked away, but she still felt him standing there watching her.

"You're a good mother," he said.

The blood rushed to her cheeks. Why was she responding like this to a total stranger? She couldn't be that starved for attention. "Thanks."

"I should know," he muttered. "I've seen enough of them."

He could only be referring to one person. She didn't want to think about whatever cat had been the mother of his Children, so she changed the subject. "How many do you have?"

"Six," he replied.

"Six! That's amazing!"

"Not so amazing." He jutted his chin at the pouch on her lap. "I'm not doing anything with them that you aren't doing with these little cherubs. You're doing this for Children who aren't even related to you. *That's* amazing."

Dina bowed her head and went back to feeding the little ones. She didn't want anyone saying that what she was doing was amazing. She didn't see how anyone could even look at these Children without trying to help them. They needed every friend they could get.

She had to tear off the meat faster to keep up with their appetites. They gobbled the food much faster and came back for more a lot more frequently even than they had last night. Their movements were becoming more deliberate and they definitely clawed at everything with more strength and more intention.

"I'm definitely going to have to get these little guys somewhere they can climb around," she remarked. "They aren't going to be happy in this pouch for much longer."

"We better get going, then. It's already getting late and the cats are gone."

"They are?" She craned her neck to peer through the open door, but she couldn't see anything out there.

"They prowled around during the night, but I guess they lost interest. Now is our best chance to get away. Finish up while I get the others out of bed."

He went upstairs and left her alone to finish feeding the babies. She probably wouldn't be able to keep calling them babies for much longer.

Troy and Link kept talking about how fast the Children grew and how active they became as they got older. These little ones would be doing that pretty soon. She could already see it in their strength and awareness of their surroundings.

Right at that moment, she felt something squirm inside her stomach. It felt like a fish swimming around in there and then something thumped against her abdominal wall. Her Children. They were in there moving around.

At exactly the same moment, a shaft of sunshine split the canopy outside, beamed through the house door, and fell on the babies in her pouch.

That beam lit up their golden fur in ways she'd never seen before. Their fur had definitely grown thicker since Fan first brought these Children to Renfroe's house.

The fur reflected the sunlight in a thousand golden rays. They spread in a halo of heavenly gold around the babies and created a dome of brilliance over the pouch.

"Aurora," Dina whispered and ran her fingertip through their silky fur. "Auroras."

It was as good a name as any, and as soon as she said it, one of them clambered over his brothers and sisters, grasped at Dina's finger with his claws, and tried to climb onto her hand.

He dug his claws into her skin, kicked out with his feet, wrapped his arms around her hand, and then sank his fangs into her knuckles.

"Hey!" she yelled and then laughed as she tried to pry him off. She'd barely dislodged him when Link came downstairs with Fitch and the others.

They rubbed their eyes, ran their fingers through their hair, and then started adjusting their weapons and supply bags.

"Are you ready to go?" Link asked Dina.

"Yeah. I'm ready." She stood up, draped the pouch over her shoulder, and handed him his rucksack. "Thank you again. They ate it all, I'm afraid. There's nothing left for you."

He laughed again. He laughed so easily. She couldn't remember anyone besides Finlie and Jude laughing this much. "I'm glad it went to good use." His smile evaporated, he shot a hard glare over his shoulder, and lowered his voice to a murderous snarl. "You better go get her."

Dina caught the others glaring at Tania, too, and Dina cringed. She was the one who had brought Tania out here and made her such a liability to these people. That made Tania Dina's responsibility, but Dina didn't want to be responsible for Tania falling down on the road—mentally or physically.

She crossed the room and bumped Tania's shoulder. "It's time to go, Tania. We're all waiting for you."

"I'm not going," Tania muttered. "You go on without me."

Dina lost her temper, yanked Tania to her feet by her arm, and shook her a lot harder than Dina meant to. "I said get up and get going! I risked my life by taking you into Renfroe's house and I risked it again on the road to bring you here. You're alive right now because of me. Now move it! I'm sick and tired of hearing your pathetic excuses. If you don't care enough to keep yourself alive, you'll do it to keep the rest of us alive. Now move it and don't make me tell you again or I won't leave you for the cats to tear apart. I'll do it myself."

She gave Tania a cruel shove and made Tania stumble, but Dina was all done playing games. She grabbed Tania's arm a lot harder than Dina would have dared to grab it at any other time.

The way the patrol was looking at both of them made Dina act. She couldn't let them think she was going along with this or being soft on Tania—not now that Dina had finally found someone who could help her get to safety.

She marched Tania over to the patrol and gave her one good hard shake to make her stand up straight. Dina mumbled, "Sorry about that," to the others and then pulled out her cleaver. "We're ready to go."

Link raised his eyes at the cleaver. "Is that your only weapon?"

"I have two other knives." She showed him. "That's enough, isn't it? It was all I could get before I left and I've fought the sentinel cats with less. These should work."

He shrugged and turned to the door. "Okay. Let's go."

Chapter 24

Link, Troy, and Salman lowered the ladder to the ground and everyone climbed down. Dina climbed down after Tania to make sure she didn't pull another scene.

Dina made herself a pledge right then not to baby Tania on this journey, and if Tania didn't behave, to put a stop to it immediately. Dina couldn't let Tania put the rest of the patrol in danger.

The group made it to the ground and the patrol left the ladder in place. They crossed the canton, slid the gate back, and advanced into the jungle.

Dina checked every corner, branch, and shadow surrounding the outer fence wall. None of the cats from yesterday were here—or at least they didn't show themselves.

The rest of the patrol paused there to survey the area, too, and Dina sent up another silent prayer of gratitude that she'd found these people. She wasn't alone anymore and they stayed as alert and tense as she did. They were ready if the cats came back.

Link murmured one more time, "Let's go," and turned off toward one of the paths leading deeper into the jungle.

Dina had only been on a few of these paths and didn't know where the patrol was taking her. She got so preoccupied with looking over her shoulder to pay attention that she didn't pay attention to which direction they were going.

Link went in front with the rest of the patrol behind him. Troy and Meredith brought up the rear with Dina and Tania between them and the others.

Dina didn't see anything, so she faced front just as Link entered the first line of trees. She prepared to turn around when something moved in the undergrowth behind Troy and Meredith.

Dina spun backward and almost hit Meredith with her cleaver. Meredith opened her mouth to protest. "There!" Dina blurted out. "They're here! They're following us!"

Troy and Meredith whipped around and the rest of the patrol darted into position. They all drew their bows, but Dina only had her knives.

The same cats from last night materialized out of the trees. Their eyes and faces appeared first and then, like something out of a bad dream, more and more of them slithered over branches and under bushes.

Dina jerked left and then right trying to keep them all in sight at the same time. "They're all around us! They're trying to surround us!"

Link bumped into her elbow. "Keep moving. We need to keep going or we'll get trapped here."

"But...." Dina didn't dare to turn around.

"Keep moving," he repeated a little louder. "Fall back!"

She kept her cleaver in front of her and scrambled to pull out the other kitchen knife she'd brought from Renfroe's house.

She kept pivoting from one side to the other, but she couldn't cover every cat all the time. The patrol backed together with their bows aiming outward, but the cats didn't rush in to attack.

Link grabbed Dina's sleeve and tugged her away. "Come on, Dina. We gotta keep moving."

She didn't see where he was leading her. She backstepped.....and again. The rest of the patrol inched a little deeper into the jungle, but the cats didn't go away.

They didn't advance, either. They kept the same distance between themselves and the patrol. Did the cats ever plan to do anything—anything at all?

She didn't dare to slacken her vigilance even for a second. None of the patrollers did, either. They wheeled their bows from one cat to another and the archers' muscles strained from holding their strings taut for so long.

Link kept pulling on her sleeve. He had to. She would never have been able to move without him directing her where to go.

They retreated a hundred yards up the same path. The jungle hung thick and hot over the trail. The vines grew right across the path so Dina could hardly see anything beyond where she and the others were standing.

Just then, Link backed everyone out of the trees into some kind of clearing. He kept guiding Dina backward to cross it. It widened and her heart dropped into her stomach when she saw fifty cats in the upper canopy.

They were all on the small side. None of them looked bigger than a medium-sized dog. Thank the stars they didn't bring out any cougars, tigers, lions, or panthers, but these smaller cats would still be able to do just as much damage with these numbers.

Her gaze riveted to the two cats she'd seen yesterday—the tabby that Link shot and the tortoise-shell Manx.

She didn't even know if he was a Manx. She only called him that because he was about Fallon's size, but this cat had a regular long wavy tail and his body more closely resembled an over-sized housecat.

Both of them followed the patrol up the path. The cats didn't climb into the trees....or maybe they'd already climbed down from there. Dina didn't see the tabby limping or injured in any other way by Link's arrow.

Her mind immediately switched to trying to find some explanation for this. Did these cats have some way to heal themselves from injuries? That wasn't possible and Dina had already proven to herself that these cats could be injured and even killed. She'd done it herself.

She faced them down with both her knives brandished between herself and them. She forgot about going anywhere, and for some reason she couldn't understand, Link didn't pull her in reverse anymore.

She couldn't look away from those two cats to see what the rest of the patrol was doing. At least the cats didn't attack the other patrollers, either. No one had moved or released any of their arrows.

Right then, another flicker of movement on Dina's left made her eyes dart in that direction, and at that moment, the tabby launched at her. That seemed to be the signal and cats imploded into the clearing from all sides.

Bowstrings twanged, cats shrieked, and then the whole clearing erupted in pandemonium as the cats collided with the patrollers in a bloody battle.

The tabby rocketed at Dina and the tortoise-shell Manx and a different cat charged her. She caught a split-second glimpse of the third cat. It was much smaller than the other two with a dusky tan coat, black markings around its face, and black tufts on its ears, but it wasn't a normal lynx. It was too small.

She didn't have time to think about that before the tabby shot off the ground and flew straight for her face. The other two launched at the same instant.

They would have all three hit her at once, but her attention became so fixated on the tabby that she only saw him. She raised her cleaver, but he ignored it. She couldn't figure out why this cat wanted to kill her so badly, but that hardly mattered right now.

She timed her swing down to the second, and when he got within range, she hacked her cleaver at his neck. She hit him and sent him crashing into the other two cats.

The tabby hit the dirt with the cleaver embedded in his neck, but the other two bounced up at the same instant. She became aware of the archers near her. None of them were shooting anywhere if they ever did.

A few cats lay dead on the ground with arrows sticking out of them. The rest of the group fought hand to hand against dozens of cats swarming the clearing.

The two cats closed on Dina from both sides. She couldn't fight them both. She jabbed her kitchen knife at the tortoise-shell only the for black-pointed lynx-type cat to land on top of her arms. He perched there and lunged for her face hissing, spitting, and slashing.

She cringed from his assault and yelled out as his claws sank into her skin. She tried to throw him off, but he was too strong and held on too tightly.

She ducked her head to get away from his fangs, and when she did, he gripped his claws into her clothes and yanked her off her feet. She toppled onto her side and a high-pitched squeak came from her pouch when she landed on top of it.

That sound set her nerves on fire. These cats were trying to hurt her Children. She rolled off the bag, grabbed the cat, and flung it away.

She'd lost both her knives and she couldn't get to her last weapon before both cats came at her a third time.

She couldn't even get up in time to protect herself before the tortoise-shell Manx pounced on top of her. She raised her arms and legs to catch him and hold him at arm's length, and in that moment, she realized that she'd fallen right next to a cat with an arrow sticking out of its dead body.

She grabbed the arrow and lifted it to defend herself from the assault. The arrow remained embedded in the cat it had shot and she wound up picking up the dead cat along with the arrow.

She didn't have time to dislodge it before the tortoise-shell Manx landed on her. She thrust the arrow in front of her and the cat landed right on top of it.

He let out a sickening groan as the arrow stabbed straight through him and then the lynx landed on top of Dina, too. She moved the Manx upward and huddled under his body for protection from the lynx.

His weight pulled all three of them sideways and she spotted her kitchen knife lying on the ground just a few feet away. She rolled toward it, grabbed it, and kept rolling until she threw both cats down next to her.

The thought that she might be fighting to protect not just the Auroras but her own unborn Children gave her all the energy she needed. She vaulted onto her knees, struck out with her knife, and pinned it through the lynx's body to stick him to the soil.

Chapter 25

The instant Dina killed the last of her three cat attackers, she collapsed on her knees and pulled open her pouch. "Oh, my God! Are you all right, little ones?" she exclaimed. "I'm so sorry! Did you get hurt?"

She pushed the Auroras back and forth inside the pouch, but they didn't seem to be injured in any way. They cheeped at her and tried to grab her hand with their claws, but she didn't see any damage on them.

"Are you okay, Dina?" Link asked.

She looked up. She'd completely forgotten about the rest of the patrol.

Sweat and blood soaked his hair and clothes. His curly hair hung in his eyes and Meredith sat on the ground not far away hugging one arm over her chest.

Link inclined his head the other way. "Is everything all right?"

"Yeah!" Dina panted. "I fell on top of them. I thought they might have gotten hurt."

"You did very well against those cats—almost like you were used to fighting them."

Dina looked away. "We should get out of here and cover as much ground as we can before they send more cats after us." She stood up and walked over to Meredith. "What happened?"

"She has a broken arm." Salman pulled a piece of fabric out of his bag and tied it into a sling around Meredith's shoulders. "You should be able to walk just fine until we get to the canton."

"How far away is it?" Dina checked the surroundings again. "How long will it take us to.....?" She froze. "Where's Tania?"

"We were hoping you could tell us," Link replied.

"I didn't see her. I was too busy facing the cats. They were over there. Tania was behind me."

"She was behind all of us," Fitch interjected. "She was behind us when we closed off to face the cats."

Dina spun around to stare at him. "Are you saying.... What are you saying?"

He shrugged and started to look away. Then he locked his eyes on her and didn't break eye contact. "I'm not saying anything except that she was behind us and now she isn't here. She couldn't have gotten in front of us without us seeing her."

Dina cast another hopeless glance around, but the more she looked, the more Tania wasn't here. Dina's mind snapped to the most logical conclusion and she cringed again. Tania better not have run away from the fight while Dina and all these others guarded her escape.

Dina narrowed her eyes at nothing as her disgust turned to rage, but Tania still wasn't here, not even for Dina to rage at.

"Come on," Troy murmured. "Let's move out. If she did run away, she'll make it to the canton before us."

"And if she gets lost in these woods and *doesn't* make it to the canton?" Lucy asked.

He shrugged that off. "Then we won't have to worry about her anymore. Come on. We've wasted too much time and too many arrows already. Get your knives back, Dina. We might need them again."

Dina retrieved her cleaver and her kitchen knife from the two dead cats she'd killed. She wiped the blood off, put them back in her belt where she had been carrying them before, and checked the Auroras one more time to make sure they really were okay.

The fight and her landing on top of them had woken them up. They were in their active phase, and when she looked into the pouch, she noticed that one of them had his eyes open.

He looked right up at her and mewed, but she didn't have any food to give him. She didn't want to stop here to feed the Auroras even if she did have anything to give him.

Right at that moment when he made eye contact with her, a rush of heat shot to her chest. Her nipples prickled and she distinctly felt something warm and wet leak down her breasts.

A pang of shame and disgust gripped her.....and then she discarded that, too. She was about to become a mother. She was already a mother to these six and they needed her as much as her own natural Children would need her.

Link had already mentioned her starting to lactate. If he knew about it, then everyone else in this community of outsiders must know about it, too. Why should she be ashamed of it? She should be glad she didn't need to find food to keep these Children healthy and growing.

The rest of the patrol didn't notice anything. Why would they? They turned away and filed back up the path in the direction they'd been going to begin with.

Everyone kept a much closer watch on the surroundings this time. The group shunted Meredith to the front and Troy brought up the rear with Dina in front of him. They occupied the same positions except that Tania wasn't here anymore.

"You fought those cats very well," he remarked after they'd been walking for an hour. "Most people who come out from Prideland have no experience fighting the cats. Some of them can't even imagine it—kind of like your friend."

Dina flinched when he called Tania her friend, but Dina let it pass and focused on the compliment. "Thanks. I've gotten in a few fights against cats before, so I guess I'm used to it by now."

"It's great to see. We can always use good fighters. The patrol will give a good report of you to the Council. They won't have any problem accepting you."

Dina spun around to stare at him. "Accepting me! You mean....your Council decides who's allowed to stay?"

"They don't usually turn away pregnant mothers, but it does happen, especially if the mother in question turns out to be a danger to the rest of us." His eyes darted forward to the path through the jungle, but he didn't mention Tania. "But you won't have that problem."

She didn't wake up from her surprise in time and he stepped around her to keep walking. She hurried after him. Now she was in the very rear.

"How did you wind up out here?" she asked. "How did you bring your Children out of Prideland?"

"My benefactor was going to turn them over to the Senate as soon as she gave birth," he replied over his shoulder. "I couldn't let that happen, so I convinced her to let me leave with them. I got lucky."

"Wow," she breathed. "I keep thinking about the mothers. I never thought what it would be like for the fathers."

"I left my wife and human children behind to get my Children out," he went on. "It wasn't easy, but I had to do it. I couldn't let my Children die."

She didn't know what to say, and a few minutes later, Link called a halt next to a stream to check Meredith's arm. Dina felt the Auroras squirming around in their pouch and she could definitely hear them complaining.

She didn't dare to take them out now. She didn't know if she would ever work up the courage to nurse them, especially not with all these other people around.

She wound up sitting across from Troy while they rested and waited. She definitely couldn't do anything in front of him, not even with the heat in her chest building to a maddening ache.

"Do you think you'd ever go back to Prideland?" she finally asked. "Not now, I mean, but after your Children grow up? Do you ever think about seeing your family again and maybe getting them out, too?"

"No, I'll never go back," he replied immediately. "I wouldn't have left at all if I hadn't had Children. I had a good relationship with my benefactor. My wife and children got good benefits from my position. I had a good understanding with the Pride and now I'm out here. I'm free and I have my Children to thank for that."

"That's incredible," she breathed. "I never thought of it like that."

He turned his gaze toward the east. "Sometimes I think about them.....my other children. I wonder.....will they ever know why I left? My benefactor might never tell them or anyone else that she was ever pregnant. My children might think I stopped caring about them. They'll never know that I cared for all my children the same way. I couldn't put any of them above the others." He turned back to face front and smiled when he saw her staring at him. "You're a good mother."

She looked away and concentrated on checking the Auroras. She didn't want anyone commenting on her mothering skills as a prelude to flirting with her. This was turning into an awkward situation she didn't see coming.

Fortunately, Link interrupted when he called everyone to keep going. The conversation between Troy and Dina ended there, but it gave her plenty to think about. She hadn't really left anyone behind in Prideland—not the way Troy did.

The only people in Prideland that Dina cared about were Tom and Renfroe. Dina couldn't really say she'd lost Tom, or if she had, she'd lost him long ago. Having these Children didn't change anything between them.

Renfroe was a different matter, but her relationship with him had been so complicated. She would have lost her life entirely if she'd stayed, though, and who knew? Maybe this life in the cantons would turn out to be even more rewarding.

The instant she thought that, she spotted more cats following the patrol through the jungle. These were brand new. She didn't see any of the same cats that attacked the party earlier. Did the patrol kill them all?

She spun around and pulled her cleaver to confront these new cats, but they didn't attack. They kept their distance.

She stood there holding out her cleaver at them for so long that she didn't hear Troy come up behind her. "Keep moving, Dina," he murmured under his breath. "We need to get back to the canton. We can't keep standing out here."

She had to choke to get her voice working. "What if they attack us on the way?"

"Then we'll fight them then. Come on." He tugged her shirt to get her moving, but he only did it once. He didn't steer her backward the way Link did.

She lost the sense of where he was, and when she glanced over her shoulder, he was already standing a dozen yards farther up the trail waiting for her.

She turned away to follow him and he started walking before she got there. She had no choice but to keep going.

She kept a constant watch on the cats behind her, but they never came any closer. They followed the patrol for hours and kept her on high alert.

The patrol walked all day until the sun started to go down. Link didn't stop again. Dina became progressively more fatigued, especially from keeping herself at a nervous breaking point all day.

She held the rearmost position behind the group and kept a non-stop watch on the cats. She never put her cleaver away all day.

By sundown, her legs ached. She didn't know how much farther she could go or if she'd be able to do the same thing tomorrow to get to the end of her journey.

The patrollers stopped looking behind them long ago. They seemed to relax considerably now that she was there to do it for them. Should she be worried about that?

She was just looking over her shoulder one last time, and when she faced front, she almost cried when Link entered another clearing and she saw the stockade ahead. The usual fence surrounded houses on stilts, but none of them stood as far off the ground as they did at Frank's canton.

Her heart leapt when she saw adults and Children running and playing in the fields surrounding the canton. This canton looked so different from the one that Dina had just left. The jungle grew thick, tall, and wild around Frank's canton. The canopy kept it in perpetual shadow.

This canton lay in the middle of rolling fields with a rim of jungle around the outer perimeter. The setting sun shone beautiful golden light on everyone and everything in the scene. Children's voices echoed across the fields along with adults laughing and talking. Smoke curled from the chimneys behind the fence.

The whole thing looked so domestic and peaceful. Dina glanced behind her and didn't see any cats. They'd vanished into the undergrowth, but that didn't put her mind at ease. They were still there, or if they weren't, they knew where this canton was. They'd followed the patrol here and the cats would come back...eventually.

The patrollers picked up their pace and a bunch of Children ran out to meet them. Three of them collided with Meredith and started making a fuss about her arm. Another two children flanked Salman, talked in both his ears at the same time, and then they started climbing up his clothes to hug him.

That was the moment when Dina realized. They weren't human. These were Children—part cat and part human.

They didn't climb like regular human children. They dug their claws into his clothes and kicked out with their back feet. Their hips bent at strange angles, but they didn't bend the opposite way like a cat's hind legs.

Dina couldn't figure out how they did it, but the Children climbed with incredible agility. Then she noticed more Children all over the village. They climbed the trees across the field and climbed up the support posts of houses to clamber through the windows and onto the roof. She didn't see any of them using the doors like human children would.

She also saw Children pouncing from ledges, tree branches, and even off of each other. They scrambled over each other, launched themselves into the air, and tumbled and tussled all over the place.

She stopped in her tracks to stare at them. Some of these children looked like they might be ten or even twelve or thirteen, but they couldn't be. The Children mutation had only occurred in the last few months.....or had it? She didn't really know when it happened or when these Children had been born.

Before she could figure it out, a different figure crossed her line of sight. Tania Barnes walked from the open canton gate to a firepit out in the middle of the field. A bunch of human adults sat around the blaze with Children and also a few normal human children.

Tania sat down with them and Dina saw her talking to the adults. What the hell was Tania doing making herself at home here?

"It looks like she really did run for it," Link remarked.

Dina snapped out of her trance and noticed that she and Link were the last patrollers left outside the fence. The rest had gone inside for the night.

Dina grimaced and tried to look away. "I better straighten her out."

Link shot out a hand to stop her. "You can't, Dina."

"I have to! You don't understand. She was a combat officer on my starship. She has no excuse to just give up like this. We were on a mission together. That's how we got stranded on this planet. I thought I owed her something. That's why I brought her with me. If she's shirking like this, it's my responsibility...."

"What she does isn't your responsibility," Link interrupted. "I heard you talking to her back at Frank's house. You've done all you could for her. If she gives up or becomes a millstone around our necks, it isn't up to you to pull her out of it."

"But...." she protested.

He silenced her with a shake of his head. "I've seen this before, Dina. We all have. If she really wants to throw her life away, you won't be able to stop her."

"But what if...." Dina's gaze migrated back to Tania. She looked so comfortable and at ease out there. "What if the Council turns her away? She's pregnant. What will happen to her Children? I don't think she'll take care of them."

He shrugged. "If you're worried about that, you can tell the Council that when they call you up to make your petition."

"What petition? What does that mean?"

"You'll have to go see the Council. Tania just got here so it is possible no one has told her she has to petition to join our community. You can explain the situation to the Council at your petition and ask them to keep her here until she gives birth. You can include in your petition that you're willing to take her Children so she doesn't have to take care of them."

Dina's jaw dropped in horror. "You're serious! You want me to take her Children away from her?!"

"Which would be worse—you taking them away from her or them dying of neglect because she doesn't care enough to take care of them?"

Dina cringed and turned away. "Jesus!"

"It happens all the time. We have mothers come out here, give birth, and then leave to go straight back to their benefactors. We have mothers who are so disgusted by their own pregnancies that they come out here and try to kill themselves to stop themselves from giving birth. We've seen it all and it isn't pretty. Tania is not unique. Believe me."

Dina found herself staring at him again. How could he say these things so casually?

Why did she find it so surprising? The Pride wanted to wipe out the Children and pretend they didn't exist. It would be only natural for the cats' most loyal helpers to feel the same way. They would be disgusted by their own pregnancies and try to kill the Children before they were ever born.

Right at that moment, Dina felt her own Children somersaulting in the womb again. Were they trying to tell her something?

Link read her mind and glanced down at her shirt. She didn't realize until right that moment that her milk had soaked through her shirt. It was wet.

"You better come with me and feed your babies before they cut their way out of that bag. Come over to the fire and you can meet the other mothers. Then I'll show you where you can stay as long as you're here."

Chapter 26

D ina sank down on a log by the blazing firepit in the middle of the field. Link crossed the circle and sat down on a different log across from her. Troy, Meredith, Fitch, Lucy, and some of the other patrollers who weren't already there showed up a minute later.

Their Children ran over. Some of them sat on their parents or cuddled up before running off to play with their friends. Others stayed and settled down by the fire to listen to the adults' talk.

More than one of the mothers nursed their Children in plain view of everyone. None of them showed the slightest shame about exposing their breasts, nor did they act like nursing non-human Children was anything out of the ordinary.

The men in the group acted like this was completely normal, too, so Dina pulled forward her pouch and opened it.

All the Auroras had their eyes open now. They scrambled, clambered, climbed, and even wrestled inside the pouch.

Dina burst into a huge grin when she saw them looking up at her. They definitely made eye contact with her and squalled in hunger. "All right, little ones," she murmured. "I'll do my best for you."

She lifted out the male who had opened his eyes first. He seemed to be the alpha of the litter and he'd been awake and squawking the longest.

She copied the other mothers by lifting her shirt and putting him to her breast. He latched on instantly with no help and starting sucking like crazy. She gasped at first and then it started to feel good. He relieved the pressure as the milk ran into his mouth.

She watched him settle into the crook of her arm and he relaxed considerably, so she took out another one of the babies.

"Ugh! Dina! What are you doing?" Tania exclaimed.

Dina looked up in surprise. "What? What's wrong?"

"Stop it!" Tania blurted out again. "What are you doing? How can you let one of them touch you like that?'

"What's your problem?" Meredith asked. "We're all doing it."

Tania turned up her nose and curled her lip at Dina. "It's disgusting! Those things aren't human."

"They're our Children," Troy countered. "What else would we be doing with them besides feeding them and loving them? That's what parents are supposed to do."

Tania stuck out her tongue and turned away with another grimace. "It's disgusting! Put your shirt down, Dina! How can you even touch that thing?"

"Leave her alone," Link interrupted. "Dina's a good mother. She's taking care of her Children."

Tania gave another exclamation of revulsion, jumped to her feet, and took off walking back to the nearest houses.

"Don't listen to her, Dina," Lucy told her. "You're doing the right thing for these little ones. Don't let her stop you."

"What's wrong with her, anyway?" Fitch asked. "She was fine sitting here while the other mothers did it. Why would she have a problem with you?"

Dina tried to shrug it off, but she got distracted by the Children in her arms. The first male finished nursing and she laid him in the pouch while she picked up another one of his siblings. The first little guy curled up, shut his eyes, and fell asleep with a contented smile on his face.

Dina got so absorbed by how angelically beautiful he and his siblings were that she almost forgot to answer. Tania and her problems seemed so far away when Dina looked at these little babies like this.

"I guess me being her old teammate makes it all a little too real for her. If Tania accepts that I'm pregnant and I'm going to have some of these Children, then she'd have to accept that she's going to be doing the same thing."

"She better not become a problem for us," Meredith remarked. "We don't tolerate mothers like her."

"Why do you help her so much?" Troy asked. "Why do you go to such lengths to protect her when she obviously doesn't return the favor?"

"I don't know," Dina replied. "Her husband died in Prideland and he asked me to help her. I can't think of any other reason. She hasn't given me any reason to make special allowances for her, but I guess I still feel like I have to."

"You aren't responsible for her," Link repeated. "You can't risk yourself to protect someone who doesn't have the courage to protect themselves."

"I know all that intellectually," Dina replied. "I guess I feel more responsible for her Children than I do for her."

Meredith and some of the others exchanged glances, but the Auroras distracted Dina from wondering what that glance meant.

She picked up the last two babies, and while she was busy switching out the ones that had finished nursing with the ones that hadn't, Lucy leaned over and smiled at them. "What are their names?"

Dina looked up. "What?"

"Their names. What are your Children's names?"

Dina opened her mouth and shut it again. "I....um....I haven't named them yet."

"You better hurry up and do it," Link called across the circle. "They'll be talking soon and you'll need to name them before that."

"Talking!" Dina exclaimed. "But....they're barely a week old."

"I'm surprised they haven't developed farther than this," Lucy remarked. "You better come up with something."

"I...uh....." Dina floundered. It had never occurred to her to name the Auroras. She hadn't let herself think that far in advance. She'd been too busy just keeping herself and them alive.

Just then, another woman walked over to the fire. She wore an ankle-length dress of handwoven beige fabric and her long brown hair hung down her back.

She carried a young Child in her arms. It was a girl who looked about four years old and the girl huddled against the woman's chest with her arms wrapped tightly around the woman's neck.

The woman walked right up to Link, lowered the girl into his lap, and sat down next to him. The woman sat down a lot closer than any random community member should have.

She beamed at him and he stroked the girl's hair, kissed her on top of the head, and then smiled up at the woman with the same beaming smile. Was that the same beaming, flirtatious smile he'd been using on Dina? Was this guy a playboy....or was that woman his wife or some significant other?

They definitely gave each other knowing looks like they shared a secret just between the two of them. They looked into each other's eyes like they had a close intimate relationship.

Just then, another two Children appeared out of the shadows. They were older—maybe seven or eight years old. The younger of the two climbed into the woman's lap and the older one leaned against her side while he murmured something in her ear.

While Dina watched, all three Children exchanged places. The girl Link had been holding stretched away from him, extended her little arms to the woman, and then climbed onto the woman, displaced the boy, and both boys went over to Link.

The boys sat down on either side of him and he put his arms around both of them. They cuddled against him and he kissed the older one on the head, too. They must have been his Children.

Dina found herself staring at them. They looked so different from normal human children. These Children's fur patterns gave them a distinctly animalistic look and their elongated pupils made their gazes particularly piercing.

The older boy had brilliant green eyes with orange lines radiating outward from the pupil. The girl had ice-blue eyes and an almost Siamese-cat fur pattern.

The older boy got tired of cuddling with Link, said something to him, stood up, and walked away. He walked upright, but he only made it a few feet before he launched himself forward, bounded on all fours, and then rocketed onto the top of the canton fence where he crouched easily on the topmost points of the logs.

His movements resembled a cat's movements so precisely that Dina couldn't help but stare. He crouched there scanning the surroundings with bright, penetrating eyes. Then he sprang down on the other side of the wall and vanished into the darkness.

"Not what you expected it is?" Link asked.

Dina snapped out of her trance to find him watching her across the fire.

"It's amazing!" she exclaimed. "I never imagined what they would be like when they grew up. It's.....it's uncanny how they have all the characteristics of both cats and humans."

"They have all the intelligence of both, too," Troy remarked. "So be prepared for them to pull out some pretty stunning arguments for why they shouldn't have to do what you want them to do."

The other parents laughed and the conversation turned to other matters.

Lucy got Dina's attention by asking, "So....getting back to the subject of your Children's names."

"They aren't actually my Children," Dina pointed out. "They're......"

Lucy raised her eyebrows. "Adopted?" She dipped her eyes to the two Children lying in Dina's arms. "It looks to me like they're yours. They're more yours than anyone else's....so what are you going to name them?"

"I never even thought about it." Dina put her hand into the pouch and stroked the Auroras that had already fallen asleep with full bellies. "I don't even know where to begin."

"It's easy," Link called over. "This is India....." He ran his hand down the girl's head and spine and then did the same thing to the little boy. "And this is Israel and his brother is Cairo. Their other siblings are Kenya, Egypt, and....."

"But don't think you have to name your Children after places or birds or trees or whatever," Troy interrupted. "Some of us give our children real names. Mine are Sasha, Shelby, Leroy, Franco, and Devon."

"I don't know...." Dina stroked the Auroras a few more times and then went through the process of putting the last two into the pouch.

"I kind of like the idea of giving them names that have something to do with who their parents are."

"You said their mother is Aurora Helion," Meredith remarked.

"Maybe I could give them names that all start with A....like Amber." Dina smiled down at one of the babies—a female. She had glowing darkish gold fur. "Yeah, I like that—Amber."

"What about the rest of them?"

"I don't know. I guess I'll just give them names that start with A, too......like Aries, Abdullah, Amir, Aldo....."

"Agatha?" Link suggested and everyone around the circle laughed.

"Or Aurelio," Troy suggested.

Dina laughed with the others. "The last one is female. I guess I'll just stick with regular names. She's much lighter than the others. I'll call her Ivory."

"Good thinking," Meredith replied. "Now you just have to remember which ones you named which names."

A yowl echoed through the jungle beyond the rim of firelight. Troy heaved himself off the ground. "That was one of mine. I better go bring him in."

"It's time everyone came inside," Link added and he stood up. He carried the little boy in his arms, but as soon as Link got to his feet, the boy jumped down and scampered off somewhere. "You come with me, Dina. I'll show you where you can stay tonight."

Chapter 27

D ina followed Link into the shadowy canton. Night had settled over the houses in a thick layer of darkness. Quite a few doors stood open and let lantern light beam from inside.

Dina hung her pouch over her shoulder, picked up what was left of her luggage, and crossed the village to its other side. Link climbed a ladder into a dark house and lit a lamp inside.

The house had been constructed the same way the houses in Frank's canton had been except that this house only stood about ten feet off the ground.

She got there just as the lamplight spread to reveal one big empty main room with three smaller bedrooms branching off from it. A kitchen counter covered one wall of the main room and handmade beds occupied each of the three bedrooms.

"Were you planning for me to live here all by myself?" she asked. "It's a little big for just me."

He smiled at her again and she could no longer deny that he was definitely smiling at her in a very intimate, suggestive way. "You won't be here alone. Tania is staying here, too, and you'll have more company than you know what to do with pretty soon." He nodded at her pouch. "Someone will bring over some more furniture in the next day or two to make this place more comfortable. They'll also include you in the sentry rotation to guard the wall and the gate. In the meantime, I live right next door so you can come and let me know if you need anything."

She raised her eyebrows at him. "You live next door? Did you plan this?"

He blushed and lowered his eyes, but only for a second. "I might have."

"That isn't a good idea when you already have a wife and six Children of your own. What would she say if she knew the way you've been acting toward me?"

He froze and his eyes glazed over. "Wife? I don't have a wife."

"That woman at the fire just now....the one you were sharing your Children with. I know what I saw. I'm not blind, you know."

He blinked once and then exploded in that infectious laugh of his. "Oh, I understand what you mean now!" He laughed some more. "She isn't my wife. She's my sister and those are her Children. Their father is a cougar from another city. I mean, they were both living in another city when she got pregnant. She ran away and came to find me to ask me to help her get her and her Children out. That's how we got here. They aren't mine—except that they are mine—if you see what I mean. We're raising them together."

Dina's jaw dropped. "Your sister! So.....you're raising those Children as your own?"

"Someone has to. I couldn't leave them where they were. She's all the family I have—her and the Children."

Dina shut her mouth with difficulty. "Oh. I see."

He took a step closer. His eyes shone with a strange light and he lowered his voice to a murmur. "I like you. I like what I see in you. We don't get people like you very often. I.....I guess I just want you to know that—that I like what I see in you. You're special. You aren't like anyone I've ever met before. I....." He faltered. "I guess I just needed to say that."

He walked around her heading for the door.

"You and Tania will need to go before the Council later tonight. They're convening to discuss accepting you and your Children. Get comfortable here and then go over to that house there—the one closest to the gate. The Council will be waiting for you."

He stepped out into the night and silence fell over the house. Dina turned in a complete circle, but the house's very size and emptiness only reinforced his words. She wouldn't be living here alone—not for long.

She and Tania would give birth here. Their Children would fill this house to overflowing until three bedrooms wouldn't be nearly enough.

Dina opened the pouch and looked down at the six sleeping babies inside. They already looked bigger, stronger, and more human than they did the first time she saw them in Renfroe's kitchen.

Six of them. She already had six Children just like Link did and that wasn't counting the two she would give birth to.

Tania. Tania would have her own Children....and then what? If Tania was that hostile toward her own Children now before they'd even been born, what kind of mother would she turn out to be?

Link's comments about taking Tania's Children away from her—Dina didn't want to think about that, but hadn't she just said a few minutes ago that she felt responsible for Tania's Children?

If Tania turned away from her own Children or called them disgusting or even abused them, Dina might have to step in and do exactly that. Then Dina would be adding Tania's Children to her already growing brood.

Brood. What a bizarre word. Dina couldn't think of these Children that way. They were innocent, helpless babies....until they grew up into those otherworldly Children she'd seen outside.

She had a hard time picturing the Auroras like that—or her own Children. How strange it would be to parent Children like that....and yet none of these other people seemed to have any trouble parenting their Children. Everyone in this canton treated their Children the same way they would treat normal human children.

These Children were children. That was the most fundamental truth. They were just as innocent and helpless. They needed love and guidance and protection. Dina had seen that with the Auroras.

They'd awoken her maternal instinct and now she felt the same way toward all Children, even those that weren't technically hers. Was that what Link and Troy and everyone meant when they called her a good mother?

She couldn't help but feel that way when she gazed down into her pouch. She'd nursed these Children with her own body. They were as much her Children as anyone's. She would do anything to protect them. They needed a mother and she would give them one.

Another bubble of voices drew her attention to the canton outside. It sounded like any normal human village. She heard parents and Children arguing out there and then Link laughed in the darkness.

She had to grin when she heard his laugh. She would never be able to forget that voice. He had a big, lively presence that spread to everyone around him.

He also didn't hold back on showing his protective paternal fury not only for his own Children but everyone else's, too. Dina had seen it in the way he talked about Tania. Link didn't like her because she didn't take care of her Children. She wasn't preparing herself to be the mother she should be.

She had no reason not to. She had Armada combat training and she'd been a martial arts champion in the Coalition. No one was better equipped to protect her Children than she was, but something had broken in her mind. She no longer wanted to protect them or even herself.

Just then, another door opened in the darkness outside. Light flooded from inside and Dina spotted Tania stepping inside the house closest to the gate. Tania was already going before the Council.

Dina couldn't stay in this house while that was going on. She climbed down to the ground, hurried over to the house, climbed up, and entered without waiting to be invited.

The house had been emptied of all furniture except for a long table against the opposite wall. Seven chairs sat behind it. Meredith, Fitch, Cook, and Lucy from the patrol occupied four of the seats. Three other men occupied the other seats. Dina didn't recognize those men. They all looked as tough and capable as the men from the patrol.

Dozens of people stood in a crowd facing the table. A few people along the outer walls sat crosslegged on the floor. Everyone else remained standing.

Tania flattened herself against the back wall with dozens of people standing in front of her. She hadn't been called up to address the Council yet. She hadn't even been able to get near them.

Troy stood before the Council giving an account of everything that had happened on their trip. Dina walked in on the part where the patrol had saved Dina and Tania at the canton.

He related the conversation where Dina revealed that she had been the one to coordinate with Frank to evacuate all the jungle people before the massacre that wiped out the canton.

Dina cringed and tried to shrink away when Troy also related the part where Dina had admitted being present during the massacre. Did these people understand what that meant?

Did they understand that the Pride had reduced the canton to get her back and to stop her from evacuating anyone? Did these people realize that she alone had survived because Renfroe wanted to take her back to his house as his special helper?

None of the Council members or anyone else asked any questions about that. No one asked any questions at all about Troy's account. He went on to tell the part of the story where Dina spotted the cats approaching the patrol from behind and then how she'd fought with the patrol to drive them cats off.

People definitely did turn around and look when he mentioned Tania running away under the patrols' protection. Several people glared at her and whispered to each other on the side.

A few other members of the patrol came forward to corroborate Troy's account. Link did the same thing, but no one questioned. The Council just listened to their stories.

The Council members waited for him to finish and then Meredith looked around until she spotted Dina. "Dina? Would you mind coming forward to address us?"

The assembled people parted to let Dina through. Every eye fixed on her when she took her place before the Council.

Meredith smiled warmly at her. "You don't have anything to worry about, Dina. We all saw the way you behaved on the patrol. This hearing is just a formality."

Dina gulped. "Thank you. I'm very grateful for your help...and your hospitality. I....I have nowhere else to go."

Meredith waved to the three men at the end of the Council table. "These are our fellow Council members, Nicholas Lockerby, Paul Frasier, Richard Shriver."

Richard nodded to Dina. "Hello, Dina."

She mumbled. "Hello," and, "It's nice to meet you," to the three of them, but then it was time to get down to business.

"You mentioned on the patrol that Senator Renfroe is your benefactor," Fitch interjected. "You mentioned that he let you leave. I don't think I have to tell you how unusual this is."

"Yes, he is...I mean, he *was* my benefactor. He said I was having twins....and he said he'd been trying to convince the Senate to incorporate the Children into the Pride all along, but no one would listen to him."

"You don't need to justify Renfroe's actions to us," one of the other men cut in. "We all know what he's capable of."

Dina shut her mouth and gulped. She shouldn't be defending Renfroe. No one knew better than Dina did all the horrible things he'd done to people over the years.

"You also mentioned on the patrol that Renfroe warned you that the Pride would come after you," Fitch went on, "and you mentioned that the Pride had already retrieved you from Frank's canton at the last massacre."

Dina nodded. "That must be why they came after me and Tania at the other canton.....but he did say that the Pride was keeping the other canton under surveillance before Tania and I left the city. He said the other canton was occupied.....I don't know why he would say that unless there was someone staying there and then they left." She shook her head to clear her thoughts. "That's just what he said.....but I also believe they'll come after us here. The cats followed us and....."

A flurry of excited talk broke out behind her back and a few of the Council members put their heads together in whispers. Dina couldn't understand why because the four Council members who had been on the patrol had seen the cats themselves.

Dina looked around her. People she knew from the patrol stood in the crowd including Link. She couldn't be the only one who put two and two together about the cats following the patrol to this canton. Dina's statement shouldn't have been a surprise to them. So why hadn't they told their people about it sooner?

The Council members straightened up and faced her. "We appreciate you coming before us to explain the situation," Meredith went on. "We've agreed to accept you and your Children, including the Children you brought from Aurora Helion. You're free to return to your house until...."

"Wait a minute," Dina interrupted. "Those cats followed us here. They know where we are, which means they'll be planning to attack this canton next. The Pride has a policy of reducing all Children no matter where they are. We have to evacuate this canton as quickly as possible and pull it back to some other less populated part of the jungle."

"That is the Council's decision to make," Fitch replied. "If you wouldn't mind stepping aside, we have another...."

"Hold it!" she blurted out. "You're just going to brush this under the rug? How can you knowingly put these people in harm's way? I came here because I thought the Children and myself would be safer here. You have to start planning to disband this canton and move your people somewhere else. Don't you get it? You can't stay here!" She spun around and called to the crowd. "None of us can stay here! It's too dangerous!"

More bursts of talking ran through the crowd. No one tried to keep their voices down. After a second, Nicholas Lockerby had to get to his feet and he yelled over the crowd. "The Council will take up this matter in due course. In the meantime, we have certain matters to settle before we go on to other business."

The crowd settled and then Meredith called, "Tania Barnes, would you please step forward?"

Everyone turned around to stare at Tania. Dina did, too.

Tania cowered behind the crowd, but she couldn't stay there when everyone parted and left a clear path for her to approach the Council.

They hadn't dismissed Dina yet and Link's suggestions came back to her, so she stayed where she was. Tania cast terrified glances at the people around her, but their expressions didn't soften. They outright glared at her.

She finally made her way to the front of the room and shuffled her feet in front of the Council.

Meredith eyed Tania with a raised eyebrow. Fitch made a face and turned away so he wouldn't be looking at Tania at all.

"Tania," Meredith began.

"Yes, Ma'am?" Tania replied in her best military tone.

"Do you deny the reports we heard from the patrol that you ran away from the fight against the cats? Do you deny that you left the patrol and even your own friend to fight the cats for you while you ran away to safety?"

Tania squirmed again. "No, Ma'am. I don't deny it."

"What do you have to say for yourself?" Meredith countered. "What possible justification can you offer for such despicable behavior?"

Tania shrugged and wound up twisting in all the wrong directions. "I.....I was scared."

"I'm sure Dina was scared, too. I'm sure all of us on the patrol were scared." Meredith waved to the people nearest her. "None of us ran away and we certainly never left our comrades in danger while we ran off to safety. If one of us had died in that fight, our blood would have been on your hands. Do you realize this?"

Tania barely whispered, "Yes, Ma'am."

"We don't accept anyone into our community who isn't prepared to fight alongside us and help us defend our Children and ourselves. Don't you even care at all about your Children's safety and wellbeing? If you don't protect them now, what makes you think you'll do it after they're born?"

Tania glanced over at Dina with a pleading look, but Dina couldn't help her. Dina also saw something else in that look—something Tania had been saying all along.

She didn't care about her Children—certainly not enough to put herself in danger for them. She had no plans to protect them after they were born.

The Council waited, but when Tania didn't answer, Meredith threw up her hands. "I'm sorry, Tania, but we can't accept you. Your behavior and attitude have been reprehensible ever since we found you. You've treated Dina worse than anyone and she's the one who saved you from Prideland. We can't allow you to stay here. You'll have to leave first thing in the morning."

Tania's expression changed in a heartbeat. She obviously had never once considered that these people might actually go so far as to throw her out on her backside. "But....where will I go? I have nowhere else to go! I can't leave! You can't do this to me?"

Meredith shrugged. "That's your business. You aren't part of this community. Maybe, if you change your attitude, one of the other cantons will take you in."

Tania cast another hopeless glance around, but she saw the same truth written on every face. The surrounding parents glared at her and many kept their arms crossed over their chests.

"Um...." Dina blurted out. "Excuse me. I know I don't have any right to address you and I don't want to appear ungrateful that you've accepted me...."

She cringed when everyone on the Council turned to her instead. Now what was she supposed to say?

"You can't change Tania's behavior for her, Dina," Fitch told her. "It's precisely because you've acted so honorably that we can't accept Tania. The contrast between you two is startling considering you both came from the same place."

"I know....and I'm not asking you to change your judgment of Tania....."

"Dina!" Tania yelled. "How can you say that? You said Matthew told you to help me! You said he put me in your care! What happened to that?"

Dina did her best to ignore Tania and concentrated on the Council instead. "I'm not asking you to change your judgment of Tania, but I would ask you to reconsider for the sake of her Children. They're as innocent of her mistakes as they are innocent of the Pride's mistakes. Why should they suffer because she doesn't know how to act?"

"What are you suggesting?" Lucy asked. "We can't take her Children without taking her."

"Not now," Dina replied, "but later, after they're born, you will be able to. Tania doesn't even want her Children. After they're born, I'll take them and raise them. Then you can do whatever you want with her."

"Dina!" Tania screamed.

Dina finally allowed herself to face the woman she once considered a friend. "You should be thanking me. This is the only way you're going to be allowed to stay here. You can take this deal or you can start hiking right now."

Tania gaped at Dina with her mouth open, but Dina was all finished making allowances for Tania. Link had dropped too many hints into Dina's ears.

Taking Tania's Children away from her the moment they were born would be the best thing for them. It would be the best thing for everyone. It might even be the best thing for Tania if she hated them so much.

The Council conferred with each other and everyone in the crowd talked animatedly about this turn of events. Dina glanced out at the crowd and noticed Link staring at her. He didn't talk to anyone around him. He seemed to be single-mindedly focused only on her.

That gave her another idea and she turned back to the Council. "I'll take responsibility for Tania for as long as she's pregnant. I'll make sure she doesn't cause any trouble or put anyone else in the community in danger. Just...please don't punish her Children for her behavior. These Children are going to suffer enough hardship in their lives. Don't make it worse by throwing them out without some protection."

"All right, Dina," Meredith replied. "We'll allow this based on the goodwill we've all developed for you." She turned to Tania and Meredith dropped her tone to an icy growl. "We're only letting you stay because of Dina. If I was in your shoes, I would start working very hard to change everything about everything I do. I would start working day and night to win back some of the good grace you've squandered so I didn't wind up getting thrown out after all. This hearing is adjourned."

Chapter 28

The Council room erupted in talk and everyone flooded onto the floor as soon as the Council rendered its decision. People Dina had never seen in her life came up to her, shook her hand, talked excitedly, and even hugged her. The Council members stood up and joined the crowd as everyone filed out of the house.

Dina pushed her way to Tania, grabbed Tania's arm, and marched her outside. The canton had fallen into deep darkness and Dina pushed Tania toward the house Link had given them.

"What do you think you're doing, Dina?" Tania hissed.

"Did you hear a word Meredith just said?" Dina fired back. "I just saved your life—again—and now I'm responsible for you. You better straighten up or we're going to have a serious problem."

Tania protested a few more times, but Dina had lost all patience with her. Dina pushed Tania into the house. Link had left the lamp burning, which was a good thing because Dina hadn't seen how he lit it.

She still hadn't figured out how anyone in this crazy place lit any kind of fires. The Pride didn't have matches which meant the jungle people didn't have them, either.

Dina picked up the lamp and peered into the three bedrooms. "I'll take this room. You can have that one over there. Now you better get some sleep."

Tania stood in the middle of the room watching Dina as though Tania didn't recognize her. Dina came back and studied her. "What's wrong now?"

"Thank you, Dina. You're right. You saved my life. I've acted ung ratefully....and I am grateful."

"I don't want your gratitude. You're going to be a mother, so start acting like one. What the hell is wrong with you, anyway? You used to be a fighter. Now you're just....pathetic."

Tania winced and looked away, but she didn't answer. Dina waited, but when Tania still didn't do anything, Dina walked away. She was getting really sick and tired of Tania.

Dina took the lamp into her bedroom and shut the door. Tania remained standing there in the middle of the empty living room. Dina really, really hoped Tania was in the middle of having a life-changing moment of realization about just how dismal her life had become.

Dina stretched out on the bed, put her pouch on the mattress next to her, and opened it. She gazed into it at the sleeping babies and another rush of love gripped her heart.

She would have liked to stroke them, but she didn't want to wake them up. These were her Children as much as any others would ever be. She could never let anything bad happen to them.

She floated in a haze of so much happiness and bliss just from gazing at them and loving them. She wrapped her arms around the pouch and hugged it against her body. She could fall asleep like this, but right then, she heard a knock on the outer house door.

She jolted upright and listened. The knock came again.

She grabbed the lamp and went back out into the main room. Tania wasn't there and one of the other bedroom doors was shut. Tania must have gone to sleep.

The knock came a third time and Dina's hand flew to her cleaver. She inched closer to the door and listened again. "Who's there?!" she called.

"It's me! It's Fan—from Helion House!"

Dina yanked the door open and gasped when the lamplight fell on Fan's cheeks and forehead She wore the same dark dress with her hair drawn back into a knot. "Fan! What are you doing here? How did you get here?"

"I followed you. It wasn't hard. The cats are keeping this place under surveillance."

"How did you get past them?" Dina grabbed her and pulled her inside. "You could have been killed."

"No, I couldn't have. I came on Aurora's orders again." Fan held out another identical pouch bag. "I brought you another four kittens."

Dina froze. "Another....four?"

"Aurora had another litter." Fan set the pouch on the floor and opened it to reveal another four babies. These appeared to be much younger than the first six that Dina had been taking care of.

"How could she have another litter so quickly after the first batch?" Dina asked.

"I'm not sure. She told me to bring them to you and then I heard from the cats that they'd tracked you here."

Dina grimaced and almost said something about the danger again when one of the little ones squeaked. He was the biggest of the bunch and he turned up his sightless eyes in Dina's direction.

Dina knew that sound too well by now. She sat down on the floor, lifted him out of the pouch, and raised her shirt.

"What are you doing?" Fan asked.

"Feeding him. He's hungry."

Fan watched her for a second and then blew out her breath. "Wow. You're really doing this, aren't you?"

"Someone has to. What did you think was going to happen when you brought them to me? I couldn't let them go hungry."

"Are you feeding the other six like this, too?"

Dina nodded. "It's the easiest way. At least I don't have to worry about finding them food all the time. You wouldn't believe how fast the Auroras are growing. They already have their eyes open and they're climbing around so much. I don't know how much longer they'll be satisfied to stay in that pouch."

Fan raised her eyebrows. "Auroras? Is that what you're calling them?"

"I had to name them. It seemed like as good a name as any."

"I guess I can't really say that you're the Auroras' mother, can I?" Fan asked.

"I'd be glad to be their mother, but I'm surprised their father didn't bring them out. There are a lot of fathers here who wouldn't let the Pride threaten their Children."

Fan didn't answer. Dina got distracted by feeding the Children, and when she looked up, she discovered Fan looking at her with a strange expression. "Is something wrong?" Dina asked.

"Their father....." Fan choked on the words and her hand flew to her mouth. "He's my husband."

Dina froze and then wilted. "I'm so sorry! I didn't know."

Fan turned right and left looking everywhere but at Dina. "I.....I should have left with them. I should have come out here to raise them. They're......I just wish....."

"Hey!" Dina murmured. "You *are* here. You risked everything to bring them here and now you're here with them. You can help me raise them. You don't have to go back."

Fan didn't answer. She fought to control her lips and ended up having to clamp them shut to choke back sobs.

Dina concentrated on feeding the new Auroras. They were just as beautiful as their six siblings. She would need to name them, too.

As soon as she thought that, their names came into her mind. She took the name Aurelio that Troy suggested. The other three were girls so she named them Opal, Briar, and Indigo.

Opal had pale, iridescent fur and Indigo had another Siamese pattern similar to Link's niece India. Dina didn't understand how these Children could have such different fur patterns when their mother was a lioness and their father was human.

Dina didn't ask those questions anymore. This whole Children mutation was beyond her scientific understanding. Besides, her job wasn't to understand them. Her job was to be their mother.

She didn't let herself think about the fact that she already had ten Children under her care and that wasn't counting her own two and however many Tania would have once they were born. Link was right. This house was going to get very, very full.

Dina finished feeding the Auroras, tucked them back into their pouch, and then placed the second pouch on her bed next to the second. Fan leaned over and looked in on the first litter. "You're right. They're growing so fast!"

"I don't feel right about putting them all together. The older ones might harm the little ones without realizing it."

"You've done amazingly well taking care of them so far," Fan remarked. "They're really lucky to have you."

Dina colored and turned away. "You can stay in the third bedroom. If you're right about the cats keeping this place under surveillance, we'll need to warn the Council tomorrow. Come on. Let's get some sleep."

She left the Auroras on the bed and showed Fan into the last bedroom. Dina was just saying, "Good night," when she heard a thump coming from Tania's room.

Dina listened and heard a scratching sound. It sounded like something scraping on the wooden floorboards.

Dina pressed her ear to the door. "Tania? Are you all right?"

No one answered and Dina heard more scuffling inside.

"Tania!" Dina called louder. "Answer me or I'm coming in!"

"I'm....I'm all right." Tania's voice quavered. "You don't need to come in."

Dina hesitated. She didn't like the sound of Tania's voice.

Dina threw caution to the wind and opened the door. Tania sat on the floor leaning against the bed. She'd taken off her leggings and pulled her tunic up to her waist. She sat on the bare floor naked from the waist down with her legs spread.

Dina caught one sight of a straight stick lying in a pool of blood on the floor between Tania's legs. Dina rushed into the room and snatched the stick away just as Tania tried to pick it up.

"What the hell are you doing?!" Dina roared and then covered her eyes and spun away when she saw Tania's thighs smeared with blood. "Oh, my God! Have you completely lost your mind?"

Tania turned her face away. "You wouldn't understand."

"You're damn right I wouldn't understand! Jesus, Tania!" Dina floundered for a second and then turned to Fan who stood frozen in shock in the doorway. "Fan—run next door and get....whoever you can get. Wake up Link Randall and tell him we need medical help over here right away—whatever these people can give us!"

Fan raced away. That left Dina to deal with Tania alone.

Dina floundered for another minute before she decided what to do with the stick. She didn't dare to put it down in case Tania tried to pick it up again.

Dina raced out to the living room and threw the stick outside onto the grass. She still struggled to believe Tania would do something this reckless and stupid.

Dina strode back into the room and took a split second to make her decision. She grabbed the deer-hide bedspread off the bed and flipped it hair-side down so the smooth skin faced upward. "Get up here and lie down. Someone is going to have to examine you to make sure you didn't perforate anything."

"I hope I did," Tania muttered.

Dina couldn't even bring herself to speak to Tania anymore. Tania really must have cracked her gasket if she would do something like this.

Dina went into her own bedroom, came back with the bedspread from her own bed, and used it to cover Tania. Tania refused to look at Dina, but Dina didn't care. She didn't want to look at Tania, either.

Dina went back out to the living room and paced around while she tried to decide what the hell she was going to do about Tania. Dina heard people talking outside and then Link came in with his sister, Fan, and Meredith.

"I'm the most highly trained medical person in the canton," Meredith told Dina. "My benefactor had me trained as a nurse in the city where I was born. How bad is she?"

"I have no idea," Dina admitted. "I didn't look very closely, but she seems lucid enough—I mean, as lucid as someone can be who would be crazy enough to do something like this."

Meredith only smiled. "How bad was the bleeding?"

"Well....." Dina stammered. "I guess....there really wasn't that much. There was just some on the stick that she used and some on her thighs and on the floor." She waved toward the bedroom. "I figured you could examine her and see for yourself."

Meredith smiled even more warmly and squeezed Dina's arm. "You're doing the right thing....and you're right. She's crazy."

"I shouldn't have left her alone," Dina exclaimed. "I should have kept a closer eye on her."

"You couldn't have known she would do this, but maybe you shouldn't leave her alone from now on."

Dina nodded and Meredith went into Tania's bedroom and shut the door behind her. Dina would have liked to pace some more, but she couldn't with Fan, Link, and his sister there. Dina kicked herself for not asking Link what his sister's name was. Now the woman had been called to an emergency at this house on Tania's very first night in the canton.

"You're doing all you can," he began. "You can't blame yourself for this."

"I hate to say it, but I really wish I could just take her Children now," Dina admitted. "I didn't realize she was this much of a danger to them."

His sister interjected. "The worst part is that, if she really wants to destroy them, all she has to do is stop eating. You won't be able to force-feed her."

Dina turned to the woman, but Link read Dina's mind before she could ask. "This is my sister Lyra. Lyra, this is Dina Dyer."

Dina stuck out her hand. "It's very nice to meet you. It was so beautiful to see you with your Children earlier. It's really inspiring to see parents raising these Children the way you and Link are. I hope I can live up to your example."

Lyra burst into a big grin. She had long dark wavy hair, large, soft brown eyes, and a round, cherubic face like her brother's. "That's really strange!" Lyra exclaimed. "I was just about to say the same thing about you! Everyone is talking about how you're raising a complete stranger's Children....and then the way you spoke at the Council meeting—you're such an inspiration! We're all so pleased you came to join us....."

She probably would have said more, but just then, Meredith came back out of Tania's room. Meredith left the door open this time.

Dina and the others turned to face Meredith when she reappeared. "How bad is it?" Dina asked and then groaned. "I don't want to know."

"It isn't that bad at all. She carved some deep scratches in her vaginal wall. That's all. She didn't do any damage to the cervix or the uterus. She's still pregnant and her Children are just fine."

Dina wilted in relief. "Oh, thank God!"

"I can't say the same for her mental state, though. You're going to have to keep a constant watch on her and then there's the question of getting her to eat."

"That's what I was just saying," Lyra interjected.

"What should I do about that?" Dina asked Meredith.

"I really don't know. I would say you should just keep offering her food or maybe leave it out where she can get to it without asking for it. I'm no expert on mental conditions, but I'd say she's about the most selfish person I've ever met. I don't think she would starve herself to the point of putting herself in danger."

"But she would starve herself to the point of putting her Children in danger," Dina corrected.

Meredith shrugged. "Like I said, there's nothing any of us can do about that. Do your best, and whatever you do, just remember that you aren't responsible for her actions. You're doing everything you can for her Children, but in the end, what happens to them will be up to her. Good night."

She let herself out.

Link squeezed Dina's arm. "Do you want us to stick around for a while?"

"I don't see what good that will do. I guess I won't be sleeping in my own bedroom....like....ever again."

He burst into a big, warm grin. "Consider this practice for when your Children get older. I'll see you tomorrow unless you need something else during the night. Don't hesitate to call me if you do. Come on, Lyra."

He and Lyra left. Dina really hated to see them go. She was starting to really like these people.

She glanced at Fan and found Fan smiling at her. "Maybe you want to stay in another house," Dina suggested. "This could get complicated."

"And leave you here to deal with this on your own? No way. She might try something while you were asleep and then you would have to go without sleep to keep an eye on her. You go to your room and sleep. I'll keep the first watch."

"Thank you," Dina groaned. "You don't know what this means to me."

"I'm starting to get an idea. Go on. I promise I won't let anything happen to her tonight."

Chapter 29

Dina went into Tania's room where Tania lay on the bed with her eyes closed. From what Dina could see, Tania hadn't moved since all night.

Fan sat on the floor sewing something in her lap. "Anything?" Dina asked.

"Nothing," Fan replied. "She's been like this since last night."

Dina studied Tania for a second, but the longer Dina stood there, the more convinced she became that Tania was awake and pretending to be asleep so she wouldn't have to face Dina about Tania's idiotic stunt last night.

Dina strode up to the bed, squeezed Tania's leg through the deer-hide blanket, and shook her. "It's time to get up, Tania. Don't think you're going to spend all day in bed."

Sure enough, Tania turned her head away and rolled onto her other side to face away from the other two women. "Leave me alone," she grumbled. "I have no reason to get up and I'm not going to."

"You're getting up because I said so." Dina grabbed the blanket and ripped it off. Tania was still naked from the waist down. "You can get up on your own or I can take you outside dressed like that if you'd rather."

Tania grumbled some more and Fan laughed. That definitely got Tania's attention. She turned around to scowl at Fan, but Tania made sure to do it while she sat up and put her feet on the floor. "Who the hell are you?"

"This is Fan Tiko," Dina replied and handed Tania her clothes. "She's helper to Aurora Helion."

"What the hell are you doing here?" Tania snapped.

"She's the one who brought the Auroras to give to me," Dina replied and she started to make the bed even while Tania was still sitting on it. She didn't want Tania to get any ideas about lying back down. "And she's the one who's going to help me keep an eye on you, so you better be polite."

"I don't want you keeping an eye on me," Tania growled while she pulled on her leggings.

"If you started behaving right, I wouldn't have to. Thanks to your little stunt last night, I have to keep you under observation around the clock which means you won't ever be alone again until you give birth. I hope you're happy with the consequences of your actions." Dina waved at Fan. "You can go to sleep now if you want to. I'll take over here."

Fan finished what she was working on and stood up. She left the room and Dina went with her into the outer living room. Dina could see Tania through the bedroom door. Tania wouldn't be able to do anything.

Dina was liking this situation less and less. She didn't want to spend the next however long babysitting some lunatic woman who tried to abort her babies with a sharp stick.

The full implications of last night's disaster kept sinking deeper into Dina's awareness. Tania might do absolutely anything to avoid her own Children. Dina no longer believed Meredith's idea that Tania was too selfish to do anything to harm herself. What better way to prevent herself from giving birth to these Children?

Fan puttered around the living room for a while and Dina opened the house door to look outside. The sun was just coming up over the jungle, but she stopped dead on the threshold when she saw the Children already out there playing, climbing, wrestling, and running all over the canton.

The gate was still closed. Archers and other armed sentries stood guard in the watchtowers and patrolled along the ground inside the fence, but the fence didn't stop the Children. They scrambled right over it, vanished on the other side, and Dina saw plenty of them climbing around in the trees along the fringe of jungle beyond the fields.

Fan walked up behind Dina. "It's incredible!" Fan breathed. "They look as fast and agile as the cats. They look even faster and more agile than the cats."

"It's hard to believe the Auroras will be like that soon." A squeak from her pouch caught Dina's ear. She seemed to be more highly tuned to their noises now.

She opened the pouch except that this time, she had two pouches and two litters of these Children to feed and tend to.

She sat down on the floor and started with the older group who were even more active and insistent than yesterday. They started crawling out of the pouch even before she had a chance to take them out.

They instantly spread out and started exploring the room, climbing onto Dina's lap, and clawing their way up her back to her shoulders. "Hey!" she yelled, but when she tried to take them off, they only did the same thing all over again.

Fan laughed at her. "You might as well bow to the inevitable. It looks like this is going to be the story of your life from now on."

Dina did bow to the inevitable and let the little ones run. Fan had to stop two of them from going straight out the door.

Dina started nursing the younger ones. The older ones didn't seem hungry enough to come straight to her or to lie quietly while they nursed.

She was just finishing with the last of the younger group when Link climbed up the ladder and entered the living room lugging a skinned deer leg on one shoulder. He dropped it onto the kitchen countertop with a thump and raised his eyebrows at the younger Auroras. "Where did they come from?"

"This is Fan Tiko," Dina told him. "She's Aurora Helion's helper. Fan was the one who brought me these wild things here." She waved at the older Auroras. It took them all of a few seconds to discover Link and they started climbing up his pant legs. Dina frowned at them. "Are they.....?"

"They smell the meat." He picked up the biggest young male and put the little one on the counter next to the haunch. "They start eating solid food pretty early after they open their eyes. Which one is this—Aldo or Aurelio?"

Dina made a face at him, but she couldn't help but blush when he grinned back at her. "It's Amir since you ask."

He laughed and ran his hand down the little boy's fur. Amir didn't even notice. He squatted down next to the haunch and started tearing into it with his teeth. The other older Auroras showed up a minute later and Link had to move Amir and the haunch down to the floor so they could all get to it.

"It looks like I'm out of a job," Dina remarked.

"It looks to me like you have enough to do." Link headed back to the door. "I'll see you two ladies around. Let me know if you run out and need some more."

Fan and Dina waved goodbye to him, but Dina couldn't stop staring at the Auroras. They gathered around the haunch and devoured it like wild animals, but she could definitely see them growing into a more human version of whatever they were. They weren't cats by a long way.

They used their teeth to tear the meat apart, but they sat up straight to eat it. They also made eye contact with each other. Once, when two of the boys pulled off the same scrap of meat, Amir told his brother, "Mine."

"Don't fight over it," Dina told them. "We can get more. Share it."

The Children turned around, pierced her with intense, penetrating eyes, and she froze under their gaze. They could mesmerize anyone with that hard, predatory stare, but a second later, they turned away and went back to eating.

Tania came out of her room in the middle of this, wrinkled her nose at the Auroras, and walked straight out the door. "Hey!" Dina called after her. "Come back here!"

Tania didn't come back and Dina had her hands full. She couldn't go after Tania or follow her around the canton to make sure Tania didn't do anything else as stupid as last night.

"I'll go with her," Fan offered. "I want to go get some water anyway and these little guys will probably get thirsty."

"Are you sure you don't want to get some sleep?" Dina asked. "You've been up all night."

"I'll sleep when I get back. I'll see you in a little while." Fan walked out. That left Dina alone with the Auroras—her Children.

She laid the four younger ones back in their pouch. They instantly curled up and went back to sleep. Taking care of them would be easy compared to their older siblings, but the younger ones would start exploring soon, too.

Almost as if he read her mind, Amir crawled over to her just then, clambered into her lap, used his claws to pull himself up to her face, and stared deep into her eyes. He tried to touch her cheek and wound up running his claws down her skin without realizing it. "Mama!" he chirped.

"Hello, little darling!" she murmured. "I don't even want to know how you learned to talk so fast."

He curled up in her arms and his eyes softened like he was ready to drift off to sleep again, but he kept them open and gazed up at her from the nest of her arms.

She hugged him close to her body and the same overpowering sense of maternal love overcame her. She couldn't stop staring into his eyes and touching his fur all over his face and body.

Three of his siblings got the same idea. They must be getting sleepy, now that they'd filled up their bellies. They all came over and piled into her arms and lap. They kept saying, "Mama! Mama!" when they looked at her and touched her face.

She petted them one after the other and then cradled them all. They squirmed into the same nest of comfort in her arms as they'd been using in the pouch. Their affection and closeness flooded her with emotion, but just then, Fan returned.

She halted right outside the house door and stood staring out for a minute. She didn't turn around when she said over her shoulder, "I think you better come here."

"What's wrong?" Dina asked. "Did Tania do something?"

"No, it isn't Tania," Fan replied still without turning around. "There's someone here to see you."

"Who is it?" Dina didn't want to get up. That would mean putting the Auroras down and they were just starting to close their eyes.

"I think you better come and see for yourself," Fan replied.

Something in her tone made Dina look up. Fan still hadn't turned around. She stood in the doorway facing outward, but Dina picked up a hint of tension in the other woman's body. "What's the matter, Fan? Why don't you tell me who it is? I'm a little busy here."

Fan finally turned around and a hint of a smile played at the corners of her mouth. "I think you better put them down for now and come and see for yourself. You aren't going to believe this."

She wouldn't give Dina any other explanation, so Dina had no choice but to transfer the older Auroras back to their pouch. They were already getting too big for it. She would have to ask Link for some other kind of bedding for them, which meant the house would be filling up even faster than she anticipated.

She crossed to the house door just as Fan stepped back inside. Dina glanced out and saw instantly what the problem was.

A cat strutted across the open field from the jungle to the canton, through the open gate, and sauntering slowly between the houses. No wonder Fan had been acting so strangely.

Every man, woman, and Child far and wide had run away at the cat's approach, which seemed comic because the cat was a tiny, fluffy white Persian with gorgeous silky, snow-white fur sticking out from her delicate face, body, and bushy tail.

She approached the nearest house, which turned out to be the house the Council had met in last night. The cat kept glancing around the village, and when no one came near her, she hopped onto a railing near the house entrance.

She paced up and down it placing her paws one in front of the other and swishing her plume of a tail back and forth.

Dina relaxed, now that she saw who it was. This cat was too small to pose a threat to anyone, but the archers and sentries treated her as one. They aimed their bows at her to keep her under guard the whole time.

The archers in the watchtowers swiveled inward to follow her movements and the patrollers on the ground surrounded the cat on all sides.

The cat examined them with her head on one side, sniffed, and went back to surveying the village with reserved interest.

Dina went over to them and waved at the sentries. Fitch was with them and seemed to be in charge. "It's all right," Dina told him. "I'll handle this."

"What does it want?" he asked.

"Did you ask her?"

He jolted and spun around to stare at her. "What do you mean?"

"Did you ask her what she wants?"

He gaped at her like she had three heads. Dina waved him away. "You can go back to what you were doing. She isn't any threat to us."

"But....she's a cat. We shouldn't allow her inside the fence."

Dina made a face. "It's because she's a cat that you wouldn't be able to keep her out of it—not without shooting her."

He scowled at the Persian. "Maybe we should."

"At least let me find out what she wants. You can see she didn't come here to attack us."

"Why did she come here, then?"

"This is getting us nowhere," Dina told him. "Just go back to the fence and let me talk to her. Okay?"

He scowled at the cat again and finally he took his men back to their positions. Dina waited until the archers turned their attention back to the surrounding jungle before she approached the cat. "Hello, Elyse. What brings you so far out of the city?"

Elyse swiveled around and strutted down the railing. "Oh, there you are, Dina dear. You can't imagine how impossible these silly slags are to deal with. Do you know not one of them would even speak to me? I've been standing here trying to get someone to tell me where I could find you. They just stared at me like they couldn't understand the words coming out of my mouth. I think they must all have the same demented brain sickness that stops them from answering when they're spoken to."

"Well, I'm here now. What do you want from me?"

Elyse glanced around the canton. A few people peeked out of their doors to watch Dina and Elyse talking, but no one dared to come out into the open.

Elyse changed her tone and lowered her voice. Dina actually thought she heard Elyse's voice trembling. "Is there somewhere we can go to talk, Dina—in private?"

"You're welcome to come to my house and sit down if you want. There's no one in there except Fan and she won't eavesdrop on our conversation if that's what you're worried about—or I can ask her to leave—but she's very trustworthy. She's a loyal helper. She won't betray your confidence." Dina frowned at Elyse one more time. "What is this about, anyway?

Elyse narrowed her eyes at the buildings around her and wrinkled her nose. "I've never been inside one of these canton shacks. I don't know that I'm ready to go into one now."

"It's perfectly safe and it's a lot more comfortable than those dirt mounds in the village. If you don't want to come in, then we have to talk here. You might as well come inside."

"Oh, all right," Elyse finally conceded and she followed Dina back to the house.

Chapter 30

Fan had retreated into her bedroom and she strategically shut the door when Dina showed up with Elyse. Dina turned around in the living room. "So here we are. What can I do for you?"

Elyse hesitated on the threshold and peered into the house, but she didn't enter any further than that. "Well...you see, Dina....."

Dina waited for her to say something. Only after another long pause did Elyse take one tentative step into the room.

Elyse took an exaggeratedly long time to scrutinize the room including what was left of the deer haunch the Auroras had left lying on the floor. Scraps of bloody meat lay scattered on the floorboards around it.

Dina considered cleaning it up and just as quickly discarded the idea. Dina didn't really want Elyse to make herself comfortable here. "Are you hungry? You're welcome to whatever we have left."

"Um....no.....thank you, though.....you see....."

Dina waited a little longer and then sat down on the floor. No one had brought any furniture to make this house more livable. Maybe they never would, but Dina didn't care.

She had to adjust the position of her two pouches on her hip. One of the younger Auroras made a squeaking noise in there, but that was all. They were still asleep, thank goodness. Dina didn't want Elyse to see them.

Elyse tiptoed up and down the room twice without saying anything. She twitched her nose at everything. She must have been incredibly nervous.

She always acted so put-together and demur in the city. Coming all the way out here to the slags' canton must have been the most out-of-character thing she'd ever done.

Dina leaned her back against the wall and prepared to make herself comfortable. In an instant of realization, she finally understood that she had all the power here. Elyse was the one out of her depth with no idea what to do or how to do it.

Dina, on the other hand, was in her element. She didn't have to treat this cat with any kind of deference or consideration. Elyse needed her for something, whereas Dina didn't need Elyse for anything.

Dina could have told Fitch to shoot Elyse the minute she set foot in this canton. Dina could call the patrols to kill Elyse right now.....or Dina could kill Elyse herself. No one would even blink and Dina certainly wouldn't face any consequences from that—not negative ones, at least.

A lightning bolt hit Dina in the head and her world tilted on its axis. She could overpower Elyse in seconds. Elyse might be a cat, but she was small, weak, and Dina would bet any amount of money that Elyse had never fought anyone in her life—cat or human.

Dina was just imagining how that confrontation would go when Elyse stopped in front of her, turned to face Dina, and sniffed again.

"What's the matter?" Dina asked again. "You came all the way out here to see me. Here I am. What is it you want?"

"Well....you see, Dina dear....." Elyse began all over again. "You see.....I've had a lot of helpers in my time.....I rather enjoy them, you see....especially the males....."

Dina snorted. "I know you do."

"Well.....you see......I've never had a male helper like Tom before... ..He's so.....well, I don't need to tell you what he's like....."

Dina froze. "You came out here to talk to me about Tom?"

"No, no!" Elyse exclaimed. "It's just....you see.....after you came... ..and he came to live with me.....well, I never had another helper after him.....he's just.....so.....well, he's very attractive....and charismatic.... .and virile......"

Dina passed her hand across her eyes. "I don't believe I'm hearing this."

"But you must see......I haven't had another male helper since Tom came to live with me.....and then.....this mutation happened......"

Dina's hand dropped.....and so did her jaw. "You.......you're pregnant......from Tom......?"

"I had no idea what to do or where else to go, you see......there isn't anyone in the city I could turn to......and Tom......."

Dina gaped at her in slack-jawed shock. She couldn't be hearing this. Tom......and Elyse......

Dina's heart flipped. She'd spent years fantasizing about the future she'd share with Tom. No one knew better than she did how attractive and charismatic and virile he was.

Just thinking that made her cringe now. She'd long since given up any hope of a future with Tom, but now.....

Dina realized a second too late that she should have expected this. It happened to Tania and Khalid. It happened to Dina and Renfroe. The cats had been carrying on sexual relations with their human helpers without any precaution whatsoever.

The instant the mutation happened, it must have produced pregnancies all over Prideland. Renfroe had been right about that. There must have been thousands or even hundreds of thousands of these pregnancies happening everywhere at once. No wonder the Pride was in such a dither about the Children.

"You see, Dina dear......" Elyse squirmed a few more times, sniffed, paced around, sat down, stood up, and sat back down. "I realize now .....I'm so silly.....I thought you of all people would understand......but now I realize how foolish it was of me to come here—to you of all people....."

"You thought I would understand what?"

"That I love him, you see!" Elyse blurted out. "I've had dozens of kittens. I don't care about them—I mean, I do—but this is different .....because they're his, you see......and I love him......my, what an idiot I am to tell you this. Of course you understand, but......I realize how insensitive it is of me to say this to you.....but I want.....I want......I can't exactly say I want to keep these kittens, you see......"

"They're Children," Dina interrupted. "Just call them what they are. They aren't kittens."

"Yes, of course....these Children.....you see......they're his, aren't they? They're his Children even if he never finds out that he had....."

Dina gasped out loud. "He doesn't know?! You haven't told him? Oh, my God!" Dina covered her eyes again.

"I can't go back, Dina, don't you see?! I can't go back to the city—not the way I am. I don't want the Children to be killed outright. Tom would never forgive me for that....."

"And you think he would forgive you for keeping this from him? Do you realize.....?" Dina broke off as she realized. Tom......He was completely in the dark that Elyse was pregnant with his Children.

She could just imagine his reaction when he did find out.....except that he would never find out. Elyse had kept so much from him already. She'd bald-faced lied to him about the true nature of the Pride—all so she could keep him for herself.

She was almost worse than Fallon and Khalid in that way. At least Fallon and Khalid were honest about their treatment and attitude toward helpers.

Neither of them pretended to be something they weren't. They never kept anything from their helpers or deceived them about anything, especially not about the way they would be treated.

"You see, Dina...." Elyse kept stammering. "I need a safe place to give birth.....and I'd like you to take these Children. I can't keep them and the only alternative is to reduce them outright....and I don't want to do that....."

"Fine. I'll take them," Dina replied. "What do you want to do? Do you want to come back when you're ready to deliver? I can't promise this community will still be occupying this canton then. We've had threats....."

"I can't come back," Elyse told her. "I'm too close to time. I'll have to do it now."

Dina froze all over again. "Um.....now?"

Elyse stood up and stretched her shoulders. "Well......sometime today, I'd say. Definitely before tomorrow morning."

"You.......you're ready to deliver now?" Dina choked.

"Is that a problem? I thought it best if we get it over with. Then you can keep the kittens.....I mean Children.....and I can go back to the city. It will be less complicated that way than a lot of going back and forth.....don't you think?"

Dina gulped as the reality of the situation sank in. This was completely out of her ballpark. Elyse must have sensed that she was getting close to giving birth.....and she came all the way out here.....to drop her Children in Dina's lap.

The next instant, Dina's mind switched gears again. These were Tom's Children, and even if they hadn't been, Dina couldn't turn Elyse away.

Dina was starting to understand her mission in life where these Children were concerned. Everyone seemed to be thrusting them on her, but she welcomed them.

Lyra's comments last night came back to her. Dina had no problem caring for the Auroras and she'd already volunteered to care for and raise Tania's Children. Why not Elyse's, too? Why should any of these Children suffer from the lack of a mother through no fault of their own?

Dina got to her feet and breathed a deep sigh—of relief, this time. "All right, Elyse. I'll do it...so we'll need to get ready for you to deliver." Dina glanced around. "Come in here to my room."

Dina went into her room and turned the deer-hide bedspread over so the skin faced up. Elyse followed her inside and watched Dina prepare the room.

"You can make yourself comfortable in here," Dina told her. "This is my room, so no one will bother you. I'm going to go out and get some water and a few other supplies. I'll be back in a little while to check on you."

Elyse hopped onto the bed and pressed her tiny white paws into the deer hide. "Thank you, Dina dear. This will be perfect."

Dina left the room, but just as she was pulling the door shut, Tania came back. She glanced around and made a face when she saw the haunch the Auroras had been eating. "What are you doing?" she demanded.

"Nothing," Dina replied. "What are *you* doing?"

Tania waved toward the open door and grimaced again. "These people are freaks. They all treat these Children like they're normal human children. It's disgusting."

Dina ignored her. Dina made a conscious decision to disconnect herself from everything Tania did, said, and thought. Tania no longer existed in Dina's world—or Dina tried her best to make it that way.

Tania went back into her own bedroom and Dina realized that she couldn't leave Tania unattended while Dina dealt with Elyse.

Fortunately, Fan came back a minute later and Dina gave her the briefest explanation about what was going on. "Would you mind keeping an eye on her again? I'm really sorry about this. I know you haven't slept. I'll see if I can find someone else to come in and...."

"Don't worry about it," Fan interrupted. "I'm not tired. I'll keep an eye on her for you."

"I really appreciate it. I'll keep watch over her tonight so you don't have to."

"Forget it," Fan repeated. "Go do what you have to do. I'll make sure nothing happens to her."

Chapter 31

D ina hurried out of the house and had to stop again. She didn't even know where to get water in this canton. That would be the first thing Elyse would need once she gave birth.

Dina still had no idea when it would actually happen. It could be hours from now or Elyse might be going into labor right this minute.

Dina would have liked to be there for the birth. Elyse was hardly bigger than one of the younger Auroras. Elyse didn't look big enough to carry even one of the Children, but she'd already told Dina that she was carrying "kittens". Elyse must know her own body well enough to know she was carrying more than one.

Dina headed deeper into the canton in search of some water source or at least someone who could tell her where to find one. She started to pass the gate when she heard a shriek from out in the jungle.

The Children were all still out there climbing the trees and playing in the undergrowth. She didn't see anything different about their behavior, but something about that noise sounded wrong. She couldn't put her finger on what it was.

None of the archers or sentries seemed to think it was anything out of the ordinary. She just happened to be passing the open gate right then and she glanced through to the fields and jungle beyond.

Children played in the grass and along a stream that ran through the field. The Children tumbled together and Dina saw one of them pouncing on an insect that kept hopping ahead of the little girl through the grass.

Just then, Link strode across Dina's line of sight. He frowned and then smiled when he saw her. "How did you manage to tear yourself away from your litter?"

She burst out laughing. She found it impossible not to blush when she saw the way he kept looking at her. "I wouldn't call them that."

"How many are you up to now—ten?"

"Cut it out," she chided and then turned back to the scene outside the fence. "This place is so idyllic. It's the perfect place for Children to grow up surrounded by friends and supportive adults."

He turned side on to follow her gaze and he smiled when he saw that the little girl pouncing through the grass was his niece India. "It is pretty nice. Life could be a lot worse."

The instant he said it, Dina caught a glimpse of a different kind of movement in the surrounding jungle. It started about thirty feet to the right of the Children.

She sprang forward and pointed. "There are cats out there! Get the Children out of the jungle! The cats are moving in!"

She sprinted through the gate and Link raced right at her side on their way down the field.

He grabbed India and pushed her toward the gate. "Get back inside! The cats are out in the trees! Get back inside!"

He grabbed a little boy next and sent him running for cover, too. Dina had half a second to recognize the boy as one of Meredith's Children. Dina didn't know his name.

Both Children took off running for the gate. They started by running upright and then bounced forward on all fours, launched themselves for the top of the fence, vaulted off it, and disappeared behind it just as the sentries grabbed the gate to haul it shut.

Dina and Link raced down the field yelling warnings to the Children in the treetops. They heard, turned to look out of the leaves, and then the Children burst out of the jungle by the dozen. Dina didn't realize there were so many Children up there until they all came pouring out into the fields.

Link plunged headfirst into the undergrowth yelling his head off. "Riyadh! Riyadh!! Get inside the fence! Riyadh!"

Dina ran under the remaining Children calling up to them. "The cats are in the trees! Get back inside the fence! Hurry!"

More Children responded, but they didn't come down to the ground. They sprang effortlessly from branch to branch, gripped the bark with their claws, and some even paused to search for the cats before the Children raced the rest of the way back to the fields.

Link kept right on running. He crashed through the undergrowth running deeper into the jungle. He kept calling for Riyadh, whoever that was.

Then Dina remembered that his nieces and nephews were all named after places. Riyadh must be Link's nephew, but Dina didn't see any other Children in here. They had all responded to the call.

Dina made it all the way to the last groups of Children. She kept calling warnings to them until she made sure they all got back to the fields.

She started to look around for Link, but she didn't see him anywhere. He'd run too far into the jungle. She turned in that direction to go find him when she saw the cats moving in.

Her hand flew instinctively to her cleaver and she snatched her kitchen knife with her left hand. When she did, her elbow bumped the pouches containing the Auroras. She should have left them in the house. If these cats wanted to reduce Children, they could kill ten of them just by taking Dina down.

She inched her way back toward the canton and swiveled outward to keep the cats in view at all times. She couldn't let them flank her from behind.

They'd closed the gap and now surrounded the area of jungle where the Children had been playing, but the cats didn't move in or attack.

They darted from branch to branch in the upper canopy and didn't descend. She searched everywhere, but she didn't see any bigger cats. These were all small ones like the patrol had seen near Frank's canton.

She paused there and let them surround her. Better for them to come after her than the Children. They didn't come after her, though. They watched her from the treetops. Did they understand by now that she wouldn't go down with taking a few of them with her?

Crashing footsteps startled her into spinning the other way. Link barged out of the undergrowth with sweat dripping from his face and hair. "That little rat has run off again!" he panted.

"Who?" Dina asked.

"Riyadh. I thought he was out here, but it looks like he's run away again."

"Run away!" Dina exclaimed. "We have to find him! It isn't safe out here for any Children."

Link only shrugged. "He's long gone by now. We'd never find him and I'm sure he's perfectly safe. He's done this before and he always comes back in one piece. He even brags about fighting cats—though I'm not sure how big they are. These Children are tougher than you think."

"Are you.....are you sure?" Dina's eyes darted through the undergrowth. "I thought the whole point was to protect the Children from the cats."

"It is—when they're younger. Once they get older, they seem to be able to protect themselves well enough. You can't keep them locked up forever. They need to get out of and roam, and once they do, they stay out. They don't really belong with humans."

Dina stopped herself from asking again if Link was sure about this. "Well....how old is he?"

"He's less than a year old. He's the same age as his siblings, but these Children grow a lot faster than human children. Some grow faster than others. He acts more like a ten or twelve-year-old human boy. You've seen how fast they grow and some of them are a lot more adventurous than others. I wouldn't be surprised if they're all like that once they get older."

"Are you saying....he's out there....living in the jungle by himself?" Dina couldn't help casting another wary glance at the undergrowth.

"He can handle it. He hunts for himself and lives in the trees like a cat. We wouldn't think it was anything out of the ordinary for an eight-month-old cat to go out on his own and live by himself."

"This isn't a cat we're talking about. Aren't you at least a little worried about him?"

"No, this isn't a cat we're talking about. He's a Child and I wouldn't be much of a parent if I didn't worry about him. I suppose I'll always worry about him even when he's fully grown." Link took a few steps closer and lowered his voice to a half-whisper. "It's really sweet how much you care about this."

Dina's heart flipped again. He was making a move on her right here in the jungle. No one could see them.

Adrenaline scorched her insides, but she forced herself to stiffen. "That isn't a very good idea."

"Why?" he asked. "I like you and you like me, don't you? What could be wrong with that?"

"How about the fact that you've known me less than three days?"

He burst into one of his big, blushing grins. "What besides that is wrong with it?"

She started to answer when one of the cats dropped out of the canopy from high above. Link had distracted Dina from watching them and this cat plummeted straight down on top of them.

It crashed through branches and hit the dirt with a thump. Link and Dina spun around and she brandished her weapons at it only to realize a second later that it was just a normal-sized tabby housecat.

He landed on all four feet, flexed his knees, and shook himself before he turned his piercing green eyes on Link and Dina. "Get back to the canton," Link hissed out of the side of his mouth and pulled a knife from his belt. He moved in front of her to block the cat from getting to her. "I'll cover you."

"Wait a minute." Dina laid her hand on his arm and then she stepped around him to approach the cat. She recognized him instantly and he didn't attack. He just stood there staring at her.

"Osiris?" she asked. "Aren't you a little out of your territory coming out here? Shouldn't you be back in the Senate?"

"I should be." He sniffed at Link and then glanced around the jungle. "I came out here to find you. Khalid is making a huge fuss about tracking you down and a few of these other cats have reported that you and Khalid's helper are staying out here."

"If you came out here to bring me back, you better bring some bigger cats with you next time. I won't go back without a fight. I have my Children to protect."

"I didn't come here to bring you back. I came to give you something."

She almost asked what it was, but some part of her already knew. He slithered into a nearby shrub and came out dragging another pouch shoulder bag along the ground. He tugged at the strap with his teeth and she heard peeping noises coming from inside.

"This is getting ridiculous," Link muttered under his breath.

Osiris pulled the bag to a stop in front of Dina and sneezed. "I don't expect you to do this as a favor to me. You and I have never been friends....."

"That's funny," Dina sneered. "You tried to kill me the last time we met."

"That was before I found out about *these.*" He nudged his nose into the pouch. "You may not want to do this to help me, but maybe you will want to do it to help them."

He looked up at her, and when she didn't move, he backed away to make room for her to approach the pouch. She only had to pull back one lip of the opening to see five Children curled up inside.

They couldn't have been more than a day or two old and they all had a beautiful brown, green, and charcoal-grey tortoise-shell patterned fur. "Where did you get them?" she asked.

"They are mine," he murmured. "The helper who gave birth to them doesn't know I'm here. I told her I was taking them to get rid of them."

Dina's head shot up, but she couldn't speak. She found it nearly impossible to believe what she was hearing. He was the first cat father she'd heard of to take this step.

"None of the other cats know I'm here, either, obviously," he went on. "I don't suppose I have to tell you what will happen if anyone finds out about this.....but then again, I don't suppose you'll ever have a chance to tell anyone, will you?"

"No, I won't tell anyone.....and I will take them. Thank you for bringing them to me. Don't worry. They'll be safe with me—as safe as they can be."

"Thank you." He hesitated for a second, glanced from Link to the canton and then out to the jungle.

She became aware of an intense silence hanging over the whole area. She glanced up into the canopy, but the cats she'd seen were all gone.

Did they realize what Senator Osiris was doing out here? Did they see him hide this bag in the bushes before they showed themselves to the Children? He must have hidden it last night before they came out here to play.

A thousand questions rushed into her mind, but she didn't have a chance to ask them before he slipped away into the undergrowth. His tabby coat perfectly concealed him in the shadows.

How tragic that Osiris and Renfroe didn't know about each other's secret opinions on the Children. Renfroe still believed he was the only Senator who wanted to spare them.

He and Osiris would probably never find out about each other. They would keep hiding their secret from each other thinking the other was their enemy.

Link stepped forward to Dina's side and pulled the bag the rest of the way open. "It looks like word is spreading about you."

"At least I'll be able to save a few more—or try to."

"You better come back inside the fence," he told her. "It isn't safe out here anymore."

Chapter 32

L ink and Dina stepped out of the jungle shade into the open field. The canton gate was still shut and none of the Children played out in the fields anymore. "So much for this place being so idyllic," Dina muttered.

"It never was," he murmured back. "The cats will always come around to threaten the Children. It's only a matter of time before they strike."

"Shouldn't we move? Shouldn't we evacuate to somewhere else?"

"Somewhere like where?" he asked. "Nowhere is safer than anywhere else. The cats will always be able to find us no matter where we go."

"We could at least move somewhere farther away from the cities."

"Moving farther away from the cities means it will be harder for new mothers to find us. It means more Children will fall to the Pride and fewer will escape."

Dina didn't reply. Of course it would mean that.

She and Link crossed the fields. The archers on watch aimed their arrows at the pair as Link and Dina drew nearer. "It isn't too late to change your mind about us having a torrid romance and living happily ever after in this jungle paradise," he murmured out of the side of his mouth.

She couldn't help but burst out laughing. "You make it sound so tempting."

He blushed and grinned at her again. "I'm glad I could tempt you."

"I have to ask you....why did you name your Children after places?"

"Lyra named them. I had nothing to do with it." He shot her another grin. "Place names wouldn't have been my first choice."

She didn't get a chance to think of an appropriately clever response before the sentries rolled back the gate, let Link and Dina inside, and rolled the gate shut behind them. Now Dina carried three pouches over her shoulder.

She wanted to get Osiris's Children back to her house so she could examine and feed them, but when she and Link stepped through the gate, they heard arguing nearby—a lot of arguing.

Children and parents yelled at each other all over the canton. Meredith was in the middle of reprimanding the little boy Dina had seen in the fields earlier. He stood up to her and she pointed toward a different house.

"What's going on?" Dina asked Link.

"It's like this all the time—every time the cats come around. Parents want to keep their Children inside the fence, and since the fence won't hold them, the parents fall back on the next best thing which is to keep the Children indoors. You can imagine how well that goes over."

Dina didn't have to imagine it. She could see the conflicts breaking out all over the canton. One father tried to grab his son's arm and march the boy into the house, but the boy broke away easily, bounced to the nearest wall, and in half a second, scrambled up to the roof where he perched out of his father's reach.

So many arguments broke out all over the canton that Dina couldn't hear what any of these people were saying to each other.

Meredith and her son exchanged a heated barrage before the boy stormed off to the house she'd been trying to convince him to enter.

He remained walking upright until he came to the ladder. Then he scrambled up it using all four limbs and his claws. He vanished inside and Meredith heaved a sigh before she followed him.

Dina hustled over to her. "Don't you think it's time to evacuate this canton now? Those cats won't be content to stay in the jungle forever."

"They haven't attacked yet," Meredith replied over her shoulder as she walked away.

"That's the whole point of evacuating, isn't it?" Dina countered. "We should evacuate *before* they attack."

"That will be for the Council to decide."

"When will they decide it?" Dina persisted. "I thought you would make a decision last night."

"We couldn't. We had to deal with your petitions first."

"Can't you decide it now? Why wait until it's too late?"

"Those are only small cats," Meredith replied. "We don't have anything to worry about from them."

"But they know where we are. They followed us here and they aren't the only ones. It's only a matter of time before they bring out the larger cats to attack us."

"That's debatable." Meredith waved her hand and walked away. "Excuse me. I have to deal with my son."

Dina halted at the ladder's base while Meredith climbed up, disappeared inside her house, and shut the door. Dina wanted to keep arguing. She wanted to force Meredith to evacuate the canton.

How long would it take the Council to make a decision? Even once they did, Dina couldn't count on the Council deciding to evacuate. They might decide to make a stand here.

Should Dina leave without them? Where would she go? She didn't even know where any of the other cantons were. Wherever they were, they might be close enough to Prideland cities that she and her Children would be in just as much danger there as they were here.

Dina couldn't leave without Tania—or at least not until Tania gave birth to her Children. Dina kicked herself for committing herself to take care of Tania's Children, but the instant Dina thought that, she recommitted herself to doing exactly that.

Dina had just taken on another five Children from Osiris. The fact that Osiris took the risk to bring his Children out here and hand them over to a total stranger—that deserved a commitment if anything did.

Her opinion of him changed in a heartbeat. He wasn't a monster or a mindless animal. She couldn't imagine what he'd been saying in the Senate to make Renfroe think that Osiris didn't care, but Osiris must have been suffering the tortures of the damned seeing his Children in danger.

He must have risked far more than any other parent she'd seen so far. He risked even more than Renfroe did.

Now she owed Osiris. She'd promised him that she would take care of his Children and she meant it. She committed herself to protecting them as much or more than any others except maybe her own.

The other parents and Children kept arguing. Some of the Children eventually went into their houses, but they obviously weren't happy about this.

Dina didn't see how the parents could reasonably stop these Children from doing anything they wanted. They could outclimb, outrun, and outmatch any human of any age.

Plenty of the Children just flatly refused to go inside. They ran from their parents, climbed on top of houses, or sometimes just kept running circles around their older human caregivers. No one could catch the Children if they didn't want to be caught.

Dina couldn't watch this anymore. Seeing these Children's antics showed her a vision of her future. The Children were turning out to be stronger, faster, and more resourceful than she ever thought possible.

Now she had fifteen of them to take care of, not counting her own, Tania's, and Elyse's Children. Link was right. This was becoming ridiculous, but Dina didn't see any reason or avenue to stop it. Taking care of these Children was so much better than the alternative.

She'd gotten herself into this position and now she didn't want to get out of it. It gave her energy, meaning, and purpose. She couldn't think of anything better to do with her life.

She went back to her house, and on the way, she spotted some other mothers pulling up buckets of water from a well behind the houses. Now she knew where to get it

She planned to get some water for Elyse, but before that, Dina sat down on the floor and opened all three pouches. These Children would be her Children's closest companions. Her Children would grow up with these other adopted Children. They would be like siblings.

They would create their own community. None of the human parents could imagine what the community would look like once the Children grew up. They really would become a law unto themselves and then no one could contain them, not even the Pride.

Dina heard a strange noise coming from her bedroom. The door was still closed, which meant that Elyse was still in there.

Then Dina noticed that Tania's bedroom door was closed, too. Fan wasn't in the house at all that Dina could see. Fan had left her own bedroom door open so Dina could see that Fan wasn't inside it.

Dina jumped up in alarm, stormed over to Tania's room, and pushed the door open expecting the worst.

The door banged into something solid and wouldn't open any further than that. It wouldn't budge until Dina shoved hard. Then whatever obstacle sat on the floor skidded out of the way.

Fan and Tania both lay asleep on the bed facing each other with two feet of space between them. Neither of them moved when Dina forced her way in.

She stood there watching the two of them before she fully reconciled that Tania wasn't in any danger. Dina pulled the door shut and then went over to her own bedroom.

She heard the noise again before she walked in. "Elyse? Are you all right?"

No one answered, but the noises definitely sounded like Elyse was in distress. Dina opened the door.

Elyse paced rapidly back and forth across the deerskin bedspread making tiny cheeping noises under her breath. She kept raising her fur along her spine, shivering, and swishing her tail back and forth.

Her eyes had glazed over and she didn't acknowledge Dina when she walked in. Dina eased over to the bed and sat down on the very edge of the mattress. "It's going to be all right," Dina murmured. Those words sounded so stupid right now.

Elyse must have given birth to countless litters in her life. Nothing Dina did or said made a difference.

Elyse didn't respond or calm down. Dina had seen cats giving birth before—or at least been around them when they did. The best thing to do would be to leave Elyse alone. Dina's role didn't start until afterward.

She left the room and shut the door behind her, but once she got back into the living room, she came up against the same problem. She wanted to get water....but how?

She left her three pouches in the living room and went back outside. From the sounds coming from Osiris's Children, it sounded like she was going to have to feed them soon. She wanted to get the water before that.

Things seemed to have calmed down outside. None of the arguments were going on anymore and none of those who'd engaged in them were outside anymore....except for the boy on the roof.

He glared at Dina when she stopped in front of her house. She was still trying to decide what to do when Link strode past.

He squinted down at her. "Are you all right?"

"Um....I'm not sure. Would you be able to tell me where I can get a bucket to bring in water?"

"Sure. Here." He went into his own house, came out with a bucket, and handed it to her, but he wouldn't stop frowning at her. "Are you sure you're okay with all of this?"

"Yeah, it's just...." She waved toward the house. "There's a cat giving birth in there."

"Oh, the Persian. Who is she? How did she find out about you?"

Dina waved at nothing again. She didn't want to talk about Tom or what it would mean for her to raise his Children alongside her own. "It's a long story."

"I'll tell you what," he went on. "How about I bring some more meat over later for your older bunch? You and Fan and Tania can cook up what's left, and if the Persian wants some, she can share it. What do you say? You haven't eaten anything today, have you?"

"No, I don't think any of us has. Thank you. I really appreciate your help."

He rubbed his hand up and down her arm in a comforting way. "You're doing great. Just keep doing what you're doing."

She couldn't ignore the intimacy of that gesture or how close he was standing to her. She opened her mouth to say something when he raised his hand, trailed his fingertips down her forehead to her cheek, and kissed her.

She didn't pull away, and when he straightened up, he looked down into her eyes with that glowing warmth she'd become so used to.

"This is a bad idea," she began. "We really shouldn't start anything between us."

"Why not?" he asked again. "I might have only known you for three days, but that will change. What do you have against it besides that?"

Dina took a deep breath, but she couldn't meet his eyes. She had to pull away and turn aside before she summoned the nerve to tell him the truth.

"When I left Prideland, my benefactor made me promise that I would go back to him when my Children got old enough to take care of themselves."

"So he made you promise under duress," Link countered. "You wouldn't have promised that if your Children's lives hadn't been in danger. Am I right? That promise doesn't mean anything, so you don't have to go back."

"It isn't just that." Dina passed her hand across her eyes trying to decide what to say.

She couldn't tell Link about Tom and Renfroe. She trusted Link enough to tell him the whole story, but it would take too long to explain everything right now.

She'd gone directly from being engaged to Tom to finding out he'd betrayed her with Elyse to living with Renfroe. All of that had happened so fast.....and now she was here.

This was the first time she'd been away from them since.....well, since before she and Tom first got together. She couldn't dive into another relationship—not now.

Link came up behind her and clamped both of his big warm hands on her shoulders from behind. "Tell me one thing," he murmured in her ear. "It isn't me, is it? It's something else—something that happened in Prideland. Tell me I'm right."

"You're right," she husked without turning around. She couldn't turn around. She couldn't face him. "It isn't you. It's something that happened in Prideland."

"All right. I can live with that." He bent down and kissed the side of her neck from behind. "I'll see you later. Let me know if you need anything else."

He walked away and left her shaking with buried emotion. She couldn't imagine a better man anywhere, but too much had happened to her in the last few weeks and months. She wasn't ready to cross that bridge, not even for him.

She warred with herself trying to decide what to do about Link. She'd tried to push him away, but she already sensed that what she said accomplished the opposite. He was already acting like they were in a relationship. She should stop that, but it may have already been too late.

Chapter 33

Dina took the bucket to the well and carried the water back to her house. The noises coming from her bedroom sounded louder and more agonized, but Dina didn't open the door. She supposed Elyse would call out if she needed help.

Dina sat down with her three litters. She really needed to stop calling them that. The older Auroras climbed out of their pouch right away and immediately spread out to explore the room. Some of them sat up on their hind legs—or their legs. Dina had to check herself not to think of them as cats.

Some of them went back to the leftover haunch from earlier and gnawed what was left of the meat off the bone. A few of them were more interested in playing with it, climbing on the kitchen counter, and even clawing their way up the walls.

Dina took out Osiris's Children one after another, nursed them, and studied their fur patterns before she put them back into their pouch to sleep. Each had a unique pattern to their fur that gave them strikingly individual appearances.

Their patterns inspired her to give them names similar to what she saw in their fur, so she named the two girls Emeral and Calliope before she realized she might be giving them pet names. She didn't want to get into the habit of doing that. She wanted them to be people—real people with real people names.

She named the three boys Keith, Dexter, and Brock. Those sounded human enough not to sound like pets. All five of them curled up and went back to sleep just as the younger Auroras woke up. Dina finished nursing them, too, when she noticed that the noise coming from her bedroom had stopped.

She waited for a while, and when Link came in with another, larger section of some dead animal, the older Auroras mobbed him. He squatted down next to them and watched them tear into it. They went at it in a frenzy and that gave Dina the time she needed to check on Elyse.

She knocked on the closed door. "Elyse? Are you all right? Can I come in?"

"I'm fine, Dina," Elyse murmured. "You can come in."

Dina walked in and found Elyse curled up on the bed licking four newborn Children with pure white fur. The four little ones squirmed closer to her body and made little mewing noises every time her tongue passed down their backs.

They started out just five or six inches long, but they seemed to expand with every minute they spent outside in the open air. Elyse's stimulation encouraged them and they clawed their way over each other to get nearer to her.

She finished licking them and sprawled onto her side so they could nuzzle into her midsection. Dina sat down on the edge of the mattress to watch.

"Are you sure you want to do this?" she asked Elyse. "You care for them so much. I hate to see you give them up."

"I'm more sure of it than ever." Elyse raised her head to nudge each baby with her nose. "It's because I love them so much that I have to give them up." She gave them each a long, rough lick. "I've decided to name them if you don't mind, Dina. This one is Nova....and this one is Naia. The two males I've decided to name Duke and Darius."

She nuzzled each one in turn. The glow of bliss and love surrounded all five of them.

Dina didn't know what to say. She'd never seen any cat act this way around her young before—much less a mother with Children.

It didn't seem right that a mother who loved her Children this much should have to part with them. Dina didn't want to be the one who took these Children away from a mother who wanted them so badly.

Elyse would never be able to keep her Children, though. She wouldn't be able to stay in the canton. That wouldn't have worked any better than Renfroe accompanying Dina. The jungle people only let Elyse inside the fence because she was so small and defenseless.

Dina watched the four Children nursing for a while, but she didn't feel right even about that. Her very presence felt like an intrusion on something holy and beyond perfect. She left the room to give Elyse as much privacy with her Children as possible. The moment would end soon enough. Dina wanted to make it last.

Link stood up when Dina shut the bedroom door. "Is everything all right?" he asked.

"Everything's fine. I just hate to see them separated. It's such a tragedy."

A feral growl interrupted her. Three of the Auroras had decided it was a good idea to attack Link. Amber gnawed at his ankle while Aries and Ivory tried to claw his pant leg to climb up him.

He laughed at them, pretended to push Amber away, and then bent down to pick up Aries. The little boy gnashed his fangs and pretended to sink them into Link's hand while Aries grappled his arms and legs around Link's arm.

Link rotated his arm in all directions in a playful attempt to dislodge the boy, but Aries hung on and yowled like he was trying to attack some wild beast.

Link laughed some more. "Keep trying, pal. You have some growing to do before you can beat me."

"Do you have to encourage them?" Dina asked.

"Yes," Link replied and laughed again. "It's good for them."

"Keep telling yourself that."

Just then, Amir and Abdullah both crawled over to Dina. They tugged her pant legs and they both called up to her at the same time, "Mama! Mama!"

"I'm here, sweetheart," Dina replied to both of them and sat down crosslegged on the floor.

They clambered into her lap and started tugging at her shirt to pull it up. "You're getting a little old for this, aren't you?" she remarked to no one in particular.

"Not at all," Link replied. "Lyra's Children are way older and they still can't get enough of their mother. We've decided as a community to keep doing it for the first year unless the Children wean themselves first."

"A year!" Dina groaned.

He laughed again and set Aries on the floor. All six of the older Auroras were more interested in Dina now than in playing with him. "You are going to have a very busy year....and that's not counting your two."

"I meant to ask you. How long do these Children usually gestate? How long does it take from conception until they're born?"

"We don't know for certain. It seems to vary based on what species the parent cat was, but most of them seem to take about six weeks."

Dina groaned again. "Six weeks......" She did a hasty mental calculation.

She'd lived with Renfroe for four weeks....or it might have been five. She couldn't exactly remember, but she must be coming due right about now.

She glanced down at her stomach, but the nursing Auroras got in the way. She didn't have a huge pregnant belly like she might be about to give birth any second. Neither did Tania and she'd been living with Khalid more consistently than Dina had been with Renfroe.

Just then, the bedroom door opened and Elyse strolled out. She tried to use her usual dignified strut, but it didn't come off as well here as it did in the city.

"Are you all right?" Dina glanced toward the bedroom. "How are they?"

"The young ones are sleeping now. Thank you for all your help, Dina. I'd best be getting back to the city."

"You don't have to rush off. You should stay here and rest. We have some food here for you."

"Thank you, but I really must be going. I don't feel comfortable staying in this canton any longer than is absolutely necessary and I have to get back before someone notices I'm gone. I....I hope I see you again someday, Dina. I'm so grateful to you for doing this for me."

She tiptoed over to Dina, ran her satiny body down Dina's side, and then strode out of the house.

"Now I've seen everything," Link remarked as soon as she left.

Dina put the older Auroras back in their pouch and went into her bedroom. The four snow-white babies lay curled in a ball in the center of the deerskin throw. They couldn't have been more exquisite.

She didn't want to disturb them, so she left them lying where they were and went back out to the living room. Link stood with his back to the room. He'd lit a fire in the hollow in the kitchen counter and he'd moved the new haunch onto the counter where he was busy cutting it up into pieces.

Dina took a few steps over there to ask him how he lit the fire when a scream startled her from the other room—Tania's room. Dina didn't have time to move before Fan yanked the door open from inside. "It's starting!" she called out to Dina.

"No rest for the wicked," Link remarked over his shoulder as Dina hurried away.

She burst into the room to find Tania writhing and shrieking on the bed. "Aarrgh!!" she bellowed. "You have to help me, Dina! You have to help me!"

Dina bent over her and clasped both hands around Tania's head to hold her still. "Listen to me! You wanted to get rid of these babies! Now's your chance. The only way to get rid of them is to give birth to them. Do you understand?"

"I can't!!" Tania roared. "You have to help me get out of this! I can't do this!"

"You have to!" Dina snapped. "Stand up and walk around. You'll feel better if you move and work out some of your energy."

"I CAN'T!!" Tania thundered. "MAKE IT STOP!!"

Dina straightened up and looked around. Fan stood off to one side and shook her head. "It was never like this with Aurora."

Dina didn't reply. The contrast between Elyse and Tania couldn't have been more striking.

Tania kept bellowing and screaming in a hysterical frenzy, but Dina no longer believed that Tania was in that much pain. She was just scared, but Dina couldn't do anything about that.

The same thought came back to her. Giving birth to these Children would be the best thing for Tania, her Children, and everyone else. The sooner they all got it over with, the better.

Dina went back out into the living room. Link was still there cutting up the meat and sliding the chunks onto wooden skewers. "Were you present when Lyra gave birth to her Children?" Dina asked him.

He caught her eye, nodded, and went right on with his work. "I was there and I helped her, but it was nothing like this. Sorry. She just has to get through it as best she can."

Dina passed her hand across her eyes. "I sure hope it isn't like this when I give birth."

"It won't be." He beamed at her again, but only for a fraction of a second before he went back to cooking. "You're far too practical to act like this. She's out of her mind. Let her rage. She won't stop the birth."

Dina didn't know what else to do. Tania's mindless screams were really starting to get on Dina's nerves, but she couldn't summon the will to go back into that room. Even Fan left the room. Tania was all alone in there yelling her head off.

Dina should have taken the opportunity to ask Link about how he started fires, but Tania's noise made conversation impossible. Fan and Dina paced around the living room.

Meredith stuck her head in to ask if everything was all right. As soon as she opened the door, Dina spotted parents and children watching the house from a distance. They must have been able to hear Tania across the whole canton.

Then Fitch came by and then Lucy did the same thing. Each person looked concerned until they realized who was making all the racket and why. Then everyone shrugged it off and left.

Chapter 34

F an and Dina went into Tania's room to check on her every now and then, but she only got more hysterically incoherent as the sun went down and night set in. She eventually stopped yelling for Dina to either stop the progress of labor or to do something to help Dina—as if Dina could do anything she wasn't already doing.

Tania completely ignored Dina's suggestions to walk around or change her position in bed. Tania stayed lying on her back and thrashing around like she was going through the worst kind of torture.

Link roasted the meat on the coals and served it to Fan and Dina on carved wooden plates he brought in from somewhere. He also brought in lighted lamps and left one in each room. Dina made a mental note to ask him where he got all this stuff and how the people in this canton did everything.

Tania's bellows escalated to an epic pitch hours after sunset. Dina finally held her down on the bed while Fan pulled Tania's leggings off, but Tania resisted even that.

The minute they got her undressed, she burst into a complete lunatic convulsion of writhing and contorting on the bed. Dina positioned herself near Tania's legs, but Dina didn't dare to get too close in case Tania kicked her by accident—or on purpose.

Dina could have helped Tania more if she'd only kept still, but Dina had to watch from a distance until the first baby's head appeared. Fan brought in a bucket of water and Dina dove in to guide the Child to safety to keep it away from Tania's kicks.

A slimy shape of solid black squirmed into Dina's hands and Fan cut the umbilical cord as soon as Dina caught the Child in her arms.

She had to lay the Child on another deerskin while the second and third Child were born the same way. All three were pure, solid black with the blackest skin and silky, shiny black fur.

"They're beautiful!" Dina murmured while she wiped them down with a wet cloth. "You have three sons, Tania."

Tania rolled away and turned her back on her own Children. "They're hideous. Get them out of here. I can't stand to look at them."

Fan and Dina exchanged glances. Dina collected the deerskin with the three newborn boys on it and carried it into her own bedroom. Fan shut Tania's bedroom door with both of them inside and silence finally, mercifully fell over the house.

Dina laid the deerskin on her bed and then went through a much more meticulous process of cleaning the three boys. Their midnight fur glistened the lamplight.

She laid them in the same nest with Elyse's four Children. The black of the newborn boys' fur contrasted so starkly with the white fur and pale skin. Even the boys' claws were black.

Link came in just as Dina was putting the first boy to her breast. Link ran his fingertips down the other two's spines. "They're beautiful," he murmured. "They look like their father."

Dina's head shot up. "You know about him?"

"Everybody knows about him, but that doesn't make these three any less beautiful. They aren't him. They're nothing like him. How different they are from him will depend on how they get raised and that's up to you. I'm sure you'll raise them to be very different from him."

"Tania will want them even less when she sees how much they look like Khalid."

"Then it's a good thing they have you, isn't it?"

She caught him smiling at her again. "I'll need to name them something."

"Three somethings," he corrected.

She couldn't stop petting each of the boys in turn. Their blackness made them fascinating, captivating, and otherworldly. They really were hypnotically beautiful.

"This one....." She stroked the biggest one in her arms. "He's the oldest and the strongest. I think I'll name him Kaiser."

"Are you sure you want to name him something that's so similar to his father's name?" Link asked.

"What difference does it make? Having a name that starts with K won't make him grow up to be like Khalid. I think I'll name this one Kenji and the youngest one Karim."

"Those are good names. I have a feeling these are going to be good boys." Just then, another knock at the door interrupted their conversation.

Link headed for the living room to answer it, but Meredith entered the house without waiting to be let in.

She grinned when she saw Dina nursing the second of Tania's sons. "You're going to need a bigger house."

Dina had to laugh. "I'm starting to think I'll just throw a bunch of mattresses on the living room floor and forget about any other furniture."

Meredith didn't laugh. "Good idea. I came to tell you the Council is meeting to discuss your proposal to evacuate the canton. You're both welcome to come. In fact, we'd appreciate your input......when you're ready."

She left and silence once more reigned after she shut the door. Dina glanced from the closed door to Link. "What do you think?"

"About what?"

"About going to the Council meeting. I seem to be tied up here."

"You won't be forever," he replied. "Finish what you're doing and I'll walk you over there."

"Are you sure?" Dina studied the sleeping Children. "I don't like leaving them alone."

"That's because you're a good mother, but they'll still be asleep when you come back."

She didn't answer. She really wanted to be there for the Council meeting, so she nursed the last of the boys, and like Link said, all three of them crashed with Elyse's four babies. They all burrowed in together and didn't move again.

Dina told Fan where she and Link were going. Tania still lay with her back to the door and didn't respond or even look up to thank Dina for her help.

Dina didn't expect her to. Dina no longer expected anything from Tania—not even a simple acknowledgment that Dina had saved her life.

Dina would have been tempted to regret that decision, but thinking about Tania's three sons banished that thought instantly. Saving Tania had been worth the effort to get the boys away from her. Dina would do it again in a heartbeat.

She and Link walked across the dark canton to the house where the Council met. Only half the residents showed up this time.

The Council was already listening to arguments for and against the proposed evacuation.

"We can't keep our Children locked up around the clock," one father exclaimed. "They need to climb and explore."

"We've all seen how impossible it is to keep them out of the jungle," Nicholas Lockerby added. "If they go outside at all, they'll be over the fence and into the trees in seconds."

"We haven't seen any big cats and none of these smaller ones have attacked yet," Lyra remarked from the other side of the room. "Maybe they're just watching us."

"They aren't just watching us," Link interjected from the back. "It's obvious the Pride is following these mothers right to us. We either need to stop these mothers from coming to us or...."

Numerous people burst out in protest at this and then another group argued back. The noise level spiked until Fitch pounded his fist on the table.

"Quiet down!" he roared. "The Pride knows where we are. There's no question about that. We're only here to decide what to do about it."

A man Dina had never seen before waved at Dina. "Why would these cats attack us if they're bringing their own Children to us for safety? They should want to protect their Children—not harm them."

"They have to attack us," Dina replied. "Any cat who doesn't join in and show loyalty to the Pride runs the risk of getting killed themselves. The cats have to go along with this....and it's only a matter of time before they send bigger cats to attack us. The Pride considers the Children their gravest threat. The Pride won't stop until they wipe out all Children everywhere, even if it means killing their own. They've already killed thousands."

The debate broke out again on all sides. Link joined in and Dina saw him talking to a lot of different people from both sides. The Council members also debated amongst themselves and with several others in the crowd.

Fitch finally banged his fist on the table one last time and called everyone to order.

"The Council has rendered its decision in this matter," he announced. "We will evacuate the canton in one week and fall back to the Riverbend canton. It's far enough away from the cities, but not so far that new mothers won't be able to reach us. Everyone in the canton should prepare to leave and take anything they can carry with them. This hearing is adjourned."

"A week!" Dina exclaimed to those nearest to her. "That's way too long! The Pride could attack before then."

"I'm surprised they ordered the evacuation at all," Lyra told her.

"You can't be serious!" Dina countered. "You must have seen the cats in the trees. They were only a few dozen yards from the Children."

Lyra shrugged. "That's nothing they haven't done before."

"The larger cats launching a full-scale massacre isn't anything they haven't done before, either."

Lyra didn't listen and the meeting broke up with everyone still talking as they walked outside. Dina tried to convince a few more people, but everyone either thought a week was fine or that the canton shouldn't evacuate at all.

"You can't be going along with this," she told Link when she finally met back up with him.

He shrugged. "It's the Council's decision and I already made my feelings clear. We have a week."

"That isn't soon enough," Dina muttered. "We should have evacuated yesterday after those cats followed us back here."

"The decision has already been made. There's no use arguing about it now. Besides, don't you have enough to worry about already? How many Children are you up to now—twenty?"

She winced. "Twenty-two and I still have my two yet to be born."

"You should concentrate on them instead of organizing everyone else's lives."

"It's because of them that I want to leave. I don't want them growing up here with the threat of an attack hanging over their heads all the time. I want to get them somewhere safe."

He stopped in the middle of the canton, put his arm around her shoulders, and gave her a sideways squeeze. "It's admirable that you want to protect your Children, but they'll be under threat at the Riverbend canton, too. The Pride can travel there just as easily as they can travel here, and once we do move, they'll be able to track us. I hate to tell you this, but your Children will always live with the threat of an attack hanging over their heads. That will never go away."

Dina sighed. She tried to ignore the fact that he was acting again like they were in a relationship. She might have dismissed that gesture as a friendly show of neighborly support.

Some part of her didn't want to dismiss it as that. Sharing the danger and all the implications and complications of this life with someone—she never thought she'd find that so quickly.

Some part of her had hoped Tania would pull her head out of the clouds and become that person for Dina. Dina would have loved to share motherhood and all the trials of jungle life with Tania.

Dina found Link instead. He'd been so helpful, kind, and supportive since she first met him. No one understood the troubles and complications of raising these Children better than he did.

He'd been the first person besides herself to say that Tania's sons were beautiful. He understood and he didn't care at all that they were Khalid's sons.

Link escorted her back to her house and they said good night. Tania's bedroom door was still shut with both her and Fan inside.

Dina went to her own room, opened both pouches, and spent hours just lying there gazing at the Children sleeping. She became more certain than ever with every passing minute that she would do right by them—all of them—including her own.

Chapter 35

Dina came out of her bedroom just as Fan and Tania walked out of the house. Fan only took long enough to say good morning to Dina and Tania didn't say anything at all before they both headed outside to join the bustling canton.

Fan left the front door standing open. Golden morning sunshine streamed into the house and Dina heard Children laughing and shouting in the distance. Their voices got mixed up with the sound of adults talking....and other sounds Dina didn't recognize.

She carried her pouches onto the front steps to see what the sound was. Once she got out into the fresh air, she decided to sit down and feed her Children outside.

The older Auroras crawled all over the place, and after she finished feeding them, they didn't go back to sleep. They kept exploring, climbing, and falling over themselves trying to do things they weren't strong enough to do.

She laughed at them and enjoyed watching their antics while she took care of the others. Tania's three boys, Elyse's four, the younger Auroras, and Osiris's Children were all the same age and they seemed to appreciate being in the same nest with each other.

They comforted each other when they curled up to go back to sleep. They even put their arms around each other and nestled their faces into each other's fur.

Dina couldn't stop staring into the pouch to watch them sleep. They fascinated her in how different they looked, but at the same time, they resembled each other in their behavior.

This bunch was growing as fast as the older Auroras. These younger Children would open their eyes soon and then no force on the planet would be able to stop them from exploring their world the same way.

The same unusual sounds made Dina look up. Link, Troy, Nicholas, Cook, and Fitch passed her house steering five double-yokes of oxen pulling heavy wagons. The men parked the wagons in the middle of the canton at strategic intervals between the houses.

The minute they showed up, people came out of their houses carrying furniture, bedding, pots and pans, and every other kind of household goods. Everyone loaded their stuff onto the wagons.

The men unhitched their oxen and steered them off somewhere else. Link spotted Dina on his way past her house. "You better load up, too. We'll be leaving in three days."

"I don't have anything. The house is still empty."

"You'll need to bring your bedding. Riverbend canton is more than a week's journey away. You'll need all your bedding on the way and to make your Children comfortable once you get there."

"Oh. Okay." Dina glanced behind her into the house and frowned, but just then, one of the older Auroras yowled and she faced front to see what the problem was.

Abdullah and Aries locked together in a death grip, gnashed each other with their teeth, and growled and hissed at each other while they tumbled over and over each other in the grass.

Aries even latched his fangs around Abdullah's neck and made his brother howl in pain as he tried to break free.

Dina put down the pouch with the younger Children and went over to the two boys to pull them apart. "Leave him alone, Aries," she told him. "Let him go."

"Let them play," Link interrupted.

"Play? You call this play? They'll kill each other."

"No, they won't. It's good for them." He laughed at the two boys when Abdullah got the upper hand, toppled Aries, and in a matter of seconds, completely reversed their positions. "See? They need to challenge themselves and who better to challenge themselves on than their siblings? See? Look out there."

He pointed through the gate to the Children playing, climbing, and moving through the jungle at the edge of the fields.

Two of his nephews, Egypt and Israel, snarled, bit, and clawed at each other in a similar death match in the middle of the field.

Dina had to admit that she'd seen Children fighting each other the same way. Some of these fights got serious with the Children coming home bleeding, but none of the parents intervened and the perpetrator never got punished. A Child who had been the perpetrator one day was as likely to be a victim the next day.

"Aren't you at least a little worried they'll get hurt?" she asked.

"I used to be. Then I saw how naturally it comes to them. They need to test their strength. They'll never threaten each other or actively try to harm each other—not the way the Pride will. These Children need to learn to fight and defend themselves. They'll never get that chance if they don't do it now while all their parents are watching."

"I guess you're right," Dina replied, but she didn't like it.

Just then, Amber and Amir came over to Link and Dina and started attacking the two parents' ankles the way they attacked Link last night.

He laughed at them some more and Dina found herself joining in, but at the same moment, Troy walked over. He'd steered his oxen away and come back. "Dina—you're on the rotation for sentry duty, which means you need to come and practice your archery skills. Report to me when you finish there and you can get started."

"Sentry duty! But I don't know anything about archery. I've never used a bow and arrow in my life."

"Then it's time for you to learn. Every adult does a rotation on sentry duty—no exceptions." He looked around at her Children. Amir had started trying to climb up Link's pant leg again.

"Go ahead," Link told her. "I'll keep an eye on these little rascals for you. I'll come and get you if they need you."

She didn't want to leave, but she could see that the Children were as safe with him as they would be with her. She'd just finished feeding them and they were far more interested in attacking both him and each other than they were in her.

She hesitated a little longer, but she wasn't really doing anything else. She had no reason not to go with Troy. He led her to the wagon nearest the gate. Three women were in the process of carrying arm-loads of bows, arrows, and a bunch of other weapons out of the house the Council used for meetings.

The women loaded everything into the nearest wagon that Cook had parked in front of the house. Troy stopped at the wagon's back end, took out one of the bows, and handed it to Dina. "This one looks like it might fit you. No, don't hold it that way."

He adjusted her grip so the string passed along her inner forearm. Then he handed her a quiver of arrows and motioned for her to follow him through the gate.

They went out into the field and he gave her a long lecture on arrow types. Then he took hold of her shoulders, turned her to face the fence, and positioned her in the right stance.

She tried not to notice him touching her. Then, when he showed her how to hold and draw the bow, he actually put his arms around her to guide her arms in the right direction.

He finally pointed at the fence and said, "Go on and practice for a while until you get the hang of it," before he walked off.

She drew the bow a few dozen times, but her muscles weren't used to this kind of effort. Weeks of doing nothing at Renfroe's house had left her weak. She had to quit after an hour.

She gathered up the arrows to take them back inside the fence. Link hadn't come to find her to tell her that the Children needed her. Should she be worried about that?

She shouldn't doubt him. He knew so much more about raising these Children than she did. She would be lucky if her Children grew up half as capable as his nieces and nephews. He wouldn't let anything happen to her Children.

She knew all that, but she still couldn't bring herself to trust that they were okay. She never wanted to let them out of her sight—ever.

She turned to reenter through the gate, but before she went inside, she stopped when she spotted a figure standing in the distance. That shouldn't have rung her alarm bells. Adults walked and worked all over the area both inside and outside the fence.

This was an adult, but they weren't walking anywhere or working on anything. They were just standing there. The figure was a woman wearing a dark dress and she stood with her back to the canton which would have been unusual on its own.

An air of silence and stillness hung over her and she didn't move either away from or closer to the canton. She stood unusually close to the jungle—right at the point where the path left the fields to reenter the trees. No one from the canton should have been standing that close to the undergrowth. It wasn't safe.

Dina watched for a second, but when the figure still didn't move, Dina made up her mind. She went back inside the fence to put her bow and quiver in the wagon.

Link sat in the grass with three of Dina's Children climbing all over his back, head, and arms while he laughed at them. He even wrestled with them by grabbing them, tussling them on the ground, and making them snarl and bite his arms and wrists.

Dina left them to their play, strode out into the fields, and headed for the path where Fan stood very quietly facing out into the jungle.

She didn't move when Dina got near her, and when Dina walked around her to peer at Fan's face, Dina saw tears streaming down her cheeks.

"What's wrong?" Dina exclaimed. "You shouldn't be out here. It's dangerous for you to stand this close to the trees."

Fan lowered her eyes, looked down at her hands, and her face twisted in misery. "I have to go back, Dina! I can't stay here. It's so beautiful here....and the people are the most beautiful of all. I wish like anything I could stay....with you.....and help you raise your Children. I would give anything to be able to do that....."

"You can," Dina choked. "You don't have to leave. You're as committed to helping the Children as anyone. You've risked your life twice to bring the Auroras to me. I'm sure the Council would accept you."

Fan shook her head and her whole body shook with sobs. "I can't! God knows I want to, but I have to go back."

Dina couldn't speak above a whisper. "Why?"

"The Auroras......their father.....he's my husband. He's been Aurora's helper for years....and then this happened. My husband and children are all back at Helion House.....and I'm pregnant. I just found out......It's his. I've never helped a cat. This baby will be human. I have to go back. I've been gone too long already."

Dina gulped down the lump in her throat. She really didn't want to lose Fan. Dina had spent less time with Fan than with Tania, but Dina had come to like and respect this woman as a friend—one of the closest friends Dina had ever had.

Fan had been so helpful through it all. She'd proven beyond anyone's doubts that she was as committed to the Children's safety and wellbeing as anyone apart from their own parents. Who would Dina count on for help and support if Fan left?

"You don't have to leave," Dina husked. "You could stay here. The Auroras.....you could be their mother......"

"You're their mother now," Fan croaked. "My own children need me more than you do....and I need them. I need my family."

Dina didn't think so, but she didn't say that out loud. She would have said anything to stop Fan from going back to Prideland, but Dina could see plainly that Fan had already made up her mind. Trying to talk her out of it would only make it harder for her.

"Will you be all right?" Dina finally stammered. "Won't you be in danger—going through the jungle with the cats there?"

"I'll be all right. Aurora told me to come. I belong there....." Fan turned her tearful eyes toward Dina. "But I'll be able to help you from there."

"How?" Dina asked.

"I don't know, but I'll try." She came toward Dina and put her arms around her. Dina fought back emotion when she hugged Fan back. Then Fan pushed her off and held Dina at arm's length. "Take care of yourself, okay? And take care of those babies."

"I will." Dina found it hard to speak. Her throat ached. "Don't put yourself in danger."

"I won't. Bye." Fan turned away and strode down the path. In an instant, the jungle swallowed her and she vanished out of Dina's life.

Dina stood silently watching, but Fan didn't reappear. Of course she wouldn't. She knew what she had to do and she did it the same way Dina did.

Chapter 36

Dina stood in the same spot where Fan had just been standing. The oppressive sadness of Fan's departure kept Dina standing there much longer than she should have. She stared into the undergrowth the same way Fan did.

When Dina left Renfroe's house, she had thought that nothing would ever induce her to go back to Prideland. She thanked Heaven that she got pregnant and got out when she did.

Now, after taking care of these Children and preparing to have her own, she understood Fan's position better. Dina couldn't think of any other reason powerful enough to compel her to go back to Prideland, but she would have done it if she had children there. She would go anywhere, do anything, and risk any hazard to be near them and help them in whatever way possible.

That thought brought her back to her senses. She should go back inside the fence and see how her Children were doing, but right before she turned around, she froze when a cat stepped out of the bushes.

It hopped down from some low-hanging branch and landed right in the middle of the path—right on the spot Fan had just crossed.

The cat glanced over its shoulder in the direction Fan had just gone and then the cat turned around to fix its bright orange eyes on Dina.

She froze when she saw the dark-orange coat and bobbed tail of a Manx cat. It was Fallon. Her heart threatened to pound out of her chest and she fought to catch her breath. This couldn't be Fallon. He was dead. Dina had killed him, but could she have made a mistake about that? Maybe Fallon had survived to come back to haunt her.

The Manx held unnaturally still for a minute and then strode toward her. The cat stopped in front of hers, opened its mouth, and spoke in a female voice. It wasn't Fallon at all, but this cat looked exactly like him. Dina couldn't tell them apart in any other way.

"Do you know who I am?" the cat asked.

Dina shook her head.

"No, you wouldn't. You humans are so stupid. You can't tell one cat from the next, but I know who you are. You're the helper who killed Fallon. Don't waste my time denying it. I know it's true."

Dina struggled to get her voice working, but she couldn't stop it from shaking. "It's true. Who are you?"

"I am Amaryllis. I'm Fallon's mate. I remember the time you came to my house with Renfroe. I never forget a person's smell and I'll never forget the way you tried to help that idiot Matthew. Fallon told me you tried to run off and that he was going after you. Then Khalid told me afterward that you were the one who killed Fallon." Amaryllis wrinkled her nose in the direction of the canton and sniffed loudly. "I heard you were here. This place is as disgusting as they say it is. All these cantons are cesspools of filth."

Dina's alarm turned just as quickly to anger. She didn't move her hand to her cleaver, but she tensed her nerves to do it quickly in case Amaryllis attacked. "If you came here to kill me, you might as well do it, but I warn you. I will fight back. I won't lie down and die just to make it easier for you."

"I didn't come here to kill you. If I wanted you dead, you would never have survived to return to Renfroe's house. As it happens, you can serve my purpose much better alive. That's why I came here to find you."

"What do you want?" Dina asked.

Amaryllis turned her head and sniffed at an enormous tree stump next to the path. The stump dwarfed her and she murmured something to it under her breath.

Dina couldn't figure out what the cat was doing until a young girl crawled out from behind the stump, got to her feet, and stood next to Amaryllis in front of Dina.

The girl didn't look much older than fifteen and she didn't have a scrap of extra flesh on her bony body. Her tunic hadn't been cleaned in weeks and, from the looks of things, neither had the girl.

Her ropey, colorless hair hung in matted dreadlocks. Mud and grime covered her face, neck, and arms. Black dirt caked her fingernails and stained the creases on her hands.

The poor girl's swollen lips quivered in a desperate struggle to control her emotions, but she didn't succeed. Her eyes burned bright red and bloodshot from crying.

"This is Anoushka," Amaryllis announced. "She is my helper—or rather, I should say she was Fallon's helper. She's going to come and stay with you here."

"Who says she is?" Dina demanded.

"I say she is. She's carrying a litter of kittens from Fallon. These are his last young and I want them to survive. I heard that you were out here taking in the Children and their mothers. All of Prideland is talking about it."

Dina's eyes widened. "They are?"

"Of course. Nearly every session of the Senate is dedicated to deciding what to do about you and your.....what shall we call them? Your *people?* Whatever they are. Anyway, yes, all Prideland is in a frenzy about the Children living and growing in the jungle. I suppose you're turning yourself into some kind of zoo out here."

"It isn't a zoo!" Dina countered. "Where else are we supposed to live? The Pride wouldn't let us live anywhere else."

Amaryllis shrugged that away. "It doesn't matter. I'm ordering you, as a helper of the Pride, to take Anoushka."

"I don't take orders from the Pride. We're a free people."

Amaryllis chuckled. "That's what you think. All right. Have it your way. You're a free people. You're free until the Pride comes along and reduces you to the ground. That's how free you are."

"If you think we're in such danger of being reduced, why do you want me to take Anoushka? Fallon had other kittens. He had them with you, didn't he? She won't be safe out here."

"None of you is safe out here," Amaryllis murmured, "but she'll be safer here than in the city with the Pride. These are the last of Fallon's young and I want them to have a chance to grow up. It might not work, but at least they'll have a chance. You killed Fallon. Now you can make it up to him."

"I have no reason to make it up to him. He tried to kill me and I killed him first to save my own life. I don't owe him or you anything. I'll take Anoushka and I'll make sure her Children grow up as well as they can, but I'll do it for her and her Children, not for you and Fallon."

"Do it for whatever reason you want as long as you do it." Amaryllis started to turn away and then stopped. "By the way, you'll have to watch her very carefully. She's already tried to kill herself more than once when she found out she was carrying Fallon's kittens. She only came out here because I made her come. She doesn't want to go to the cantons at all."

The girl stole fleeting glances at Dina before lowering her eyes back to the ground. "Let me guess," Dina growled. "She didn't *help* Fallon of her own free will. He took her because he wanted her."

"What difference does that make? She's carrying his kittens. That's all that matters."

"They aren't kittens," Dina snapped. "They're Children."

Amaryllis didn't answer. She only walked away through the trees. She'd almost passed out of sight before she turned back one last time. "One more thing. You might want to move your......*people* somewhere else. I didn't come all this way to have my efforts wasted when the Pride comes to reduce all of you."

She stalked off into the undergrowth and vanished. Anoushka cast one desperate, agonized glance over her shoulder, but Amaryllis wasn't there anymore.

Dina stepped forward and extended her hand to the girl. "Are you okay? Come inside and we'll find something for you to eat."

The girl went through another spasm of misery. Her watery eyes darted all around the area and eventually landed on the canton behind Dina's back. Dina didn't need to follow Anoushka's gaze to know what the girl was seeing back there.

Adults worked all over the area. Children played in the sunshine, climbed, ran, and shouted in the fields in plain view of anyone who happened to be close enough to see them.

Anoushka took one look at the scene Fan had just said was so beautiful and the girl whirled away to bolt into the jungle.

Dina made a dive for her, but Anoushka could move incredibly fast when she wanted to. She came perilously close to breaking through the foliage before Dina got near her. Dina lunged for her, but the girl slipped out of reach.

Right before Anoushka made her break for freedom, a twig snapped somewhere and Amaryllis landed right in front of the girl. The cat must have been lurking in the canopy and she dropped directly into the girl's path.

Anoushka screamed in terror, but she couldn't get away before Amaryllis launched straight into the girl's face. Amaryllis tackled her flat onto her back and Anoushka toppled into Dina.

Anoushka screamed again. Dina staggered backward, caught her balance just in time, and Anoushka slammed down in the dirt at Dina's feet. Dina tried to grab her to help her, but Amaryllis gripped her claws into Anoushka's tunic and rode the girl to the ground under the Manx's weight.

Anoushka didn't stop screaming as they both went down. Amaryllis remained balanced there on Anoushka's chest until the girl landed flat and lay still.

The cat immediately yanked her claws free from the tunic, slashed her Anoushka across the cheek, and sprang away before Dina even realized what was happening.

Amaryllis landed fifteen feet away, turned back, and glared at both women with cold, cruel eyes. Dina scrambled to pick up Anoushka, but Amaryllis stayed where she was at a distance. She didn't attack again.

"You go," she snapped as soon as Anoushka got back on her feet. "I told you to go, and if you don't, I'll kill you right here."

Anoushka burst into loud sobs mixed with horrified screams. Her insane eyes raced around the jungle and then out to the canton. She didn't stop crying and screaming when she turned away and charged onto the field.

Dina hurried to keep up with her, but Anoushka didn't look back. She ran across the field toward the canton and her sobs got louder and more hysterical when she got close enough to see the Children.

Some of them stopped what they were doing to stare at her. Only a blind person would have missed the concerned looks on every small, furry face.

Their attention terrified her even more and she ran faster in no particular direction. She dodged in wild courses trying to avoid every single Child. She would have run straight past the gate and all the way to the jungle on the other side, but Dina caught her in time. "This way! Come this way."

Dina steered the girl into the canton. Just before Dina passed through the gate, she glanced back toward the path, but Amaryllis wasn't there anymore.

Dina had to go in to make sure Anoushka didn't run away again. Dina guided her as kindly as possible toward the house where Dina had been staying with Fan and Tania.

"It's all right," Dina kept murmuring. "Everything's going to be all right. You'll be safe here. Come inside and we'll clean up that scratch. You can get something to eat and lie down. No one will bother you here. Don't worry about them. They're just Children. You'll have some of your own soon."

Anoushka was crying too hard to answer and Dina didn't ask her to. Link still stood outside while the Auroras played. They didn't seem to be slowing down any despite how long they'd been outside.

Link raised his eyebrows at Anoushka when Dina showed up.

"I really appreciate you keeping an eye on them," she told him. "Come this way, Anoushka. You can stay in this house and I'll give you something to eat. This is Link Randall. He lives next door with his sister and their Children."

Link nodded and smiled at the girl. "Hello. Welcome. I'm glad you made it."

Anoushka burst into a fresh flood of tears, and right then, at the worst possible time, Tania strode over from somewhere and looked Anoushka up and down. "What is she doing here?"

"None of your business," Dina snapped. "Her name is Anoushka. She's going to be staying in Fan's room."

Tania snorted and walked away toward the house without another word to anyone. Dina couldn't pay any more attention to her. She steered Anoushka toward the ladder leading into the house and paused to lower her voice to Link.

"Would you mind keeping an eye on the Auroras a little longer? She's another suicide case and I need to go find Meredith and the other Council members."

"What do you need to find them about?" he asked.

"We just got a warning from the Pride. I think they might be closer than we thought."

Dina turned away to take Anoushka inside, but at that moment, a deafening roar and a piercing scream echoed across the landscape.

That sound set Dina's hair on end and she spun backward. She wasn't the only one who did. Adults and Children all froze and turned to look out through the gate.

Dina's blood ran cold as ten cats erupted out of the dense jungle canopy and these were no small house cats. Three fully-grown lions dropped from the branches, landed on the ground, and charged onto the field followed by two panthers and three tigers.

Dina had a split second to realize that none of the tigers was Renfroe and then another spine-chilling shriek ripped the world apart as a jaguar plummeted out of the high canopy, collided with an older male Child who happened to be climbing in the trees in full view of the canton, and crashed to the ground clamping his jaws around the boy's throat.

Link sprang for the gate bellowing at the top of his lungs, "Riyadh! Riyadh!"

Dina took a step in that direction, but she changed her mind as another twenty large cats erupted from the undergrowth. They came from the whole rim of forest and streaked across the field heading straight for the open gate.

Chapter 37

D ina rushed to where the Auroras were still playing in the grass. She snatched Amir and Aries, stuffed them into their pouch, and scrambled to get hold of the other Children before the cats attacked the canton.

She couldn't make up her mind between saving the older Auroras and picking up the pouch containing the younger ones. She ran to the pouch and then noticed Aldo and Ivory. They'd migrated farther away from the rest of their siblings.

Dina ran to catch them and then remembered the pouch with the younger Children in it. She grabbed it, slung it over her shoulder, and then raced to grab the rest of the Auroras. They'd all gone off in different directions.

That distance didn't seem like a problem when they'd been playing safely with Link watching them. Now the Auroras seemed dangerously far apart.

She got hold of Amir to push him into the pouch, but he didn't see the danger and struggled to get away from her. He shrieked and clawed at her hand. She had to stuff him into the pouch harder than she meant to and he instantly started trying to climb out of it.

She only had to glance toward the gate and her heart exploded out of her chest. Screams and bellows stabbed into her brain from all over the canton. It was happening again. The cats would massacre this canton down to the last helpless baby and leave no one alive this time, not even Dina.

She didn't want to be left alive without the Children. She tried not to see cats pouncing on them and tearing them apart in front of her eyes, but scenes of horror and destruction surrounded her on all sides.

The men who had been on sentry duty rushed to the gate and formed ranks to block the cats from getting inside, but more cats scrambled over the fence from all directions. They were all big, powerful predators—lions, tigers, jaguars, pumas, leopards, and a few lynxes.

They launched themselves into crowds of fleeing families, brought people down, and the crunch of bone floated on the breeze. Dina couldn't watch anymore.

She looked around for the last Auroras and finally managed to collar Amber and Abdullah. The commotion infected Aldo and Ivory and they'd scrambled even farther away in opposite directions.

Dina dashed over to grab Ivory when a massive tiger pounced right in front of her, landed on the crawling Child, and crushed the baby in its jaws. Dina froze in horror staring at it. She couldn't move as the tiger crunched through the little body with no effort.

Ivory's blood gushed down his chin....and then he looked up at Dina. Her ears rang. She couldn't be seeing this. She couldn't be standing here face to face with the monster that killed her Child.

The tiger licked his lips, and in that surreal moment, Dina's mind played a trick on her. Was this Renfroe? Was he coming back to haunt her nightmares the way he did after he helped to slaughter everyone at Frank's canton?

The jaguar straightened up and left Ivory torn in half on the grass, but Dina couldn't look away from the cat's eyes. He held her spellbound.

She even saw him coiling his legs under him to spring at her next, but she found it impossible to move even to grab the weapon from her belt.

The cat pulled his bloody lips back from his fangs and her mind snapped. She was still carrying the pouches with the rest of her Children in them. She had to protect them.

The instant she thought that, an unstoppable force collided with her from the side and Link tackled her away from the tiger. Link handed on top of her and they rolled thirty feet before he pulled her to her feet. "Come on!" he roared. "We gotta run for it!"

"What about.....?" She turned back and stopped when she saw the scene of death and catastrophe spreading all over the canton.

She couldn't see Aldo anywhere. Was he gone, too? Dina's eyes skimmed the scene just in time to see Lyra out there at the edge of the trees where Riyadh had gone down. Dina didn't see the boy, but she did see Lyra fighting the jaguar that attacked her son.

Lyra faced the cat holding a kitchen knife in one hand and some kind of club in the other. The instant Dina noticed them, the cat leapt for Lyra with his jaws spread wide open. He landed with his forepaws on her shoulders and his weight knocked her flat onto her back.

She hit the dirt and his mouth closed over her face. Dina didn't see if she landed any blows with her weapons before Link pulled Dina away. "Come on!!" he yelled again. "RUN!!"

He shoved her away, grabbed her arm, and pushed her between the houses heading for the back of the canton. Dina didn't see how they could get out that way, but when they passed another house, she realized that the fence had collapsed on that side.

She didn't see whether the cats had somehow managed to pull it down, but a huge breach gave a perfect opening for the cats to get inside the canton from multiple directions.

Adults and Children raced that way only to meet another wave of cats rushing them from the jungle directly ahead.

The Children broke away, sprinted through the grass on all fours, launched to the top of the fenceposts, and rocketed into the trees where the cats couldn't follow. That left the human adults alone on the ground.

Dina's resolve hardened. She'd already lost one Child today—maybe even two. She wouldn't lose any more of them. Her Children needed a mother and she was it.

She drew both her weapons, but she never stopped running. She charged into the thickest knot of cats and slashed and stabbed any of them that even looked at her. Link and the other adults had the same idea and rushed in wielding any weapon they could lay their hands on.

Dina hit a tiger, a puma, and a lynx, but she didn't stick around long enough to find out if she did any damage. She plunged through the breach. She was outside the canton now, but she heard more people screaming, bellowing, and the sound of bodies being torn apart behind her.

Link grabbed her one more time. "This way! Come on!"

Twenty adults surrounded them all heading in the same direction and they all plunged into the jungle running for their lives. Children streaked through the canopy overhead....and then cats materialized out of nowhere. They closed around the fleeing adults and more cats converged in the treetops.

Link, Dina, Meredith, and a bunch of other people from their patrol turned backward to guard the Children's retreat, but none of the adults could help the Children in the canopy. Screeches, crashes, and tearing branches ripped the jungle apart, but Dina had to face the cats in front of her.

A dozen archers ran up behind her to join their defensive line. The archers fired at the cats, and when the cats shrank back, the archers unleashed barrages of arrows into the canopy.

A puma screeched in agony, plummeted from the highest treetops, crashed onto the ground, and all the cats confronting Dina's party spun around to stare at him.

"Come on!" Link roared at the cats and threatened them with a knife of his own. He didn't have a bow. "Come on and take us if you think you can!"

His challenge sparked a similar reaction from the other parents. They darted toward the cats jabbing with knives, spears, and hand-made axes. Dina joined in and the cats retreated even farther.

The noise in the canopy receded behind their position as the Children fell back deeper into the jungle. Dina couldn't see them anymore and the only screams she heard up there were cat screams.

"Let's go," Fitch ordered. "We have to keep moving."

Dina had no idea where they were going. She didn't dare to turn her back on the cats until Link grabbed her arm and pulled her away by force.

The group hiked for what seemed like hours with no sign of any Children. Dina long since lost track of where she was. She didn't want to think about it. Whenever she thought about anything at all, she found herself reliving the moment of Ivory's death.

Dina gulped down despair. This couldn't be happening again. What was going on back at the canton? What would she find if she ever went back there? Why would this handful of refugees ever even go back there? Why would they want to see their loved ones killed and their homes destroyed?

She didn't see who was in line in front of her until the group broke through into a clearing. It surrounded a wide pool at the base of a waterfall where a stream fell over some rocks.

Dozens of Children jumped up when the adults arrived. The Children charged the group, grabbed their parents, and excited talk broke out all over the place as everyone hugged and some cried.

None of those Children were Link's nieces or nephews. He observed the other families from a distance, but Dina couldn't read his expression. Were they all gone? Was he completely alone now with no one left in the world?

Dina swallowed hard and shrank away from the group. She didn't want to be a part of this, but it was too late for that. She was one of the bereaved. She couldn't even be glad that she'd saved the rest of her Children.

The sight of all these parents petting their Children's cheeks, gazing into their eyes, and hugging them in relief made Dina feel sick. How much longer did these people have left to live and love each other before the Pride hunted all of them down?

She sat down on a rock by herself and opened both pouches. The older Auroras had finally settled down to sleep. There were four left of the original six.

All the younger Children lay asleep in their nest together. They never even realized the attack had happened. How long would it take before the older Auroras realized that two of their siblings were dead? Would they ever find out if Dina didn't tell them?

The clearing settled down as people lowered their voices and started to make themselves comfortable. No one asked what would happen to them next or where they would go.

No one here had any food or supplies to spend the night, but at least the fear and alarm of the attack was starting to fade. Dina couldn't tell anymore how much time had passed since the group left the canton.

Just then, another scream pierced the stillness. Everyone spun around and Dina's stomach dropped into her shoes when she saw Anoushka plastering herself against one of the tall rocks.

Dina had completely lost track of the girl until right now. Dina didn't see anything wrong with her, but Anoushka wouldn't stop screaming. Her wild, terrified eyes darted from one face to another and all around at the surrounding jungle.

Link rushed over to her and got in her face. "You have to be quiet! You could draw the cats right to us!"

She completely ignored him and kept shrieking her head off. Meredith hustled over there to reason with her, too, and when that failed, Link grabbed the girl, wrestled her under control in his powerful arms, and clamped his hand over her mouth to silence her.

"You have to be quiet!" he hissed in her ear. "You could get us all killed!"

She thrashed even harder to get away, but he overpowered her.

"What's wrong with her?" Fitch asked.

"She's just terrified out of her mind," Meredith replied.

"That can't be right," Dina interjected. "She was fine when we first got here. She was quiet for at least ten minutes and we weren't under threat when she started screaming."

"Who even is she?" another man asked. "I've never seen her before."

"She just showed up a few minutes before the attack," Dina replied. "Her cat benefactor brought her out here to save her Children. I was just bringing her inside when....."

At that moment, a burst of clear fluid gushed from under Anoush-ka's tunic and spattered on the stones at her feet. She erupted in a fresh bout of struggling, but Link held her firm.

"She's in labor!" Meredith exclaimed. "Sit her down, Link."

Link had to fight his hardest to overcome Anoushka's kicks. She jerked back and forth in his arms, but he eventually dragged her to the ground, sat down with her positioned between his legs, and Meredith pushed up Anoushka's tunic.

Dina turned away. She didn't need to see this and she didn't want to see Anoushka going through an ordeal she considered so nightmarish and horrific.

Chapter 38

Dina retreated into the rest of the group. The Children and remaining adults clustered by the waterfall and quite a few Children crawled into their parents' laps for comfort, but no one built a fire. No one shared any food because no one had any.

Muffled sounds kept drifting across the clearing coming from Anoushka. Dina could hear Meredith and Link talking to her, but Dina couldn't make out the words.

After more than an hour of continuous struggle, Meredith leaned back and looked down at something in her hands. Link let go of Anoushka and she crawled backward still sobbing her eyes out. She huddled against the rock as far away from everyone else as she could get.

Dina went over to them. "Is she going to be all right?"

Meredith didn't hear her. She stared down at four tiny boys in her hands. "They're Manx."

"Fallon is their father," Dina replied.

Meredith's head shot up and her eyes fell out of their sockets. "Why didn't you tell us?!" She shoved the four babies at Dina. "Get them away from me! We have to get rid of them!"

Dina scrambled to grab the four newborn boys before Meredith dropped them on the ground. "Hey! No! We can't get rid of them!

These are helpless Children—just like all the others. I'm sure someone somewhere would have said that about your Children, Meredith."

Meredith still didn't even seem to hear. "We can't take in any Manx! They're deadly!"

She whirled away and hurried back to her own Children where Meredith sat down with the other parents, gathered her Children into her arms, and didn't look in Dina's direction again.

Dina looked down at the four babies in her hands. They were tiny, but she could already see them stretching out, now that they were out of the womb.

Meredith was right. All four had Fallon's distinctive coloring, stubby tails, and blunt brutal features. The four babies also looked absolutely angelic with wide, round faces, orange fur patterns surrounding their faces, and tiny fangs and claws.

Fallon had been her worst enemy second only perhaps to Khalid himself, but Dina couldn't bring herself to hate these Children any more than she could bring herself to hate Khalid's sons. Was it an accident that both of them had litters of all males?

Dina squatted down and opened the pouch with the other young ones. She would need to find some other way to carry them. There were too many of them in there already.

Just then, one of the Manx boys twisted his sightless eyes up to her and let out the tiniest, high-pitched squeak of protest.

"You should feed them before you put them down," Link told her.

She looked up to find him standing right next to her. He didn't shrink away from these Children because they were Fallon's sons.

Link sat down next to Dina when she crossed her legs to feed the four boys. She no longer considered it unusual that she would be the one to take on the role of being their mother.

She put the first two to her breast and relaxed into the process when another wave of sickening nausea swept over her. She couldn't ascribe this to fear or devastation from the attack.

She shut her eyes and groaned. "Dina?" Link asked. "Are you okay?"

She forced herself to open her eyes. "I don't feel so good."

He laid his hand on her forehead. "You don't feel feverish. Did you get hurt in the attack?"

She shuddered as the wave passed. "I'm okay. I feel all right now. It's gone."

He sat down in the same place, but he wouldn't stop frowning at her. Five minutes later, the same thing happened and another grotesque surge of nausea hit her like a freight train, but it immediately passed.

"I think you might be going into labor," Link told her after the third time.

Her eyes shot up. "Here? I can't be going into labor *here!*"

Her gaze raced around the clearing. The sun was going down and everyone sat around on the bare dirt or on the rocks. The waterfall's spray made the air cool. It would get even colder once night fell.

"You'll be all right," he told her. "You're strong. This is the moment you've been waiting for. It will happen and then you'll have your own Children."

She tried to respond, but another brutal wave made her bow her head and groan again. She couldn't even speak. Her mind shut down until she found it difficult even to think.

She kept her head screwed on straight just long enough to finish feeding all four boys. Link had to take the pouch with the older Auroras in it. Dina couldn't concentrate on controlling them right now.

She lost all awareness of what was going on as the surges got stronger with every passing minute. She couldn't call them pain ex-

actly. They just felt like overwhelming attacks of unbearable intensit
y.......almost as if she might explode into a million pieces at any second.

She couldn't sit still. As soon as she put the younger Children back
into their pouch, she hung it over her shoulder and paced around the
clearing. She had to stop every now and then, rest her hands on her
knees, and pant to keep her mind from shattering.

Meredith came over once, but Link was the one who stayed by
herself through it all. He didn't talk much. He spent most of the time
raking his fingernails up and down her back.

She couldn't even bring herself to care that he was acting like they
were in a relationship. Nothing mattered but surviving this moment.
Every other thought evaporated out of existence.

She paced back toward the group and turned around to go in
the other direction when four people from the canton staggered into
the clearing. One of them was Richard Shriver and blood soaked his
clothes from multiple gashes all over his body.

"They're coming....." he stammered. "They're coming.....We gott
a.....get out of here.......Pack up.....move out....NOW!!"

He herded everyone out of the clearing and parents grabbed their
Children. No one asked any questions. They snatched what luggage
they could carry and some of the parents picked up their Children to
carry them, too.

Dina could only stand there hunched over at the waist and stare as
everyone dove into the undergrowth following a different path. Lucy
ran over to Anoushka, grabbed her by the wrist, and pulled her along
with the group.

Dina couldn't move. She couldn't go anywhere right now. She
couldn't even think.

Link pounced on her and wrapped his big arm around her shoulder. "Come on! I'll help you!" She braced herself to resist and he

changed his tone to a razor-sharp order. "Come on, Dina! You can't stay here!"

He steered her out of the clearing, but she couldn't move faster than a stumble. She kept buckling as the surges came closer and closer together. She would have stopped after only a few steps if he didn't keep forcing her to continue.

She lost all awareness of where she was. The rest of the group outpaced her. Branches swung closed across the path. She couldn't see anything beyond a few inches in front of her face.

She groaned and whimpered under her breath. Link kept yelling into her ear. "Keep going! Come on! We have to keep moving! You can make it!"

She couldn't tell anymore if she was making it. Her knees gave out every few steps until a catastrophic blast hit her and she slammed down onto her knees.

She couldn't get up. Link stuck his face in front of her eyes. "Dina! You have to get up! Come on! We don't know how far the cats are behind us! Do you want to let them find you here like this? Do you want to let them find your Children here like this? You can't let that happen!"

She heard him, but she couldn't stand up. She buckled again under a brutal wave of mind-blowing intensity. She couldn't even form the words to tell him that she wanted to stand up and couldn't.

He stood up straight and looked at something behind her. She wouldn't have been surprised if he'd left her there alone, but instead, he bent over and picked her up in his arms.

She shouldn't have been surprised by that, either, but her brain no longer functioned well enough to think anything about it at all.

She felt him running. The impact of every step exploded her being apart and she screamed out loud as another punishing wave tore her in half. She couldn't take this.

Link came to a steep hill. He panted and sweated trying to struggle up the rocky path. Dense undergrowth surrounded them on all sides. He tripped and winced when he slammed down on one knee.

Dina swam out of her haze and summoned all her mental power to lock her eyes on him. "Link......."

"It will....all right....." he panted. "Everything.....will be.....all right.......We'll....get there....you'll be....safe there......"

"Link....." she husked. "Put me down."

She couldn't say anything more than that, but she must have communicated the gravity of the situation through her eyes.

He gulped, glanced behind him down the steep slope, and then scanned the bushes on both sides of the path. The two of them were totally alone in the middle of the jungle.

He swallowed again and nodded. Then he walked on his knees off the path into the thickest undergrowth.

He crawled a long way on his knees still holding her up in his arms. His breath came in tortured, wheezing gasps and sweat dripped from his hair by the time he put her on the ground deep in the brush.

"We'll....be safe here......for now....." he gasped. "We.....won't be able to....stay here forever.....If the cats make it out this far....they'll still be able to smell us....."

She couldn't answer. She scrambled onto her feet, but she had to squat under the low-hanging branches.

She fumbled getting her leggings off, but even then, her tunic got in the way. Link helped her pull it over her head. She couldn't think clearly enough to care that he was seeing her stark naked and squatting in the bushes to give birth like an animal.

None of that mattered right now. She had to marshal all her courage and resolve just to get through the next few minutes.

Wave upon wave of shattering intensity and pressure exploded her out of her mind. She couldn't even tell what was happening to her and she didn't try to stop herself from screaming it all out through her mouth....and then to channel it between her legs to give birth to these Children.

Link kept his hand on her back and she heard him yelling in her ear, but she went so far out of her mind that she couldn't understand what he was saying.

She thrust her hand down between her legs and felt the first baby's head emerge. Link laid his hand on top of hers and helped her guide the Child out into the world.

He immediately took it from her and cut the umbilical cord, but she couldn't even look at her first Child. The second one was coming just as fast and she caught it in her hands.

Everything swirled in a tornado of emotions and foggy confusion after that. Link put both Children in her arms and she got lost staring down at them. She had to struggle to get her brain working when Link tried to put her tunic back on to keep her warm.

Her two Children consumed her whole attention and the rest of the world vanished. The boy had been born first and he had a dark orange coat with deep, black stripes like Renfroe's. The girl had very pale yellow-white fur. Only very slightly darker golden stripes showed up against the light background.

Dina couldn't stop touching and staring at them. Her Children. They were finally here. She didn't even care about the way she'd given birth. She didn't care about anything but them.

She put them to her breast and completely forgot that Link was still there until he did something behind his back and handed her a jug full of water. "Drink some of this. You might not be hungry yet, you need to stay hydrated."

She took a gulp and handed it back to him. She almost went back to looking at her Children when she caught his eye. "Thank you," she breathed. "I couldn't have done it without you."

He cracked one of his grins. "I think you could have."

She took her hand off her Child and squeezed his arm. "Thank you, Link. You're a godsend."

He blushed and looked away. "Don't thank me yet. We aren't safe here. You can rest for a while, but we need to move out as soon as you can walk."

She gulped and glanced around the bushes nearest her. She didn't know when she would ever be able to walk again. The lower half of her body felt pulverized and her legs trembled just from sitting up.

Link swiveled around and sat down next to her. "Take your time. They aren't here yet."

"How do you know where they are?"

"I don't. That's why I want us to move."

She fell silent, but his words brought her back to her senses quicker than anything else could have. She, Link, and her Children weren't safe here. The cats would still be prowling the jungle looking for any stragglers left behind when everyone fled the canton.

"I'm.....I'm sorry, Link....." she whispered. "About.....your family......."

He stared down at the dirt and stabbed his knife into the soft moss. "Yeah. Me, too."

She didn't know what else to say, so she crossed the last barrier and rested her head on his shoulder. He'd been there for her since day one. He would always be there.

Why did she resist getting involved with him? He was right about her promise to Renfroe. She'd made it under duress—under the threat of her Children's lives. Why did she think she owed Renfroe anything—especially her promise?

She made that promise so she could get out of Prideland. That was nothing compared to what she'd been willing to do to escape from him the first two times. Why should that promise hold any power over her at all?

Link bent his head and kissed the top of her hair. It was the same kiss he'd given his nieces and nephews—his Children. If any of them were still alive, he was all they had left. Lyra was gone. They were his Children now—his alone.

He would need as much help with them as she needed from him. Why should she push him away?

She'd lost every other friend she had in the world. Fan. Tania. Renfroe. Tom. Frank. They were all gone. Only she and Link were left—them and their Children.

She must have fallen asleep on his shoulder because, when she opened her eyes, it was dawn again. He didn't hurry her to get up and start hiking again, but she couldn't stay here. She'd already wasted the whole night.

She glanced back down at her Children. They'd both fallen asleep in her arms. "What do you think you'll name them?" Link asked.

"I've been thinking about that a lot. I think I'll name the boy after my brother, Adrian. The girl I've decided to name after my grandmother. I was always close to her. Her name was Iona. Iona Dyer."

"They're good names." Link leaned over and ran his fingertip back across the top of Adrian's head. "They're beautiful."

He kissed her hair one more time. That signal ended the moment for Dina and she sat up. Every move made her ache, but hers and Link's safety and the safety of these Children came first.

She put her two Children into the pouch with the others. It was too small for all of them, but it would just have to do until she found somewhere safe to take them out of it.

Her legs trembled even more when she put on her leggings. "Are you sure you really want to do this?" Link asked. "We could stay here a little longer. We could even spend another night here."

"No, we have to go. Where are we going, anyway?"

"We'll meet up with the rest of the canton at the rendezvous point. Anyone who's still alive and able to travel will be there. They'll spend two nights there before they send scouts back to the canton to make sure the cats are gone. If they are, we'll go back and get any wounded out before we fall back to Riverbend canton."

Dina didn't argue with that. She didn't care what she did as long as she met up with the others and got out of the cats' range.

Chapter 39

Link pivoted onto his knees and checked the undergrowth outside their hiding place while Dina finished getting dressed. The foliage grew too thickly overhead for her to stand, which was a good thing because she didn't even know if she *could* stand, let alone walk.

The hillside on which they'd taken shelter had been very steep, rough, and rocky. Could she really climb that? She would have to.

She finally pushed herself onto her knees and nodded. "I'm ready."

Link didn't move. He cocked his head and studied her. "I don't know about this. You look really pale. Are you sure you can do this?"

She almost repeated that she was ready, but she stopped herself when she made eye contact with him. She hesitated for a split second and then kissed him.

She let that kiss linger. She could have let it linger for a long, long time. She could have tackled him into the bushes right then and there, but now wasn't the time for that.

She pulled off and let the intense intimate depth of his eyes overwhelm her in ways she hadn't felt in a long time. He started to smile and the color flashed to his cheeks.

"Just promise me one thing," she told him.

"What's that?" he asked.

"Promise me we won't have any more children—human children, I mean."

He burst out laughing. "Okay. I can live with that."

A flood of affection welled up in her—for him, this time. She'd been going through these life-changing torrents of emotion ever since she came to this planet. Now she felt it for him.

She dove in and kissed him again, and this time, they both put their arms around each other and held each other while they kissed.

She pulled off all too soon. "Let's get out of here. Let's get to the rendezvous and see if any of your Children made it. Then we'll know what to do."

He crawled back the way he'd come to the trail. Dina followed him, but she already felt her own weakness. She wouldn't be able to keep up with him the way she'd kept up with the patrol.

He straightened up on the steep path he'd been climbing when she told him to put her down. He waited there while she struggled out of the bushes, but he had to catch her when she tried to straighten up and nearly fell over.

"Maybe I should carry you—just to the top of the hill," he suggested. "You'll exhaust yourself if you try to climb that."

She followed his gaze up the steep incline. It rose in a seventy-degree angle with gnarled tree roots knotted around sharp rocks. Each one created the stairsteps of a near-vertical ladder that vanished into the undergrowth. No way could she climb that.

"Here. Get onto my back," he went on. "Then I'll be able to use my hands to help pull myself up. I couldn't do that before."

He turned his back to her and she gave in, wrapped her arms around his neck from behind, and he pulled her legs around his waist when he straightened up to lift her weight.

She still drained the last of her strength holding onto him. He couldn't keep her secured when he grabbed the nearest tree roots with both powerful hands and used every scrap of his muscle power to carry her up the slope.

He panted, sweated, and gasped for air the way he did before, but he didn't stop until he made it to the top. He lowered her to the ground and collapsed at the base of a tree.

Now it was her turn to open the water jug and hand it to him. He gulped down a mouthful and sank back still breathing heavily. Dina didn't interrupt him or remind him of the danger.

She looked over the side at the jungle floor far below. Now she understood why the people from the canton used this place as a retreat point. The cats would still be able to get up here, but maybe this hill would slow them down if the cats ventured out this far.

Link rested his head against the trunk and shut his eyes while he caught his breath, but he didn't stay there for long. He struggled to his feet and shot Dina another hard look from under his sweaty hair. "Are you sure you're okay?"

"I'll make it. I might have to go slowly at times, but I don't want to stop until we get there."

He only nodded and led the way onto another winding path. This one still went uphill, but at least it wasn't as steep.

It was steep enough to slow her down. She had to stop and rest a lot more frequently than he did and then she had to stop and feed the Children.

Once she did that, the older Auroras absolutely refused to go back into their pouch. They kept escaping. She got some of them in there and turned away to capture the others. Then the first escaped again while her back was turned.

"Give them to me," Link interrupted after the fourth time this happened.

He took the pouch, grabbed Amir and Abdullah, and held them by the scruffs of their necks while he collared the other two.

He put them in the pouch a lot more roughly than Dina ever would have dared to, but instead of pushing them all the way down to the bottom, he left their heads sticking out. He used another piece of string to lash the pouch closed with their bodies inside.

Dina laughed at all their little heads poking out of the top. Their wide eyes raced around the jungle looking at everything, but they couldn't get away.

Link tied the bag over his shoulder and carried the bundle on his back. "I'll take these four," he told Dina. "You have enough to carry already."

She didn't argue. The Children definitely responded to him in ways they didn't respond to her. They couldn't get away with as much when they tried to test him and he had the strength to enforce his will on them in ways she didn't.

He gestured for her to go in front while he brought up the rear. He matched her pace that way so he didn't leave her behind.

She didn't see the Auroras from this position, but she heard them squeaking and even yelling out back there. Link occasionally had to reprimand them to stop biting each other or to keep their voices down, but they always sounded like they were enjoying themselves.

Link and Dina hiked for most of the day until they came to another downhill slope that ended in a creek. Link followed it upstream to another pool where everyone from the canton waited for them.

Everyone crowded around to question Link and Dina about where they'd been. Link started to explain when four Children charged out of the group and collided with him.

He grabbed them and hugged his remaining nieces and nephews one after the other. They all talked at once and he wrapped them in his arms choking back tears. "Oh, thank God, you're safe!" he rasped. "I thought I'd lost you all!"

He sat down on the ground and India and Israel got into a fight over which of them was going to sit in his lap. He hugged them both and kept stroking their fur and kissing them all over.

Israel leaned back and looked up at him. "I want Mama, Link! I want Mama!"

Tears streaked down Link's cheeks and his lips spasmed all over the place. "I know, baby. I want Mama, too."

"What happened to Riyadh and Paloma?" India asked.

Link pressed her forehead to his lips and tears streamed from his eyes when he shut them. "I don't know, baby. I really don't know. I wish I did."

Dina's throat constricted watching them. She would have liked to comfort them, too, but she didn't want to intrude.

She sat down a short distance away and distracted herself by finally letting the older Auroras out of their bag. They had gotten hungry and cranky again on the journey, and after she fed them, they let her put them back in the bag to sleep.

She and Link arrived at the rendezvous in the evening of the second day, and after everyone finished questioning her and Link, they settled down to spend the night here, too.

No one mentioned lighting a fire, pitching a tent, or using any other kind of structure or comfort. A lot more people from the canton had made it this far than made it to the waterfall and a few more people straggled in during the night.

Dina saw Lucy taking care of Anoushka, but Tania wasn't here. Did she survive the attack? Dina wouldn't know that until the scouts came back and everyone went to look for wounded at the canton.

By morning, four men she'd never seen before walked up the path and held a quick conference with the Council members.

"It's time to go back to the canton," Meredith told everyone. "No one has to go that doesn't want to. You can stay here and we'll collect you on our way back through to Riverbend."

Everyone got up to leave and Dina looked around. "Where's Anoushka? Has anyone seen her?"

"She was right next to me all night," Lucy exclaimed. "She went to sleep right next to me."

"We don't have time to look for her," Meredith cut in. "We can look for her on the way back, but we need to go now while the canton is clear. We don't know if the cats will come back looking for survivors."

Dina had no choice but to go with the others. Link used a long piece of cloth to create a sling to carry India and Israel. His other two Children, Egypt and Cairo, were both big and strong enough to walk on their own.

Dina repeated the procedure of wrapping up the older Auroras with their heads poking out of their pouch so they could see what was happening. Some of the younger Children already had their eyes open. They would be active enough to climb around and explore in a day or two.

Dina wanted to hurry up and get to Riverbend canton where she could hopefully settle into a more stable life, but she needed to stay with the group. She wouldn't have gone back to the site of the attack otherwise. She didn't want to find out how bad it was.

Not even the promise of finding out if Aldo had survived offered any temptation. Going back could just as easily mean finding out that he was dead.

The journey back to the canton took another two days. Scouts and hunters kept splitting off from the group to bring back food and the group lit fires that night to cook it.

People kept their talk subdued, especially on the second night. "We should make it back to the canton tomorrow," Link remarked.

"Is it worth going back for survivors?" Dina asked. "It's been almost four days. If anyone got critically injured in the attack, they'll be dead by now."

"It never hurts to go back and check. Someone could still be alive. We couldn't leave without them."

Chapter 40

No one in the group spoke at all when the sun came up the next morning. They hiked the last few miles and emerged from the jungle on the path below the open fields.

Most of the fence had been knocked down and some of the houses had been burned to the ground. Bodies lay all over the field and the oxen from the barn had been dragged into the open and slaughtered.

Dina saw from a distance the small ball of glowing fur lying where the tiger had killed Ivory. Dina didn't need to go over there to see.

Parents put their Children on the ground to walk around by themselves while the adults went into the canton to check for any injured survivors.

Link let his Children down and walked straight past Dina on his way toward the jungle. He kept his head down as he approached the spot where Lyra had fallen.

Dina followed him and found him squatting down next to her body. She lay on her back with most of her face ripped off. Her sightless eyes stared into the jungle and her throat had been torn out.

She'd fallen on top of the body of her daughter Paloma. Dina hadn't seen during the attack that Lyra had been protecting Paloma from the jaguar that killed her. Lyra's body bent over backward in a bridge over Paloma's torso. The little girl's head had been completely crushed beyond recognition.

Link's hunched shoulders quaked with sobs as he ran his hand down what was left of Lyra's cheek. He picked up her limp, grey hand and kissed her knuckles. There wasn't anything left of Paloma for him to touch.

Dina put her hand on the back of his neck, but she didn't say anything. There was nothing to say that would ever help him get over this. Now he was stranded with four orphaned Children.

He'd already made untold sacrifices for Lyra and her Children. His job just got infinitely harder.

He sobbed over her for a long time. Dina didn't try to comfort him except to stand next to him with her hand on his neck, back, and shoulder the way he'd taken care of her when she gave birth.

She didn't try to get him to leave his sister. Dina let her gaze migrate back to the canton while she waited for him to be ready to move on. She didn't want to go in there even to find out if Aldo was still alive. She never wanted to set foot in that canton again.

Link finally ran his wrist across his nose, stood up, and strode a dozen yards into the jungle where he stopped next to the fallen remains of his nephew Riyadh.

The boy had collapsed on his side with his arms and legs bent at strange angles in front of him. Blood covered his face and matted in his fur. One ear had been torn off when some cat had mauled the side of Riyadh's face.

Link stood over the boy and stared down at Riyadh for a long time. It took him ages before he shuddered, squatted down, and grabbed Riyadh's shoulder to turn the boy over.

Link flipped him onto his back and Riyadh exploded off the ground. His eyes snapped open and he yelled out in fear and surprise before he realized who it was.

Link jolted back to get away from him and the two stared at each other in breathless shock for a second.

Riyadh looked even worse from the front. Bloody gashes covered his face and the whole side of his face had been flayed open, but he was still alive.

"Link?" he whispered. "Link.....you're here....."

Link attacked the boy in a frenzy, fell on his knees, and grabbed Riyadh in his arms. "Oh, my God, baby! You're alive! I can't believe it! You're alive! I thought you were dead!"

Both of them started crying and Link wouldn't stop sobbing as he lifted his nephew into his arms. "It's gonna....be all right....." He kept choking and he covered Riyadh with kisses. "Everything...is gonna...be all right.....I've got you.....I've got you...."

Dina's eyes swam with tears. She touched the back of Link's neck one more time, but he didn't notice. He kept stroking Riyadh, looking at all his wounds, and then hugging and kissing him again.

Dina couldn't watch this. It hurt too much. She walked out onto the field, but the only other place to go was toward the canton.

Ivory's body blocked her from going near the front gate. The other patrollers crisscrossed the canton's interior. She didn't see if they found anyone.

Dina started to turn away when a different figure strode out of the canton. Dina had spent so much of the last few days away from Tania that she looked strangely unfamiliar to Dina now.

Tania halted outside the gate, scanned the fields in both directions, and spotted Dina watching her. Neither woman moved for a second.

Dina barely recognized Tania anymore. Dina struggled to remember any connection between them at all.

Where had Tania been all this time? Did she run away from the attack? Did she hide somewhere inside the canton?

Tania didn't have a scratch on her. She was totally unharmed. Even that seemed like the worst insult to these people who had fought so hard and lost so much.

Tania would never care about that. She would never even try to share these people's suffering or their trials. She'd done everything possible to separate herself from them and she'd succeeded beyond her wildest dreams.

Some part of Dina's innermost being understood that Tania wouldn't be coming to Riverbend canton with the rest of the group. The Council didn't have to throw Tania out. She would leave on her own. She didn't belong with this group and no one understood that better than she did.

That thought alone gave Dina the energy to walk over to where Tania stood. Dina wouldn't have said a word to Tania if Dina thought there was the slightest chance she would ever see Tania again after today.

Dina halted next to her. Tania locked eyes with her once and then went back to looking over the fields—anywhere but at Dina.

"Where are you headed?" Dina asked.

"Fitch gave me directions to one of the other cantons. It's north of here."

Dina looked Tania up and down. "You aren't taking any supplies."

"I'll be fine." Tania said those words in a short, clipped, harsh tone and she looked around her with hard, narrowed eyes.

How ironic that Tania's fighting spirit should come back to life now of all times. She didn't fight for Dina. Tania didn't fight for her Children or to save the lives of any other helpless, innocent Child.

She came back for herself, though. Dina never doubted for an instant that Tania would be just fine on her own in the jungle. She'd always been a fighter. She'd always been much stronger and tougher than Dina had ever been. She could have taken any cat if she really wanted to.

"Have a safe journey," Dina said, but those words meant absolutely nothing. She didn't care about Tania anymore. Dina didn't care about anything but her own people—her own family. "Maybe I'll see you again sometime."

Tania nodded. "You, too. Good luck."

She walked off without a word, went back to the path, and disappeared into the jungle. Dina felt nothing but relief that Tania was finally gone. Now Dina could get on with the business of caring about the people who actually mattered.

Dina couldn't stay this close to the canton, so she turned away to follow the stream. She wanted to get away from all this horror, but she didn't want to lose sight of the group.

She hiked up the streambed to the other end of the field. The sun shone on the rolling grasslands between the fence and the jungle. She might have been able to trick herself into reliving those beautiful, idyllic moments, now that she looked at the canton from a distance.

No Children laughed or played or wrestled or ran around in those fields now. None of the voices of adults talking floated on the breeze. A cloud of death hung over the place.....just like Frank's canton.

The peace and tranquility of those days would never come back. This war was just getting started and the Pride would never rest as long as even one Child remained alive.

The older Auroras squawked in her ear and struggled to get out of their bag. They got excited when they saw their old familiar home, but she couldn't let them out to play here—not ever again.

She turned away to scan the jungle. Her eyes automatically searched every branch and shadow for any cats coming back, but she didn't see any.

That would change soon enough. They could travel so much faster than people. The group would have to travel more slowly than ever, now that they had to take care of their wounded. Riyadh's injuries looked severe. He might die from them yet.

Dina couldn't let that happen. She couldn't let Link suffer any more loss. Two of his closest family members lost in one day was bad enough.

She would help him. She knew now that they would join together in one big extended family. She would become his Children's adoptive mother just as he would become her Children's adoptive father.

That was what these Children needed most. A father and a mother committed to raising these Children would be almost as important as protection from the Pride and these Children would get all of that from Link and Dina. They just wouldn't get it here.

She turned away one last time to push on to the end of the field. She wanted to make sure the whole jungle was free of cats before she turned her back on it again.

She came to a bend in the stream. She couldn't go past this without losing her line of sight to the canton. She spotted Link coming out of the jungle carrying Riyadh, but before she turned back, she saw something lying in the stream around the corner.

She went over to it and stood on the bank staring down at Anoush-ka's body. She lay in the water so the trickle had to dam up behind her before it bubbled down its bed again.

She stared up at the sky without blinking and four round puncture marks dotted her neck where some cat had strangled the life out of her. Did Amaryllis come back to finish the job?

Dina's mind played strange tricks on her. First, the bite looked too big to be a Manx's mouth. Then she thought it might be too big.

She couldn't think about that anymore. She had too much work to do and too many people still depending on her. She hiked back down the stream just as the rest of the patrol came out through the gate.

Dina met up with them on the path so she wouldn't have to go near the canton. Link carried India and Israel in their sling and Riyadh in his arms. Link had wrapped another piece of cloth around Riyadh's head. Only one of his eyes remained visible.

Dina evaluated Link's burden. The group had some hard miles to cover before they found any shelter. Link would exhaust himself more by carrying those three than Dina had exhausted herself by hiking after giving birth.

She didn't say anything to him about it, though. She didn't want to take any of his Children away from him—not yet. He needed them as much as they needed him.

She rested her hand on his shoulder while the group filed down the path leading back into the jungle. His eyes and cheeks had become puffy and blotchy from crying and all five of his children still sobbed and sniffled as they walked away.

Link glanced over at Dina and managed to smile at her. "Are you okay?" he asked.

She nodded, but she didn't want to talk. She just wanted to leave.

"Aldo is over there by the fence. Do you want to go see him? You might not get another chance."

"No, let's get out of here. We need to fall back to the jungle while we can. I don't want to stay here any longer than we have to."

No one said anything else. A few people supported injured relatives to leave the field or carried wounded Children on their backs or in their arms.

Dina didn't plan to look back, but when she got to the bottom end of the field, her attention swiveled toward the broken-down fence. Ghosts and memories would live on in this canton the same way they lived on at Frank's canton.

Death and destruction would follow the Children wherever they went. Every enemy of the Pride would have to fight just to stay alive and now Dina was one of those—again.

She turned away for the last time to follow the group into the jungle. Whatever the future held, she would meet it and do everything in her power to protect these Children until they grew up to meet their destiny.

<u>End of book 2.</u>

Keep Reading

Prideland Series: Book 3: Children of the Pride

Prideland isn't what it used to be, now that a new race of Children is rising from the jungle to challenge the cats' dominance on this planet. The Children are stronger, faster, smarter, and deadlier than the cats themselves and the Children are growing up at an accelerated pace—not just in strength but in their boldness to confront the cats on their own terms.

The Children struggle to find their place somewhere between the human world that rejects them and the cats trying to wipe out every last Child on the planet. It's only a matter of time before one man comes forward to unite the Children into the formidable army that can defeat the cats and win the Children a home where they can live in peace.

This man is none other than Lieutenant DinaDyer's son, Adrian—a hybrid who combines all of Renfroe's power and charisma with human intelligence and strategic cunning. Adrian's leadership and tenacity will sweep the planet and embroil Dina in a vicious war to the death between two unstoppable forces that refuse to make peace with each other—the cats who still want to annihilate all the Children down to the smallest babies and the Children who will fight to their last breath to grow up and make a world safe for the next generation.

You can find it at your favorite book retailer.

Sign Up Once--Get all Theo Mann's free books including brand new releases

Sign Up Once--Get all Theo Mann's free books including brand new releases

Humanity on the brink of annihilation.

A mysterious package, a corrupt officer, and a conspiracy that goes all the way to the top? What could possibly go wrong?

When a routine mission goes horribly wrong, Warrant Officer Ewing Archer and a handful of faithful friends get trapped in a battle to save the last survivors of Earth.

The human race has abandoned the ecological disaster of Earth. Now all that remains is a network of interconnected ships, stations, and satellites surrounding the planet.

But when war breaks out, Archer becomes a firebrand that could destroy it all....or save it.

Sign up at www.theomann.com to read it for free

About Theo Mann

I write 70 books per year—and yes, before you ask, all these books are my original creative work. Nothing written under my name is AI-generated or ghostwritten because I write better than AI and any ghostwriter out there.

People don't read fiction for entertainment or to escape from reality. People read fiction to see their humanity reflected in another person's character and story.

This is my promise to you. When you read my books, you'll see your own humanity reflected in the characters and stories. I take this commitment to my readers very seriously. My books are an intimate form of communication between us. I would never disrespect my readers by turning that over to a machine or another writer. This is my bond between me and you as my reader.

I write 20,000 words per day as my daily work output. If anyone with a public platform would like to challenge me to prove this in a controlled environment, feel free to contact me on this website's contact page.

I worked as a professional ghostwriter for fifteen years. Now I'm on a mission to set a Guinness World Record by writing 700 books over the next ten years and 1400 books over the next twenty years, all originally written by me. See my website for the full book list.

I'm also the author of *Proof for the Existence of God* and the *Crimes Against Fiction* blog. You can find all my nonfiction work at www.crimes-against-fiction.com.

If you have a story idea, or if you would like me to explore a series in more depth, or if you'd like me to explore a character by writing a spinoff series about that character or world, leave me a message on my website's contact page. I answer all reader emails, so ask me anything, tell me what you liked and didn't like, and let me know where you'd like your favorite series to go. I would love to hear your ideas and find out what you'd like to read next.

Find out more at www.theomann.com.

Also by Theo Mann (so far)